The Stage Was Set—
FOR MURDER!

Early in her career one reviewer had described Claudia Milotte as the "ten most beautiful women in the world." Another newspaper man had said, "Meeting Claudia Milotte is not the encounter of journalist and star. It is an *event*."

She had been particularly praised for her work in *The Capri Affair* by critics who admired her capacity for stripping away all the frills in this, a fiendishly difficult role.

Appreciation of her artistry had been as thunderous at every Broadway performance of the hit play as it was on opening night. But tonight the audience appeared even more enthusiastic than usual. And this was a night Claudia Milotte needed all the support she could muster—from any direction—for this was the night she became a widow.

Also by David Hanna:

THE OPERA HOUSE MURDERS
THE LOVE GODDESSES
THE VACANT THRONE
THE GRABBERS
CAPITAL PUNISHMENT

A CRIME COURT MYSTERY

THE CAPRI AFFAIR

DAVID HANNA

Book Margins, Inc.

A BMI Edition

Published by special arrangement with Dorchester
Publishing Co., Inc.

Copyright © MCMLXXX by David Hanna

Printed in the United States of America.

Part One

At exactly nine-fifteen on Saturday night, November tenth, Alice Dunne put aside her paper work, left her small, immaculate office in the basement of the Grand-Plaza Hotel and walked across the corridor to the bank of rear elevators, where she pressed the button of one of three elevators marked "private."

Mrs. Alice Dunne was a medium-sized woman well into her fifties whose age showed only in her efficiency, the seriousness with which she took her work, and her old-world impatience with the occasional sloppiness of her staff. Her trim figure suggested a woman who took care of herself and preferred activity and physical work to the tiresome business of maintaining records. Her unlined face was crowned by silver hair, carefully coiffured to give her presence authority and dignity.

Alice Dunne, with her warm Irish glow and readiness to smile, worked hard to accomplish the austerity she

5

brought to her job. Her "people," as she called the small cadre of night duty regulars in the housekeeping department, were devoted to her.

Officially, Alice Dunne's duties as night housekeeper for the elegant landmark hotel on Central Park West began when she ascended to the penthouses located atop the thirty-story building. There were two apartments, facing north and south—hence their names, Penthouse North and Penthouse South.

They commanded more magnificent views of the New York skyline than any other residential building in Manhattan. Each enjoyed three panoramas. Both looked west to the Palisades and east across Central Park, over the skyline of the East Fifties to the East River, Rockefeller Center, the Chrysler Building and south to the famous old bridges, the Brooklyn and Manhattan; north, to the Queensboro.

Penthouse South, inevitably, was the more dramatic of the two, dazzling the eye with the spectacle of downtown New York, an unparalleled tapestry of concrete encompassing names of buildings known around the world: the Empire State, the Woolworth Building, the Triangle and/or Flatiron Building (depending on your generation) and finally the supreme monstrosity, the Twin Towers, that almost negated the cluster of older skyscrapers immortalized on millions of postcards for half a century.

None of the Grand-Plaza's elevators had been accelerated to the speedy ascent found in New York's office buildings. Not that they creaked up and down; rather, they rode at a leisurely pace which the management considered appropriate to the Grand-Plaza tradition.

The ride offered Mrs. Dunne ample opportunity to consult her clipboard. Penthouse North was being held

6

for Billy Jo Harris, who was expected quite late from Houston. Miss Harris, a wealthy young lovely, was described by the gossip columnists as "the madcap oil heiress." Alice Dunne knew better. She was a lonely young woman, hoping that somewhere between Penthouse North and her family's ranch in Texas she would find a man capable of loving her as a woman, regardless of her wealth. Mrs. Dunne also knew that was never going to happen as long as Billy Jo remained "Daddy's little girl." At thirty-four, Billy Jo was way out of the "little girl" range. But no one would ever convince Colonel Willie Harris, self-styled King of the Wildcatters, of that.

Mrs. Dunne intended checking Penthouse South first. It was occupied by Richard Franklin Winston IV, a name that had been on the registry from the day the hotel opened in 1909. Newspapers covering the event looked up at the half-filled building and estimated that the fifty-odd "old family" names already in residence on the Park side of the building represented an aggregate fortune of five hundred and fifty million dollars. Richard Winston, Jr. was one of those names.

The Penthouses were an afterthought, having been added to the hotel during the thirties when construction in New York was at its height, offering speculators a once-in-a-lifetime opportunity to take advantage of cheap-quality materials and a cheaper labor market composed of master craftsmen, victims of the Great Depression.

It was from Penthouse North that Richard Franklin Winston III had masterminded the reorganization and growth of Winston and Associates. Mrs. Dunne, then a teen-age maid, had spent many nights being baby-sitter for his son, Richard Winston IV—whom everyone called Ritchie, a nickname that stuck.

Ritchie moved out of the Grand-Plaza when he married. His father had died six years earlier and his mother had died when he was five. Thus the Winston dynasty at the Grand-Plaza ended.

But Ritchie, now the heir to the family fortune and a dynamic business entrepreneur in his own right, still remained loyal to the Grand Old Lady of Central Park West. Winston and Associates used the hotel for all its social functions, and a convention of executives of the company from the far corners of the globe had gathered there this week for a series of conferences. Ritchie took over Penthouse South as a matter of convenience and as a meeting place for the numerous private conferences typical of such conclaves.

For the last three nights Mrs. Dunne had found the suite in such a shambles that she had been obliged to call a porter and a maid to clean up. She imagined it would be no different tonight.

From the elevator, the entrance to Penthouse South lay to the right of the service section, which was separated from the guest hallway by double doors. Mrs. Dunne slipped the clipboard under her arm and fished into the pocket of her smock for her keyring. She easily found the passkey by touch.

She rang the bell of Penthouse South, heard the chimes, counted to eight and rang again. Hearing no sound, she counted to ten before turning the key in the lock.

The door opened onto a hallway at whose center lay the double doors to the living room. They were wide open; the handsome, high-ceilinged room with its lovely chandelier and French provincial furniture was ablaze with light. Alice Dunne stepped back. She had smelled it

8

many times before—the bitter, fearful odor of death.

Only a few feet beyond the double doors lay the body of a man, lying face down in the thick carpet, surrounded by a pool of blood, much of which had already caked.

The smell made Alice hold her breath as she walked backward out of the suite, careful neither to touch nor to disturb anything. Outside in the hall, she nudged the front door shut with her foot.

Mrs. Dunne breathed deeply. She'd learned the trick from another Irishwoman who had trained her many years ago. Death, her instructor had warned her, was no stranger to the world of hotels, however grand or luxurious. Rich people died no differently from poor people—and murder was often the ugly companion of death.

That the dead man in Penthouse South was Richard Franklin Winston IV was absolutely certain. Mrs. Dunne knew his clothes, the shape of his trim body, and that crop of unruly black hair which had just begun to be touched by flecks of gray. That he'd fallen into his own blood was obvious even in the quick glance she'd allowed herself.

Mrs. Dunne neither screamed nor held her hand to her mouth to cut off the terror that suddenly hit every nerve of her body. She began to tremble. Instinct and experience told her to allow the shaking to ride through to its natural conclusion. This was not the first corpse she'd met in more than thirty-five years of service at the Grand-Plaza, but that did not make the experience less horrendous.

Ritchie Winston was more than a guest. He had once been close to her—even if he'd been an uncommonly nasty child. Mrs. Dunne continued to breathe deeply, slowly, composing herself so that she was fairly in control by the time she got to the service area. She found the key which opened the room, a combination bar, pantry and linen closet. She flicked on the light and went directly to the telephone.

She dialed the night manager's office and fortunately found him at his desk. When he answered she gave the coded message for death or a serious situation. "Mr. Drexel, this is Alice Dunne. There's been an incident in Penthouse South."

Like Mrs. Dunne, Laurence Drexel had put in years of service at the Grand-Plaza. He understood her message and realized instantly that this was an incident of immense significance. Ritchie Winston was one of America's richest men and the Grand-Plaza's most important guest.

There was no mention of the guest's name as Drexel said, "Stay there, Mrs. Dunne. I'll be right up." There was no need for him to inquire about the housekeeper's wellbeing. She was in control—that was how Alice Dunne always handled herself.

He glanced at the list of security officers employed at the hotel. Tonight's duty was being taken by Pat Donovan. He could be found in the Crystal Room, where the Winston people were holding their Grand Ball.

Drexel chose to speak directly to Donovan. He left his office, crossed the main foyer, ascended the steps leading to the Grand Ballroom and slipped in a side entrance which was being protected by a bellboy. "Good evening, Mr. Drexel," the youth said, as he opened the door for the night manager.

Drexel smiled automatically. But he was upset. He hated "incidents",—they affected the reputation of the hotel, and the Grand-Plaza should be above them. At this time of evening, with the guests just arriving, Drexel suspected he'd find Donovan close to the reception area. He was right. There was no mistaking the detective's boyish good looks or the flare Donovan possessed for appearing to be one of the crowd. Drexel had often remarked that Donovan was the only security officer he'd met in thirty years in the hotel business who could wear a tuxedo and not look like a cop.

He eased over to Donovan's side. "Pat," he said, "there's been an incident in Penthouse South. I'll meet you there. Mrs. Dunne is on the floor."

Laurence Drexel left the Grand Ballroom as he had come. Pat Donovan moved slowly and gracefully through the throng of guests presenting their invitations at the door and walked briskly down the hall to the rear of the building and the service area. He pushed the button of the private elevator and had already appraised the scene by the time Drexel, who took the guest elevator, got to the Penthouse.

"Mr. Drexel," he said, opening the door just a few inches. "There's no need for you to look too closely. But, of course, you must glimpse the body. It's Mr. Winston, all right. Either shot or stabbed. From the odor I'm almost certain it was a gun. I'm going to call the precinct."

Drexel looked into the room. The color drained from his face but otherwise he showed no sign of emotion. Like Alice Dunne and Pat Donovan, who'd been trained for security work in an intensive program sponsored by the hospitality industry, calm and control in the face of emergency, even murder, had been inculcated into his professional personality.

"Do you think there's anyone else inside?" Drexel asked.

"No, that's most unlikely. From the way the blood's

11

congealed on the carpeting, I'd say the incident took place two or three hours ago. Whoever was involved has long since gone."

Donovan walked briskly down the hall to the service room, giving Drexel an opportunity to speak with the housekeeper. "Are you all right, Mrs. Dunne?"

"Thank you, Mr. Drexel. Yes, I am. A little wobbly, that's all."

"Why don't you go into Penthouse North and lie down? I'll call you when the police arrive."

"Thank you, Mr. Drexel."

"Can I get you something to drink? A little brandy?"

Alice Dunne frowned. "Before the police arrive? No, thank you, sir."

Bless Mrs. Dunne, Laurence Drexel thought. She could be counted on to lighten even the grimmest situation with that marvelously unyielding personality. To her the rules of the hotel were as sacred as the Ten Commandments. No drinking while on duty—and heaven forbid that liquor should be noticed on her breath when talking to the police!

Alice Dunne started toward Penthouse North.

"Mrs. Dunne," Drexel asked. "Isn't Miss Harris expected tonight?"

"That she is, Mr. Drexel, but quite late."

Drexel sighed, "I'll have to put her somewhere else. She'll scream bloody mur..."

Drexel stopped the word in mid-syllable. "Wrong word," he told himself.

Alice Dunne shrugged. "By then she'll understand there's no other choice. It's going to be splashed all over television, you know."

Drexel shuddered. He'd been trying to avoid that thought ever since the call from the Penthouse.

"I suppose so," he said, chastened and worried. "You go ahead now, rest a bit."

In the service room, Donovan picked up the phone and dialed an internal number which connected him with a private line in the security office.

"Please disconnect the house phone," he told the operator.

When the private line buzzed, he dialed a number from a list he carried in his pocket. It connected him directly with the administrative office of the Central Park West precinct.

"This is Pat Donovan," he said. "Is Lamark on duty tonight?"

"Yes, Pat. I'll get him for you," a friendly female voice answered. He recognized it as Laura Morgan's.

Seconds later he heard, "Lamark speaking. What's the trouble, Pat?"

"Richard Franklin Winston IV—he's dead. I'm pretty sure he's been murdered, Lieutenant. The identification is ninety percent positive. I did not enter the suite."

"Has anyone else?"

"Alice Dunne, the night housekeeper, discovered the body. She's an old pro. She walked out immediately, closed the door and called Laurence Drexel, the night manager. Everyone's followed the house rules."

"Good. I'll be right over. Probably the service entrance would be best."

"We'd be obliged, Lieutenant. I'll meet you downstairs."

Lamark spoke slowly, "There's a big convention of the Winston company going on, isn't there?"

"Yes. They're having their Grand Ball tonight."

"How soon will they miss him?"

"They must be missing him now."

There was a pause. "I'll call the homicide detail and the Medical Examiner after I get there. We don't want a panic when this gets out."

"There would be a wild mess here—I'm sure of that."

"Have Drexel think of someone close to Winston whom we can use to tell the people quietly."

"Will do, Lieutenant."

"Good. See you in five minutes."

Pat Donovan found Drexel nervously pacing the hall. He felt sorry for the older man. Donovan understood how managers reacted when anything involving the police touched their establishments. To Drexel, it was as devastating as a scandal in his own home.

That Lamark was on duty would reassure him. They were old friends.

Drexel smiled when Donovan told him. "That's fortunate—but I'm thinking of all those people downstairs—the newspapers, television—Ye Gods!—it's going to be a madhouse."

"If you'll excuse me, sir, I'm going downstairs to meet Lamark. He asked if you would locate someone close to Winston who can be told first and help handle the others."

"That would be Donald Laine. Besides being a vice-president and Winston's closest friend, he's a top-flight lawyer."

"Good. After Lamark has seen the premises, we'll find him."

"Whatever the law wants," Drexel said.

For Laurence Drexel, slight, balding, the personification of an unctuous hotel man, a night of horror had begun. His poise was not the match of Alice Dunne's. As soon as Pat Donovan headed for the elevator Drexel raced to the service room and poured a double scotch.

He glanced at the TV camera placed directly across from the pantry at an angle which was supposed to encompass the elevator doors, the hallway and portions of the doors to the penthouse suites. It had never worked. For that matter, neither did any of the elaborate closed television protection, installed at a cost of thousands of dollars. The Grand-Plaza, an old building whose floors had been remodeled time and again, contained too many corners, nooks and crannies to be adapted to television surveillance. Drexel knew the owners had been warned by the installers, but they chose to go ahead anyway. Drexel poured another drink. At least Lieutenant Frank Lamark understood the problem and wouldn't pillory him as that nasty detective-sergeant had done when Norma What-shername's jewels had been stolen.

The sergeant had made himself such a hero at Drexel's expense that the next day, when he came to check the missing items again, he spent several hours in Norma's bed. Cops, Drexel knew, "cooped" in some of those hotels downtown—even reputable ones—but never at the Grand Plaza.

The elevator door slid open. Pat had reached the basement and the service entrance of the Grand-Plaza Hotel.

His instincts told him that whoever had killed Richard Winston IV had long since vanished from the premises. He was equally sure that the killer's traces had been carefully covered.

*   *   *

At ten-thirty, Claudia Milotte had just taken her solo curtain call at the conclusion of her performance in *The*

15

Capri Affair. The play would be ending its long run at the Fiske Theatre on West 49th Street with a matinee at three on Sunday afternoon.

It was a packed house and they had adored Claudia's performance as a vibrant career woman who, engaged in a battle of wits with her elderly mother, becomes a gracious loser, thus emerging with her integrity and dignity intact. It was a fiendishly difficult role, calling for a wide range of moods and abrupt personality changes. Claudia found especially challenging the obligation to keep the character totally under control.

Appreciation of her artistry had been as thunderous at every Broadway performance of the hit play as it was on opening night. Tonight the audience appeared even more enthusiastic than usual. She distinctly heard cries of *Brava*!—and this was a night when Claudia Milotte would need all the support she could find from any direction. She had recently become a widow.

She exited at stage right, walked through the back to take up her position behind the French doors of the set—the living room and patio of a villa at Capri—which she would enter for the ensemble and the last of the curtain calls.

During every one of the more than three hundred performances *The Capri Affair* had played at the Fiske, Claudia gritted her teeth as the final solo curtain was taken by her co-star, Stella Morell, who swept it up like a Neanderthal creature enveloping a cyclone in its arms.

Stella's was the lesser of the two roles and even the Italian star conceded that the finesse with which she was able to dominate her three key scenes would never have been achieved opposite an actress with less strength than Claudia Milotte.

Besides her talents there was Claudia's exquisite beauty. She was a statuesque brunette, five feet six, with lovely, porcelainlike skin. Her green eyes were haunting in their radiance, marvelously expressive when they raged, tempting when they laughed. Her chiseled face was a photographer's dream—she had no bad angles. Her lips were sensuous, completing the picture of the Hollywood Love Goddess she had once declined to become.

At thirty-seven her figure was the envy of women ten and fifteen years her junior. But even with the extra poundage that crept up on her now and then, Claudia's carriage and the gracefulness of her walk appeared to melt it away.

Early in her career one reviewer had described Claudia Milotte as the "ten most beautiful women in the world." Another newspaperman had said, "Meeting Claudia Milotte is not the encounter of journalist and star. It is an *event*."

She had been particularly praised for her work in *The Capri Affair* by critics who admired her capacity for stripping away all frills, avoiding mannerisms that might have crept into a character with so many moods and faces. One reviewer enthused, "Not since Laurette Taylor have we enjoyed an actress so capable of filling the theatre with the presence of her character."

Stella Morell was an exact opposite. She played with all the stops wide open. Her beautiful voice raced up and down the scale, accomplishing effects that Claudia would never have believed possible. She could rage like a lioness without drawing a giggle; and when she purred like a kitten, she wasn't playing to her audience. She was making love to them.

Stella's curtain call was no less dramatic and

overstated than her acting. It was accomplished in the European style, she strode deep into the apron of the stage, bowing to the orchestra section, first the left, then the center section, and finally the right.

When she moved to stage center and flung out her arms, Stella's dark, piercing eyes rose to the mezzanine and swept over the entire audience, expressing her joy to each of them individually. It was a triumph of stagecraft. In spite of being upstaged, Claudia stood in awe of Stella's brazenness. It was like a ballet, staged with such artistry that each move Stella made increased the volume of applause.

Stella was close to sixty, if not already there, but she was still a long distance away from the septuagenarian she portrayed in *The Capri Affair*. In Europe, where Stella had created the role of the Contessa La Monte, she often tore off her gray wig and let a cascade of dyed red hair come flying down over her shoulders. Wisely, to prevent mutiny among his players, producer Reginald Wuthering had forbidden Signora Morell this excursion into circus, even including a clause to this effect in her contract.

Stella accepted the restriction cheerfully when it was pointed out that in the American theatre visiting foreign artists were accorded, by tradition, first billing and the final solo curtain call.

So night after night as Claudia joined Stella and the others for the last company call, the warmth with which she embraced the Italian was as sincere as her admiration for her.

Claudia Milotte had been away from the limelight for too many years to care deeply about the specialness of being a star. She was conscious enough of her value as an actress and a boxoffice personality to insist on the

18

prerogatives of her position, but she abhored the fawning, the obligation of being so patently insincere in her relations with fellow artists and the necessity for maintaining cordial relations with the press.

Of the obligations, she found that getting along with newsmen was quite the easiest. Both in her early years and during *The Capri Affair* she'd been frank and friendly not as a calculated gesture but because that was her nature. She'd made personal friends of many newsmen and women and sometimes wondered why she'd never thought of journalism as a career. She enjoyed people but, of course, she'd never put her writing skills to any tests beyond those required in her school days. "And they weren't many," Claudia frankly admitted.

As an artist, Claudia preferred to think of herself as a custodian of her talent, that it was a special gift, having little to do with the caprices of ladies like Stella whom she personally adored but hadn't the slightest desire to emulate.

There were special and compelling reasons for Claudia to return to the theatre and for these alone she was deeply indebted to Stella Morell. Without her there would have been no American production of *The Capri Affair* and if Stella Morell had not been an avid reader of gossip columns and scandal magazines in a variety of languages, she might never have thought of Claudia for the part of Catherine, Contessa La Monte's daughter by her French lover.

*   *   *

Although *The Capri Affair* had one more performance to play in New York before touring, this *was the final*

19

Saturday night. So ushers began appearing at the side aisles carrying bouquets of flowers for the two women stars, who deftly picked out single stems to offer the male members of the small company: Robin Haywood, the juvenile, and Keith Rodgers-Byrne, the character actor.

The gesture was the handiwork of Reginald Wuthering, who had not only produced *The Capri Affair* but had also directed it. Wuthering, a tall, spare, white-haired gentleman of seventy, who had never worked at any profession but the theater, took pride in his reputation as one of the "old guard"—producers who preferred taste to corn, and who believed in treating their associates, from star to office boy, with respect.

"How sweet of Reg to think of this!" Stella said to Claudia as the final curtain fell.

"Yes, he's such a dear!" Claudia's answer sounded hollow, even to her.

Standing in the wings, obviously waiting for her, was Donald Laine. At his side Claudia noticed a darkly handsome man of average height whose inscrutable expression was a dead giveaway. He was a policeman.

"But an awfully good-looking one," Claudia thought, as she walked closer and noticed his clean-cut features, gray eyes and sturdy physique. There was a good deal of muscle, strength, and, damn it, animal attraction in that solid body. By the gray in his dark lustrous hair, Claudia fixed him at about forty-four—the same age as Ritchie.

As she embraced Donald, resorting to one of those backstage clichés, "How sweet of you to come!" Claudia's mind was actually centered on her renewed interest in men. It had been a long time since she had allowed herself to think about them in any but vertical positions. Lately she had imagined herself being intimate with Donald

Laine, in spite of the platonic nature of their long friendship. It wasn't a caprice. Donald Laine was a very desirable male, someone a lonely woman would be unlikely to pass up, given an opportunity. He stood well over six feet, with wide shoulders and a physique which he kept fit by exercising regularly. He looked like a football player turned businessman and attorney—at least that was his story. Perhaps it had been colored through the years, but whose background hadn't—her own included?

Regardless, Donald stood out in a crowd. His body, she'd known from days around the pool, had the graceful muscular lines of a swimmer. Nature had been helped in maintaining the sheen of Donald's golden locks. He explained the dark, silky patina of his skin as the product of an "intrusion on an English family by an Italian grandmother—bless her!"

Besides his looks and charm that often seemed too calculated for comfort, Claudia liked Donald and admired him. He had a reputation as one of the most skillful corporation lawyers in the country and Claudia believed what had been common rumor for years, that Winston and Associates would never have survived Richard Winston's impetuousness without the restraints imposed by his vice-president and close friend.

Donald had been chosen for his role in the Winston conglomorate by Ritchie's father, who met him when he was a young man attending college on a sports scholarship. Donald was Ritchie's roommate. Winston took him into the firm at the same time that Ritchie started his training.

"You'll balance each other. Ritchie's a speculator, a gambler like his grandfather," the older Winston told Donald. "There are going to be times when you'll have to pull him out of the clouds and bring him down to earth—before he brings down the company."

Claudia bussed Donald warmly and the tall man flung his arm protectively around her waist as he introduced Lieutenant Frank Lamark.

"This is an honor, Madame Milotte," the detective said, as his eyes turned to Donald as if to signal a cue for him to explain their presence.

"Claudia, may we go into your dressing room? We have some news for you."

"It sounds ominous."

"I'm afraid it is," Donald said, guiding her toward the short flight of steps from the stage which led to her dressing room. Lamark followed.

Inside, Claudia offered the men the choice of an armchair or a chaise lounge. Donald closed the door. Lamark, however, opened it, looked outside, then half closed it again. He slipped a hand into the inside pocket of his jacket, pulled out a wallet and flashed the badge of his office before Claudia's bewildered eyes.

"Sorry, Miss Milotte," he said, "but this is police procedure." He looked at the closed door of what obviously was the bathroom.

"May I?" he said.

"Of course," Claudia answered.

Lamark opened the door, walked inside, came back and again left the door ajar.

Lamark's gray eyes again turned to Donald.

"Claudia, I have shocking news. Richard is dead."

Claudia's hands flew to her mouth. "Richard! Dead? It's impossible. I saw him yesterday. He was the picture of health. I told him so. He hasn't looked better in years..."

Then, remembering that she was a bitter woman, she

22

added, "Of course, when you think of the sort of woman he's been running around with, anything could happen... burning the candle at both ends... still... I find it hard to believe...."

Lamark interrupted, "Miss Milotte, Richard Winston didn't die of natural causes. He was murdered. He was shot at close range in the chest and heart. He died instantly. The crime took place in the penthouse at the Grand-Plaza."

Claudia fell back to the dressing table, holding on to it for support. Donald moved to help her into a chair. She brushed the attempt aside, found her own way.

"Murdered!" She whispered the word. "How ghastly! What a dreadful way to die!"

Donald took the armchair; Lamark remained standing. "If you don't mind, Miss Milotte, there are some questions I am required to ask you—in privacy."

"Of course I don't mind, Lieutenant. Will you excuse us, Donald?"

A querulous look crossed Laine's face.

Lamark caught it. A faint smile twisted his lips. "Counselor, I intend asking Miss Milotte the same questions I asked you. Very simple ones—there's no need to worry. No one we've talked to so far is even faintly implicated in the crime. Before we get around to reading constitutional rights, police usually have a suspect. Miss Milotte hardly fits that."

"I'm sorry, Lieutenant. Of course, I understand."

He turned to Claudia, whose head was buried in her hands. "I'll be waiting outside."

When Donald closed the door this time, Lamark allowed it to remain shut.

Claudia dabbed at her eyes as she pulled herself back to

an upright position. "This is horrible, Lieutenant. I'm terribly upset. Such a dreadful thing to happen. I should be crying, I suppose, but I'm afraid that's impossible. I'm too numb to react emotionally. Richard and I have been—I imagine you know this—we've been separated for two years. For many years before that there was no marriage in the true sense. Our relationship has been anything but friendly. To be blunt, it's been extremely bitter. However, that doesn't mean I won't mourn his death...not...not after so many years. To imagine Ritchie murdered is so horrible! Why? Who would want to kill Ritchie?"

Lamark seated himself on the chaise lounge. "Miss Milotte, your friend Donald Laine has explained your relationship with the victim. I'm not here to inquire into that at present."

Claudia eyed the detective warily.

"I have only two or three brief questions to ask and I hope you'll answer them simply—for your sake. You're distraught, my presence unnerves you. You're right, you'll mourn your husband. There's going to be a delayed reaction to his death. It happens all the time."

"Thank you, Lieutenant."

"My first question is, when did you last see your husband?"

"Yesterday afternoon."

"Where?"

"At the Grand-Plaza Hotel."

"In the Penthouse Suite?"

"Yes, Lieutenant."

"Was there a particular reason for the meeting?"

"Yes. We close here tomorrow and a week from Monday we open in Boston, the first stop on a tour across

24

the country. We know we'll be on the road throughout the winter; hopefully, well into spring. Then we may go to London. Because I would be on the road, Richard wanted to see me privately about arranging a settlement for either a legal separation or a divorce."

"Was any decision reached?"

"No, Lieutenant. It wasn't the first time he tried to separate me from my lawyers, but I followed their advice. I refused to decide anything without my attorney's approval."

"A fortune is involved, is it not?"

Claudia's laugh hung in the air, a bitter, angry sound.

"Millions and millions and millions—none of which I need."

"I can imagine that."

"May I ask you something, Lieutenant?"

"Of course."

"Your name? You're French, aren't you?"

"Yes, by descent. Both my parents were born in France. But I'm a native New Yorker."

She laughed, and this time the sound was light and airy, as though it were planted in a script. "An actress in New York becomes well acquainted with the police. They help get us through storms to the theater and we entertain at Police Benevolent Association performances. We do lots of things for one another. I've met some policemen's families. I even have their names in my phone book. Names of Irish cops, Italian, Jewish and Hispanic officers. You're the first Frenchman I've met."

Lamark smiled. It was a dazzling smile, Claudia thought.

He shook his head. "We're not that rare, Miss Milotte, but to tell you the truth I've come across only one other

Frenchman on the force. He works in Brooklyn but we meet now and then." He glanced at his watch. "I don't want to hold you up. Let me ask this—was your parting friendly?"

"Friendly? Yes—for us, that is. He didn't throw me out of the apartment. We shook hands, he wished me good luck on the tour and even opened the door for me."

"And afterward?"

"It was only six o'clock. I had a bite to eat at the coffee shop on the mezzanine and walked to the theater."

"Isn't that quite a walk?"

"You're joking, Lieutenant. Ten or fifteen blocks. That's not much."

"But with the crowds?"

"I enjoy them. They make me feel alive."

"Do people recognize you?"

"Today? No, only occasionally. If they do I stop and talk, sign their autograph books if they have them. I enjoy being friends with people who say they enjoy me. I gave up my career when I married Richard . . ."

"When was that?"

"Twelve years ago."

"Now I have only a few more questions. Can you describe your movements today?"

"Of course. Today is Saturday. We have a matinee at two thirty. I arrived at the theater at twelve thirty and got ready, leisurely to do the show. Generally I stay in my dressing room between shows when there are two performances. Today I was here except for a half hour or so when I went across the street to Ginny's for a light supper. I stopped at the boxoffice to ask about some tickets for friends who are coming tomorrow afternoon, and then I came back here."

26

"I've heard that actresses stayed in their dressing rooms as you said, but I didn't believe it. A theater without a performance—like now—it seems big, cold, empty."

"Not at all, Lamark. Not when it's your life—your work. I feel quite differently. An empty theater is part of the magic. You see it now—dark with only a work light on the stage—and you know that in a few hours it'll be transformed into anything you choose to make it. And in the auditorium there will sit several hundred people, sometimes two thousand, waiting for the artist to lead them out of their hundrumlives into other worlds. That's why I enjoy this play. It's *real* theater—and I imagine that's why I'm always eager to give it my best. You must see it."

"I hope to."

"Well, tomorrow's your last chance, unless you come to Boston. Anyhow, to clarify your question, an actress my age isn't equipped to stand in front of all that light without some assistance. My make-up is complicated, and it has nothing to do with vanity. Time ages the eyes. I need them to express moods, and they must be so cleverly made up that they can be seen in the farthest corner of the theater. Then my hairstyle belongs to the character. It's not my choice, it's much too elaborate. Making sure it's in perfect order takes an hour. On matinee days, then, I stay put. If I go out I protect my hair with a scarf against the wind. Even a light breeze can ruin all that work."

The police officer pointed to a wig on the dressing table.

"Don't you use that?"

"You haven't seen the play, dear Lieutenant. I wear the wig for just a few minutes in the last act. It attaches to a hat. It's here to be combed some time next week so that

27

it'll be presentable when we open in Boston."

Lamark's smile sent a shiver up her spine as he rose, saying, "Thank you for your time, Mrs. Winston. I regret having intruded—especially with police business. I hope you understand that the questions were necessary."

Claudia stood up to open the door. "Have you any idea...do you know...oh, I suppose it's a ridiculous question...."

"Who killed your husband? No, I haven't. But I imagine I'm going to find when I return to my office that a vast amount of information has been accumulated by my staff and the medical examiner's office. A man of Richard Winston's importance! Miss Milotte, every detective and patrolman in New York City will become involved in the search for his killer."

"A regular manhunt," Claudia ventured.

Lamark's tongue touched his lips ever so slightly. "You could also describe it as a woman hunt, couldn't you?"

Claudia's voice turned harsh. "Yes, you could. There were women in Ritchie's life...many women."

There was a slight pause. "You'll find that out, Lieutenant. Anyhow, thank you for your thoughtfulness. But then, we're both French and we understand courtesy...especially...well...in a situation like this."

Claudia extended her hand. Lamark held it gently and brushed his lips against it.

Claudia pulled back her hand and clasped it with the other. "Lieutenant, can you imagine what they would think of this on Centre Street?"

Lamark's face lighted up in that devastating smile. "*Oui*, Madame. Several times. Thank you."

* * *

With the dressing room door closed, Claudia walked wearily to the make-up table. Whatever else they ask of me tonight, I must get out of this make-up, she told herself, holding out her hands and discovering they had begun to tremble. Not enough to worry about, but she'd prefer that it not be noticed. She closed her eyes, fixed her mind determinedly on the task in hand, getting into street clothes. In a few seconds the trembling stopped.

Lamark found Donald Laine and Reginald Wuthering standing by the light board talking earnestly. At the stage door entrance the doorman and crew were pushing the door closed and bolting it against an onslaught of reporters, photographers and television newsmen. Richard Winston's murder had broken in the press. It was amazing that it had held for so long.

Lieutenant Lamark drew Laine's attention by tapping the attorney on the shoulder. "I'm leaving now. Thanks for your help. I have your card and will probably call in the morning. The body will have to be officially identified after the autopsy.

"We'll need to have Miss Milotte present at some point. I don't know when. As for our short meeting, I can assure you it went extremely well, considering the conditions. The sudden shock of hearing of the murder of someone close totally destroys many women, they become hysterical. I can understand it—even men aren't totally immune. Miss Milotte is a remarkable person."

"I've always thought that, Lieutenant. I appreciate your kindness. I'll be available any time you need me."

Wuthering spoke up. "Lieutenant, if you'd rather not talk to the press you can avoid them by using our tunnel. It crosses under 49th Street to the Forrest theater and you can leave by the stage entrance there. I have the keys."

Lamark expressed astonishment at the existence of a tunnel connecting two major theaters smack in the middle of Manhattan.

"Of course you wouldn't know about the years when the basements of the Fiske and Forrest served as a sort of storage center for the underworld. We call it our 'arsenal.'"

"It's a new one on me."

"I'm not surprised," Wuthering said. "Not many people knew about it then, and we haven't been eager to publicize its existence after the fact."

Wuthering, a raconteur of considerable skill, settled himself in his chair, ready to recall some facts of ancient Broadway history which in many respects were as dramatic and colorful as the plays found on the stages of the Great White Way.

Donald, realizing this was hardly the time for a blow-by-blow account, interrupted the old man and gave a capsule summary of the tunnel's history.

"It was the Great Depression, Lieutenant, and money was hard to find. Producers turned to the underworld which, even as it is today, was overloaded with cash. And the biggest of them, Frank Costello, Joe Adonis, Jack "Legs" Diamond—they all backed shows. They got some of their kicks by hanging around the stage doors ogling the beauties. Even the great Florenz Ziegfeld had to deal with hoods to get the last shows of his career as far as opening night.

"With their producers indebted to hoods, the theaters were also expected to pay tribute. The alternative might be a stink bomb tossed into the auditorium during a performance. So the property owners cooperated. In this theater, for example, the syndicate hid their firearms—

everything from machine guns to whatever they called the 'Saturday night special' back in the thirties.

"Anyhow, in digging around the cellars the hoods found a tunnel that led across the street to the Forrest. They installed steel doors on either side, probably figuring they might use the route one day as an escape hatch. I don't know whether they did or didn't.

"And no one knows the 'why' of the tunnel. Most likely it was once a spur line, carrying material to the men who were digging the subway. That would be at the turn of the century. Old subway maps show the existence of several spur lines. A few of them have even been uncovered, but quickly forgotten because no one knew what to do about them.

"Lieutenant Lamark, believe me, archeologists of the future will never understand when they try to figure out what lies under the cement of this extraordinary city. Even the diggers today aren't sure whether they're patching the right places or simply working on pipes that begin nowhere and end nowhere."

"It sounds fascinating," Lamark said, "but I'm going to have to go out the way I came—through the stage entrance. I have to tell the press what I know, which, unfortunately, is very little. Perhaps tomorrow, when I hope to see your play, Mr. Wuthering, you'll show me the tunnel."

"Delighted, Lieutenant. Are you sure you're coming?"

"Quite sure."

"Then I'd better find a pair of tickets for you. We're literally sold out, but there's always a house seat or two held until curtain time."

"One ticket will do, thank you."

He shook hands with the two men and walked to the stage door, which the doorman opened just far enough for

31

the detective to step outside and hold up his arms to the press.

They recognized Frank Lamark immediately. Questions popped like firecrackers. He remained silent until the questions died down. It was an old trick and no one accomplished it with more finesse than Lamark. His skill at handling the press, even in the touchiest situation, was widely admired. Lamark managed where other officers flubbed because of his reputation for honesty, he never fooled around with the facts or held back any details that could be revealed without prejudicing an investigation.

Occasionally consulting his notes, Lamark began, "Richard Winston IV was found dead in his penthouse apartment at the Grand-Plaza Hotel this evening at approximately nine-fifteen. He had checked into the hotel earlier in the week because of a convention of the Winston and Associates company, of which he was the president.

"Mr. Winston's body was discovered by the night housekeeper, Mrs. Alice Dunne, while making her evening rounds. She saw the body lying face down as she entered the apartment. Noting the pool of blood surrounding it, Mrs. Dunne immediately got in touch with the night manager and the hotel's security officer, Pat Donovan. The police and the Medical Examiner's office were promptly notified.

"At this point I can only say that Mr. Winston's assailant used a revolver and the victim was shot at close range. We believe the killing took place between six and seven P.M., while Mr. Winston was preparing for the Grand Ball which concluded the convention tonight.

"During most of the day the suite was seldom locked, since Mr. Winston used it for numerous private conversations with executives who had received invitations from the company's vice-president, Donald Laine.

We have reason to believe, however, that the door *was* locked at five o'clock, when Mr. Winston went downstairs to a conference room where he made an address to the new executives of the company. His movements afterward are still unconfirmed so I can't comment on them at this time."

"What about the visit of the mystery woman?" a reporter yelled.

"I have received no information to that effect."

"Was there any special reason why you came to the theater?"

"Yes. We knew that Mrs. Winston—the actress Claudia Milotte—was performing tonight. I accompanied Mr. Laine, who requested that notification of Mr. Winston's death be withheld from the press until it had been given to his widow. This is common police policy. We try, when possible, to notify the next of kin first in all cases of death under unusual circumstances."

"Do you consider Miss Milotte to be Winston's next of kin, Lieutenant Lamark?" shouted another voice.

"So far as I was aware, she was still his wife."

"Did you speak to her?"

"Yes, we spoke at length about matters which at this time remain unconfirmed. I am afraid, gentleman, that about sums up the information available tonight. There will be further details available in the morning after we have obtained the report of the medical examiner."

"Would you say that Mr. Winston was shot by persons known or unknown?" asked a young voice.

Lamark answered the question seriously. Cubs, he knew, often became top reporters. "I imagine that's the best way to describe the tragedy. Now, if you'll excuse me. . . ."

He made his way to a waiting police car and popped

inside, and in a second the car, siren screeching, whirled eastward, headed in the direction of the office of the Medical Examiner.

At Third and Lexington Lamark dismissed the driver. "Take the car in, Officer," he said. "They'll be working on this autopsy all night. You're not going to get a word out of that office for hours—not with a corpse as important as Ritchie Winston. I'll get off here and have a bite to eat. My place is down the street."

"Okay, Lieutenant, whatever you say."

"Goodnight, Officer," Lamark mumbled, as he stepped out of the car, his mind trying to juggle the impressions he had received about a murder which, as far as he could see in the murky present, was going to lie in the "unsolved" file for a good long time.

Lamark could find no rational reason for his hunch. It was born in part from experience and in a larger sense from instinct.

He worried. His instincts were usually right.

*　　*　　*

Claudia, beginning to show the after-effects Lamark had predicted, decided against the tunnel.

"I went through it once. A stagehand took me. I wonder why Wuthering wanted to bring that up with the police."

"It seemed natural enough," Donald said.

"He's foolish sometimes. Well, the damage is done. I'd better face the press now, maybe you can persuade them to lay off at the apartment. Will you try?"

"Of course," Donald said, as he went outside and negotiated a deal with the reporters. It was late, so there was little resistance to his quid pro quo suggestion. They'd

34

call off the newsmen who were staking out Sutton Place and the ones here promised not to follow her car.

When Donald returned, Claudia's room was filled with her fellow actors and members of the crew. Billy Briggs, the stage manager, stood at the door, ushering them in and out with quiet authority.

It was a tense and awkward situation for everyone, but it seemed the thing to do. Everyone realized that Claudia's marriage to Richard Winston had soured, but there were old friendships involved.

Richard Winston, to all outward appearances, had fallen into none of the excesses of the young millionaire, and everyone approved his marriage to Claudia, a beautiful but sensible, no-nonsense young woman who unhesitatingly abandoned a career which had not yet peaked in favor of marriage. There were a few snide remarks that the American girl, reared in France, had traded her career for the security so prized by the French. But these comments came from sources who knew very little of the love affair. By all the signs, Ritchie and Claudia had entered into a marriage which promised more than security; it offered love and mutual respect.

Stella was the last one of the cast members. "My dear," she said, "they should never have written that song *Che Sera Sera*. It makes an old truth sound banal: What will be, will be. There's a reason for this tragedy and one day it will be made clear to you. Hold fast, *cara*, there are people who need you."

Donald entered the room as Stella was leaving. Her dark eyes appeared to look straight through him to some point in the world *beyond*. It was chilling. Stella placed a bony hand on his shoulder. "Take good care of our Claudia, Mr. Laine. She is a very special person. We must protect her."

35

Billy Briggs closed the dressing room door, stationing himself in front of it to ward off any more visitors.

Donald Laine never felt comfortable in the presence of Stella Morell. She was an overwhelming woman who dominated any room she entered. She was chunky in figure now, but the patrician beauty of her face had not faded. She was an elegant woman who carried herself with the regal bearing of a queen.

In Europe's post-war jet-set gossip, Stella had been linked with consorts who ranged from deposed monarchs to American movie stars and an occasional chauffeur. Like Anna Magnani, to whom she was often compared, Stella had come to stardom the hard way. She was born into a famous circus family but, lacking physical agility, she moved into the field of Italian revues as a singing comedienne.

Nino Bellafiore, the only man she married, encouraged Stella to become a dramatic actress, a metamorphosis that proved successful. When Stella's age and girth ended her credibility as a leading lady, Nino wrote plays and films in which he created *Grand Guignol*-type roles which produced a whole new audience for the actress. *The Capri Affair* was Bellafiore's last work. He had directed the first production of the play, with Stella as the contessa, five years earlier, a decade after their marriage.

It was a triumph, maintaining Stella's prestige as Italy's first actress, but the success was bittersweet. Bellafiore died a year later. His death was called a suicide, but there were rumors that another woman had come into his life and killed him in a fit of passion.

In Italy's scandal press, Stella was quoted as having vowed revenge against the unidentified mistress, but privately the actress conceded nothing to the suicide verdict.

To intimates she said quietly, "His health was failing fast. We both knew it. Truthfully, I was not surprised."

Stella's somber words reminded Donald briefly of the coincidence in the lives of Claudia and Stella, two women apparently thrust together by fate, luck or destiny, in a human drama which one had survived and the other was about to face.

Donald's voice cracked when he said, "I've talked to the reporters, Claudia. It's Saturday and it's late. They appear to be quite satisfied with a statement. There may be some stragglers or diehards at the apartment...."

"I expect so," Claudia said. "We'll face that problem when we get there. How do I look?" she added.

"Marvelous, under the circumstances. What an awful day! I wonder if I'll ever forget it!"

"You won't darling," Claudia said quietly. She walked toward the tall blond man and kissed him affectionately on the lips, touching his hand and stroking it affectionately.

"Let's hold on—as Stella says."

She took his hand, opened the door and led him to the stage door. "Hold it a second, Charlie," she told the doorman. "Put your arm around me," she said to Donald. "The more fragile I seem, the sooner this thing will be over."

When the stage door opened Claudia stood before it leaning on Donald's arm, achieving the effect of fragility she hoped for. Like Frank Lamark, she'd experienced enough meetings with the press under dramatic circumstances to wait for silence instead of trying to field wild questions. She stepped away briefly from Donald's protection to shake hands and talk with a *Telegram* reporter she'd known for years.

This stopped the clamor.

Given the opportunity, Claudia spoke quietly and calmly.

"I am deeply distressed by the death of Richard Winston who, in the several years of our marriage, showed me happiness that I had never known before or that I have since enjoyed. Our separation over the last two years may have diminished the emotional impact of this sudden horrible news, I don't know. I might collapse right now, or maybe tomorrow. The horrendous experience of having a beloved human being snuffed out by murder isn't easy to adjust to. I know that I echo the words of everyone who knew Ritchie Winston when I say we've lost a wonderful human being, a great gentleman, a quiet philanthropist—oh, yes, I know much more about his generosity than you'll find in those foundation reports— and a giant in the business world."

She paused. "What else can I say? Nothing. The shock is too deep. I am sorry...."

There was silence for a few seconds. When Claudia and Donald began to move, the newspapermen made a path to the limousine waiting at the curb, its motor running. She thought she had conquered.

Almost—but not quite.

The last cries she heard came from reporters at the rear, who shoved their heads into the car as Donald and the driver tried to shut the window.

"Were you the mystery woman, Miss Milotte, who visited Winston this afternoon?"

"Is it true, Claudia, that you're going to be the richest woman in America?"

Claudia buried her head in her hands. Donald pushed the men away and finally managed to close the rear door. The driver quickly spun the car into the quiet traffic of Broadway after midnight.

* * *

No reporters were visible at Sutton Place. Andy, the doorman, was seated directly behind the locked glass doors. He had opened them before Claudia stepped from the car. She walked out of sight of the street while Donald and the driver decided whether he should wait for Laine or call it a night.

"Tell you what, Michael," Laine said, "I'll call down in ten minutes, if you don't mind."

"Not at all, sir," Michael said. He was the driver for the company, usually assigned to Claudia. "And, sir," he said, "please tell her how unhappy I am that she's been so upset. A lovely lady, Mr. Laine. Everyone loves her. It's always the good people who get struck by these awful tragedies."

"Miss Milotte will appreciate knowing how you feel."

He loped across the pavement, joining Claudia at the elevator.

"Bless that wonderful Rose," Claudia said, "she heard the news on the radio. Evidently it didn't break in time for the eleven o'clock TV news. Anyhow, Andy tells me she hopped into a cab and is upstairs."

Donald smiled. "As Michael said, everybody loves you, Claudia."

They stepped out at the fourth floor, where Claudia had chosen an apartment which seemed to lie right along the bank of the East River. It was unexpected and, as people said when they noticed the effect, "So charming. Everyone expects you to be hung way up in the sky on Sutton Place, looking at the view. But what kind of view is there on the East Side? You never look down at the river, but here it is, almost in Claudia's living room."

Rose opened the door at the sound of the elevator.

"Good evening, Mr. Laine," she said, and as she took

39

Claudia's bag, her big eyes brimmed with tears. "I'm so sorry, Miss Claudia. I hate misery."

The tall, handsome black woman, dressed in a smart suit, brushed the tears away with her fingers. "I just got here, Miss Claudia. All I had time to do was to get out the ice and set up the bar. May I get you something to eat?" She continued, as she opened the living room door and started for the kitchen.

"Not yet, Rose. A little later, perhaps. You'll stay the night, won't you?"

"Of course, Miss Claudia."

Donald headed for the bar. "Excuse me, Claudia, but I need this. You know my male chauvinism—Adam and Eve, Mr. and Mrs., and women and children last." He poured a shot of bourbon into a glass and knocked it down straight. Then he turned to Claudia. "Now, may I offer you. . . ."

Claudia laughed for the first time since she'd heard the news. "A gin and tonic, please. My throat is dry and parched. You know, the nerves are running together—the performance, talking to Lamark and all the others, then the press. It seems to me I've been on stage forever."

She fell into one of the easy chairs, kicked off her shoes as Donald brought her the drink.

He spun back to the bar, mixed a strong highball and fell like a lump into the chair opposite Claudia.

"What happens now, Donald?"

Laine took a long drink. Then there was silence while his eyes roamed through the room, settling on the ceiling for what seemed an eternity. Finally he put down the glass, bent over, placed his elbows on his knees, folded his hands and said, "I was afraid you were going to ask me that."

"Why, Donald? Is it so horrible?"

"Death is never pleasant for those who survive. It's an agony for those who have endured the horror of a crime. Murder is not a private affair, dear Claudia. It's public—very public. The state is now in charge. Ritchie's body is in the custody of the Medical Examiner. We are at the disposition of Lieutenant Lamark and eventually of the District Attorney."

"You make it sound ghastly."

"More ghastly than what happened to Richard Winston?"

"You know what I mean," Claudia said, instantly regretting the gaffe.

"Of course, dear Claudia. Who's sure of what he's saying tonight?"

Donald stood up, walked into the hall and picked up the house phone. "Andy, this is Mr. Laine. I won't be using Michael any more tonight. Will you tell him that, please?"

Then Donald headed for the bar, mixed another drink, glanced at Claudia's glass.

"I'm nursing this one, Donald."

He flopped back into the easy chair.

"Are you sure you want all this now?"

"I'm going to have to know about it eventually," Claudia answered.

"A murder investigation is complicated," Donald began. "It involves a lot of people besides those who are close to the victim. First, as you saw, the police were notified. Lieutenant Lamark appears now to be in charge of the case. As soon as the Grand-Plaza security man notified him that a body had been found dead under conditions that could not be certified by a physician, he reported the fact to the office of the Medical Examiner.

"Both the police and a team from the Medical

Examiner's office go to the place where the body has been found. The Medical Examiner or one of his deputies 'takes charge of the body.' This is the law. He must fully investigate the essential facts concerning the circumstances of the death, and take the names and addresses of witnesses, if there are any, before leaving the premises. He also takes possession of anything found on the body or in the area that might prove useful in establishing the cause of death.

"If a simple examination of the body can determine the cause of death, it ends there. In the case of a crime, an autopsy is performed.

"That, I imagine, is what's happening now. It will be a through autopsy, I can assure you, because of Ritchie's importance. An autopsy reveals the exact cause of death. It can also determine with some degree of accuracy when death occurred. An autopsy can be very revealing. Often it leads the police straight to the murderer.

"The Medical Examiner speaks for the dead to protect the living. It's a job filled with pressures—from everybody. Insurance companies are involved, so are relatives and business associates of the deceased. The police and the District Attorney also have a stake in what comes out of his findings.

"When they're assembled, the medical facts are put together with whatever information the police have accumulated. In a case like Ritchie's where no doubt exists that a man's been murdered, the D.A. will take his information to the Grand Jury and press for a finding of murder."

"But against whom?"

"Nobody. At least none that I know of at this moment. It will simply read that Richard Winston was killed by some person or persons unknown. Acting on this, the police will pursue an investigation. All of us, I imagine, will appear before the Grand Jury. You, me, some executives of the corporation, the housekeeper, the hotel's security man and night manager, Lamark—well, just about everybody."

"When will that happen?"

"In a day or two. We go inside one by one and tell what we know. You say exactly what you told Lamark tonight. I do the same thing."

"Do you know about this 'mystery woman'?"

"I'd laugh if I could, it's so ludicrous. Mystery woman! Mystery *women*! That would be more like it."

"I know."

"Claudia, you realize that in the years you've been separated from Ritchie I've told you many confidential things, but I was careful never to betray him or give him a reason to distrust me. The affairs, the violent mood changes, his tempers and tantrums, deep depressions—all that I told you—were facts known to many of us. I wanted you to be aware of the truth. I felt that was part of my job. I owed it to Richard and to the company. You were still his wife and, for reasons which I never questioned and do not now understand, you refused to agree to a divorce."

"Yes, Donald. I know these things and I've appreciated them. I often wondered why you provided me with so much information. Thank you for explaining. You were hoping that I would understand him better."

"Yes," Donald said. "That was it—in part."

"And the other part?"

Donald nervously finished his drink, headed for the bar again and mixed a highball. "That's for some other time, not tonight."

When he sat down, Donald resumed, "There were so many women around in the last year that even I couldn't keep track; I don't believe Richard could, either. They were everywhere and they employed all sorts of ways to get to him. Usually I found out they were doing exactly what he'd told them to. He had a passion for appearing to keep that superactive sex life of his a secret. It was impossible. No man in public view as Winston was could possibly have expected to—unless he were the President and enjoyed the protection of a loyal staff, Secret Service and the United States Army.

"Yesterday, around six, when we were in the Green Room and Richard was talking to the young executives, a bellboy came in with a note for him. He read it, stuffed it in his pocket, pulled out the key to Penthouse South, gave it to the bellboy. 'Tell the lady to go right up, I'll be there shortly. No need to accompany her, she knows the way.'

"That's the mystery woman. That's how a lot of mystery women showed up—through little notes, by telephoning, sometimes by taking another room in a hotel while Richard was traveling.

"There's very little to go on with respect to yesterday's mystery woman. No one remembered her very well. She asked the head porter to deliver the note to Mr. Winston. She believed he was in the Green Room. It didn't take a magician to discover that fact. The meeting was posted on the convention schedule at about five different points in the hotel. It stated clearly that Winston was going to speak.

"The porter recalled she was wearing tinted glasses. She struck him as being about twenty-eight or so, blonde hair, nothing distinguished about her. She had on one of those vinyl transparent raincoats. Nothing unusual about that. They were predicting occasional rain, as I recall.

"If the mystery woman turns out to be the killer they're going to have to find some specific piece of evidence

44

linking her to the crime right away. Either that or go through Ritchie's little black book, and I don't believe that would help. He didn't need to keep telephone numbers. A man as attractive as Ritchie—on the loose, easily available—the chicks came crawling out of the woodwork for a crack at him."

"To me it sounds very sad," Claudia said.

"You're right, it *was* sad. Everyone knew that—except Ritchie."

"Why would a strange woman want to kill him?"

"Claudia, I don't believe it was a woman. If the mystery woman is ever discovered, it's my guess she was used as a plant—sent into the situation simply to get hold of the key and divert attention from the real murderer."

"The way you say that makes me think you know who the real murderer was."

"Be careful, Claudia, don't read a different meaning into my words."

"I'm sorry . . . I didn't mean. . . ."

"Forget it, baby. Let's not be naive. Winston and Associates has many enemies. Old man Winston and his father had enemies. Ritchie created a whole new group of enemies."

"So there are men who would have liked to see him dead."

"Yes, Claudia. You know some of them. You probably entertained them when you and Ritchie were living together. You recall those big parties out on Long Island—people came from all over the globe. Just as they did this week to attend the convention at the Grand-Plaza."

"Yes, Donald, I remember it all. I know who you're talking about. The police never catch up with men like that."

45

"And that's a good place to end our speculation. It's a job for the police—not for us."

"Donald, do you really believe I'm going to be the richest woman in America?"

"Maybe not the richest, but you're going to control a helluva lot of money, stock, and God knows what else. Even under the widow's third of an estate mandated by law, you can buy and sell most people in this fancy apartment house of yours."

"I don't like that idea, not one bit. Donald, have you seen the will?"

"I'm going to take a nightcap for that one, Claudia. How about you?"

"If you would, please."

Donald mixed two drinks, handed Claudia the gin and tonic, and remained standing.

"Claudia, I stayed as far away from Ritchie's will as I could. It wasn't difficult, he didn't want me near it. It was handled by another firm, a big law partnership, Jameson, Dodge & Sawyer. I haven't the faintest idea of what's in it, what it does to me or for me. I know that it's going to be complicated because you're his legal widow. Maybe it means you'll have more than if you'd taken his offers of a settlement. Maybe you'll have less. But you make complications, that's for sure. And since we're being so candid, why in God's name didn't you give in and take one of his offers?"

"I know you won't believe this," Claudia said very slowly. "It was because one day I knew he'd come back to me."

Finally tears streamed down her cheeks. The delayed reaction hit—and it hit hard. The sobs grew into hysterics, drawing Rose from the kitchen.

She wrapped Claudia in her sturdy arms and held her

46

like a child. "Just let it all out, baby, let it go. You've got to, that's the only way."

The black woman nodded to Donald. "She'll be all right, Mr. Laine. You go ahead, leave me to take care of this. Call me any time tonight if you want to. I'll have the phone on in my room."

Claudia's sobs began to subside as she heard the apartment door open and click shut. She waited for the sound of the elevator doors.

"Good," she said, then pulling herself away from Rose's arms. "Thank you, dear. Now let's have something to eat. I'm famished. How about some French toast?"

"Fine, Miss Claudia," Rose said, as she walked, without questioning Claudia's behavior, into the kitchen.

*   *   *

Frank Lamark missed the old Automats where he had been able to sit and think out a case over a cup of coffee—or even several cups, when the Automat people got fussy about customers lingering on their premises. He disliked coffee shops, they were too utilitarian for his taste. He might have enjoyed bars, but they'd never given him an opportunity to judge their facilities as "think tanks." New York bartenders took a dim view of quiet men who sit for a couple of hours over two glasses of red wine. So Frank had measured need with facility and compromised by patronizing a couple of delicatessen-restaurants on Third Avenue which served fine, but expensive, coffee, although you were also expected to order something edible. But a piece of cake or pie satisfied the management, though Frank could have done without either.

At Murray's Deli the corner booth he usually occupied

47

was empty. Almost as soon as he sat down, Frank was brought a steaming cup by a heavy, middle-aged waitress with dyed blonde hair who'd introduced herself as Sondra when he first became a regular, more than a year ago.

"I'll try cheesecake tonight," Frank said.

"You didn't touch it last time, Mr. Lamark. Try the apple pie. Not sweet—I promise you. Had it myself."

"Fine, thank you."

He knew it would be sweeter than a birthday cake but this was no time to argue: it was difficult enough sorting out the Winston case by his usual yardsticks. Some crimes Lamark—and every detective, for that matter—knew were going to be solved according to the record. All the information would be there—staring out from the pages of old police blotters, charges, dispositions, time served, probation report and all the documents that trail a criminal from the date of his first arrest to his death.

Then there were the cases which newspapers dote on. They enlist the help of the public, and it's rough going. You track down hundreds of crazy leads, many of them from crackpots. Sometimes you get lucky and the nuttiest tip turns out to be the right one.

Then there was the jet-set case. You walked on hot coals in a society so filled with skeletons that the line between fact and gossip was often as fine as a strand of silk. And just as difficult to break. The code of silence among the upper crust of society enjoyed far more respect than in the area of its birth, the Mafia.

"Nice people simply don't discuss their peers—certainly not to the police," was the typical attitude.

Richard Winston's murder obviously was going to lead him into the upper echelon of society, business and politics. Lamark had access to a key which unlocked many of these doors, he'd come upon it accidently several

48

years earlier when he was transferred to the Central Park West precinct.

Lamark had been assigned what the newspapers called the "Case of the Golden Girl." She was a topless dancer whose name came from the fact that for her performance she painted her entire body with gold. In her spare time Miss Golden Girl was serving as mistress to a pair of prominent New York business partners. Neither man was aware of their mutual bedmate. When one of them discovered Golden Girl's duplicity, he hired a hit man to dispose of her.

Twenty-four hours after the girl's horribly mutilated body was discovered in a vacant lot, Lieutenant Lamark summoned both partners to the police station. They were family men of impeccable reputations, and it was assumed that the detective had taken leave of his senses. Privately, Lamark thought so himself. He was accepting without reservation information supplied him by an untested source.

An hour after they so willingly submitted to questioning, one partner had clammed up, demanding that his lawyer be present.

Lamark's informant was Sal White, Publisher and editor of *The Lowdown*, the third-ranking tabloid at the supermarket checkout counters, a scandal sheet whose circulation of a million was enough to keep Sal in the seventy-five thousand dollar a year bracket, an income that supported a lovely wife, a beautiful East Side apartment and two sons, both in college. Sal's domestic bliss struck Lamark as an extraordinary contrast to that of the jet-set figures he wrote about.

Subtlety was hardly Sal's style. The page he showed Lamark carried the banner: HOW TOPLESS DOLL SERVICES TOP BIZ TYKOOKS! *She's Secret Mistress*

Sal spared readers few of the juicy details of how the Golden Girl managed to keep the two businessmen happy for more than a year without either aware that they were sharing—and supporting—the same "bundle of love."

Lamark especially appreciated Sal's 1940's language.

"She gave me the whole thing herself—every damned word—and a lot that I couldn't print. Maybe some day I can. The tricks she used in getting the boys up. Interestin' psychological stuff like that."

Pointing to photos of the Golden Girl, Sal shook his head. "This dame isn't her. It's a model. But she's the girl all right—the one they snuffed."

He fished into his pocket, pulled a slip of paper out of his wallet. "These are the partners. Naturally I didn't use their real handles in the story."

And what did Sal expect for this extraordinary service? Nothing beyond seeing that justice was done. That accomplished, he was able to haul out his old story, slap it on the front page for a re-run to remind readers they'd read it first in *The Lowdown*. The Golden Girl Case was the first of several cases which strengthened the friendship of White and Lamark.

Frank Lamark wanted badly to talk to Sal but he was finding it difficult to get Claudia Milotte out of his mind. His imagination ran riot. She was the kind of woman a man would climb mountains for, or forge a raging river to rescue her during a flood. She'd kindled fires in the detective that he'd thought long since extinguished by one unsuccessful love affair that followed too quickly on the death of his wife in a car accident, several short years after they married.

It was all so long ago. Time was supposed to heal. Since it hadn't, Frank settled for the occasional waitress, a fancy call girl when he felt flush, or nothing at all. There had been a woeful absence of lust in either his heart or his eyes until tonight. Why a fool like Richard Winston rejected this magnificent beauty, a rich, ripe woman like Claudia, was beyond his imagination. She was the embodiment of all the wet dreams of fifty million Frenchmen, and right now Frank Lamark was ready to prove it.

From snippets in the newspapers he knew enough about Ritchie and Winston and Associates to suspect the police were dealing with a shabby conglomorate whose international ties had been subject to investigation after investigation. Governments, on this continent and others, had won a few, lost a few. Winston and Associates, however, survived them all and seemingly grew stronger.

Where did Claudia Milotte fit into the picture? He knew how her image fitted into his mind but how did she affect others? Certainly anyone could see, Lamark dreamed on, that her eyes had been hewn from some rare jade known only to the Creator. As for her lips. . . .

Sondra's huge presence, with a voice to match, did little to deepen the mysterious art of contemplation.

"Mr. White just called. I said that I didn't think you were here. You know, I figured maybe you wanted to be alone—just to think. So I told him I'd call him back. Are you here?"

"Sure . . . sure, I'm here, Sondra."

"Then I'll call him back. He'll be right along. He's up the street in his office."

"I appreciate that. Thanks."

Sondra lumbered to the phone. She kept looking his way as she spoke, waving now and then to indicate conversation was in progress, finally rounding her fingers in an "o" sign to assure Lamark that Sal was on his way.

51

Although Sondra was a pest, she was a likable pest, and her ability to make the simplest act dramatic fascinated Lamark.

Sal must have flown. Lamark took advantage of Sondra's preoccupation with another customer to visit the men's room. When he returned to his table, Sal was already there, in a not unusual state of high excitement.

"Lamark, I caught your show on the radio. Can't wait to see it on TV. That voice—your personality—Christ, you come through like John Travolta, Tony Bennett, Clark Gable! Sex appeal, that's what it is. You've got it. But in your job it's wasted.

"Now, about this Winston caper. I got exactly what you're missing—the real facts about all those blind items in the regular papers. Only I couldn't print them. Why? Winston and Associates is the majority stockholder in the paper. *My* tabloid and *every other* tabloid. They got a piece of the distributor and so on and so on. What can I tell you? Nothing good. But it's all yours.

"It's in this folder—stuff I copied from my originals. Foreign stuff mostly. My guy translated it. I keep it for the record; it's a habit. So maybe it pays off. I wonder who got the s.o.b.

"Take this Donald Laine guy. You know his real name? Gianni Daniele—Johnny Daniels. I got nothing against a guy changing his name; in my own Naples I'd be Salvatore Bianco. But I admit it—this guy doesn't, he hides it. He even goes to an Episcopalian church. He's supposed to be gay. I got nothing to guarantee that. If anyone knows, it's Claudia. They're thick as thieves. Even when the marriage was going good, Winston never minded their being together—but let any other guy come near her in those days and he'd cut off his balls."

"So he *was* jealous of her. I didn't get that impression."

"How could you? You gotta go on the premise that things are never what they seem. Take that program you got there in your pocket. It says Claudia was born in Washington, D.C. in 1943. True. It also says that her mother was an attaché at the French Embassy who was stranded during World War II and that her father was an American businessman. It's crap. Just the opposite. The kid's dad was a clerk at the Embassy, the mother was a hooker. It was the father, Maurice Milotte, who took Claudia back to France after the war. She was about five.

"He dies a year later and the kid disappears for ten years, locked away in a medievel orphanage down near the Pyrénées. It's the mother's mother, Claudia's grandmother, who rescues her—not whoever they say in the program."

"Frankly, Sal, I haven't read it yet."

"Anyhow, she was a lady with class and some money. Her name was Monica O'Reilley. She was as surprised as anyone to find out that her daughter had turned hooker. When she discovered she had a granddaughter in France—and that's a long story—she traced the kid. And that's it. Overnight we have Claudia Milotte, all-American girl. Mrs. O'Reilley gives her a fine education. Claudia turns out a devoted grandchild. Better than that, she's bright, an honors student all the way.

"When the old lady dies, Claudia inherits a respectable piece of change, which she uses to go back to Europe, where we discover her at the Cannes Film Festival. So the all-American girl becomes an overnight movie star in French art movies—which, as we all well know, is just a euphamism for skin flicks.

"Great stuff! Better than the crap they make up about her. But nobody can use it—the Winston people would slaughter me."

Finally he paused. Lamark was speechless.

"Hey, Lamark," Sal shouted, "wake up! Am I being useful? Tell me, I gotta know!"

"Sal, you're one wonderful guy! You've opened windows I would never have been able to see. How can I repay you?"

Sal thought for a second. "You can. When I'm ready I'll let you know. For now this is it—it's all there in the clips. Read 'em—it's storybook stuff. Beautiful, really. Just like the lady. Christ, a man's a sucker to split from a dame like that. Why? There's a grubby answer, but I won't bore you with it tonight. But with a dame like that I can't figure it out."

"Nor I—and I only met her tonight. We weren't together more than twenty minutes but she hit me like magic. It's crazy."

Sal squinted and looked close into Lamark's face. "Yeah, that's it. She's supposed to hit guys like that—even detectives."

Part Two

Boarding the train to Boston brought an end to a week which Claudia found even more horrible than Donald Laine had predicted.

The newspapers kept her name in big black headlines, with rumors and theories that originated either from kooks or the imagination of reporters. At midweek, however, "the mystery woman" angle quietly disappeared. Claudia suspected that Lieutenant Lamark was responsible. In a television interview he stated that no evidence existed linking the "so-called mystery woman" with Richard Winston's murder. Fingerprint experts, he said, had gone over the penthouse thoroughly. The few prints they were unable to match with persons having a legitimate reason for visiting Richard Winston were old and had not been dusted.

Lamark, however, conceded that the assailant had obtained access to the apartment while Winston was absent. The position in which the body was found, the close range at which the gun was fired, ripping a hole straight through his heart, suggested that the financier had been shot without warning on entering the penthouse.

Lamark stopped his official remarks at that point, claiming that the Medical Examiner had not yet completed his examination. Meanwhile, police were involved in an intensive investigation of Winston's professional and personal life, hoping to find a motive.

"It's an extremely complicated case," Lamark observed, in an unusual lapse into his private feelings. "We have here a busy, active man who sees many people in the course of an ordinary business day. His activities are extremely hectic because of the convention. The people who contact him during this period are double those he usually encounters. Beyond this, we have to probe his private life."

Lamark had not yet issued his statement when Claudia arrived at one o'clock to play the Sunday afternoon matinee, the final New York performance of *The Capri Affair*. She entered the theater from the front to avoid the crowds milling around the stage door. Moreover, unless a security guard was on duty, the alleys leading to many older Broadway theaters had become "unsafe areas," havens for drunks, shopping bag ladies, and, often, muggers.

Reginald Wuthering's lawyers had been engaged in a year-long battle with building inspectors to seal off the Fiske alley but plans had met opposition because they conflicted with fire safety regulations.

The curtain was up. As Claudia strode down a side aisle she saw Lamark and Wuthering huddled together on the stage. Reg was pointing out various sections of the historic theater. By the bunch of keys in his hand she assumed the elderly producer intended showing Lamark the secret tunnel of the Prohibition-era gangsters.

There was only a work light on the stage. Silhouetted against it, Lamark struck her, as he had last night, as an exceedingly handsome man. His profile was chiseled and somehow he seemed taller than she had thought. It puzzled her until she realized Lieutenant Lamark was wearing a smart tailored suit, styled to show a man to his best advantage. This certainly was one for the books—a New York cop wearing his Sunday best to see her show.

Claudia managed to slip backstage and into her dressing room unnoticed. Sunday suit or not, Lamark made her nervous. What did he expect to find in the tunnel? She couldn't believe he'd chosen this particular day to satisfy his curiosity. It must involve Ritchie's murder.

She forced herself to sit quietly at the dressing table, drawing deep breaths to steady her nerves. She jumped at the first knock. It was Billy Briggs, the stage manager, who would never make her feel uncomfortable even if he noticed she'd been startled. In her state of mind, Claudia was quite sure he did. She turned on her most ravishing smile.

"Surprised to see me?" she asked, her eyes twinkling.

"Of course not," Billy said. "Being the stage manager, I asked Wuthering if I should find out if you were up to the performance. The old man glowered over his Ben Franklin spectacles. 'In my companies we don't insult stars with questions like that. If Claudia Milotte is indisposed, she will notify us.' How about that?"

"He knows his people. No wonder the old boy's survived so well. I'm a little shaken up, but the worst thing I could imagine would be to duck the performance. The press would have a field day. I'd appreciate it if you'll keep the visitors down. Except for Lieutenant Lamark. He's in the theater."

"Yes, Wuthering's giving him the tourist's tour of the tunnel and the arsenal."

"Bully for him!" Claudia said.

Billy noticed an edge to her voice. It surprised him.

"Anyhow," she went on, "if the cop asks for me after the show, I'm going to have to see him."

"I guess you do, Claudia," Billy said. "But I'll take care of the others. The house is packed—standing room only and the mobs growing deeper at the stage door."

Her tone was bitter. "It follows—after all, I'm this week's star of the tabloids. There's always the chance that I may turn out to be that 'mystery woman.'"

"Knock it off, Claudia," Billy said. "This must be tough to take. Don't make it harder on yourself."

"You're right, Billy, I guess I jump at everything. But being calm isn't exactly easy when you land in the middle of a murder."

The performance went extremely well. Interest was centered on Claudia as it never had been before. She drew strength and support from the audience, feeling that the majority, having bought their tickets in advance, were impressed with the courage of an artist who respected the tradition that the "show must go on."

At her solo call, the ovation was tremendous. When it subsided, she moved into her position behind the scrim and waited for Stella Morell. The Italian actress walked briskly to stage center, extended her arms, held the position briefly. Abruptly, she turned her back to the audience, walked to the scrim and extended her hand to Claudia.

The gesture was dramatic and totally unexpected. In the firm hand of her friend, Claudia found security and love. It had not been a theatrical trick. Stella Morell, like the audience, felt deep admiration for a woman willing to perform her job under such grisly circumstances. She intended showing that to the audience—and to Claudia.

The gesture had its lighter side. In becoming Stella's partner, Claudia discovered that those fancy curtain calls weren't as hokey as they looked. It required deft footwork to keep up with the Italian actress as she raced Claudia through the routine—stage left, stage right, stage center and finally to that magic moment when the stars swept their eyes across the mezzanine and the rear of the house, embracing every member of the audience in a display of pure love.

Long after the house lights went up, the audience continued to stand, applauding and cheering. But Billy Briggs, aware that Claudia had drawn on every ounce of energy to get through the performance, kept the curtain down and, with Stella, escorted Claudia to the dressing room.

She murmured, "Thank you" and closed the door.

Billy's unmistakable knock roused her about five minutes later. He was carrying a bouquet of flowers and a note. Claudia wasn't sure whether she was pleased or annoyed that Lieutenant Lamark had not delivered them himself.

The note read: "*Cher Madame*, this has been a thrilling afternoon in the theater. Your performance was exquisite. Thank you for a memorable event in my life." It was signed simply, "Frank Lamark."

"You mean to say that's it?" She looked at Billy mischievously, handing him the note.

"For now, I guess." Billy laughed. "I have to admit it—Lamark is the only cop I ever met that you'd call a 'charmer.'"

* * *

On Monday Claudia received a subpoena to appear on the following morning before the Grand Jury which would consider the evidence in the Winston murder. Donald had been served with a similar summons.

On Tuesday the lawyer and Claudia descended into the cavern of downtown New York where city, state and national office buildings huddle together as cold, impersonal symbols of the majesty of government. The average New Yorker for generations has come to associate them only with those moments in life described as "evil."

For many, the downtown visit involved nothing more annoying than hassling over a traffic ticket. For others, Criminal Court at 100 Centre Street was an address all too familiar to the city's poor and underprivileged, who streamed into its filthy corridors day after day, offering their fate into the hands of judges, attorneys and court personnel who, if triple in number, could only manage an equitable hearing for half the accused.

The building around the corner housing the District Attorney of Manhattan and his cadre of young, ambitious, status-conscious assistants struck Claudia as dirty and neglected, having little in common with the awesome processes of the law. At the entrance a policeman in uniform presided over a desk where he looked up her name on a list lying in front of him. Having found it, the policeman asked Claudia and Donald to sign a register.

"The Winston case is on the seventh floor. Take the elevator. The officer there will direct you. Pleased to meetcha, Miss Milotte."

At the seventh floor a hall led into a waiting room lined with benches, where she encountered some familiar and some unfamiliar faces. She recognized Laurence Drexel, the night manager of the Grand-Plaza, and assumed the tidy Irishwoman at his side was the housekeeper who had discovered the body. She extended her hand to Drexel, who rose and introduced Mrs. Dunne and security officer Pat Donovan.

"We want you to know, Mrs. Winston, how deeply we regret this tragedy."

Donald led her away. She was taken aback. She was unused to being addressed by her married name. Funny to feel that way, she thought. She used the name for charge accounts, for checking, for a hundred different things. Yet being reminded that she was the widow of a murder victim struck her as unseemly.

Two severe-looking men arrived and were ushered into a position close to the door leading to the Grand Jury room. Donald whispered, "They're from the Medical Examiner's office. They'll read their findings first."

"What about Lamark?"

"He may appear personally or submit a deposition," Donald said. "Those fellows are the big guns. We're just window dressing. The District Attorney wants to put on a proper show, let the public know he's doing his duty, leaving no stone unturned, that sort of thing."

Donald identified one of the Medical Examiner's deputies as Dr. John Thorn. "About the best pathologist in the country," he said. "They've put the top talent on this one."

The Medical Examiners testified for about twenty

minutes. When they left, Donald drew the attention of the Assistant District Attorney in charge of the interrogation. To Claudia the gangly young man looked as though he'd just made it through high school. She mentioned this to Donald.

"You may find out different when you get inside," Donald warned.

Donald succeeded in getting Claudia and himself placed ahead of the other witnesses. Claudia's name carried weight and the gawky youth knew that uppity ladies could cause trouble for underlings merely by putting in a call to their lawyers who, in turn, would complain to the District Attorney. Going out of his way for a Broadway star never damaged a politician's image.

When she was called inside Claudia found that the Grand Jury room resembled a theater or a movie set. She was seated in a witness chair on a raised platform before a group which she estimated was composed of twenty or thirty people who made up the Grand Jury and its alternates.

The gawky youth was the only attorney. However, Donald had explained to Claudia that if she had any difficulties with the questions, she had the privilege of leaving the room and asking his advice.

Then he laughed. "But that's the way the hoods handle it. I very much doubt you'll be needing me."

She didn't. The young deputy simply asked Claudia to explain her movements on the day of the murder. She repeated what she had told Lamark. Consulting his notes, he asked about her visit to Winston the day before. He required nothing more in the way of information than the time it had occurred and how long the visit had lasted.

Donald was the next to testify. He went through the details of his entire day at Winston's side, aided by the program of events which he was permitted to consult. At the time the murder was believed to have been committed, Donald was attending to the facilities in the Grand Ballroom. He was surprised that no questions were asked about the "mystery woman." Forty-eight hours ago she had seemed the cornerstone of the investigation. Something must have happened to change that attitude. Or perhaps the newspapers made more of it than the circumstances warranted. His lawyer's mind, however, told him that a lid had been put on the "mystery woman." By whom? Only Lamark carried that sort of clout. Why had he done it?

The cop in charge of the seventh floor stopped him. "Excuse me. You Mr. Laine?"

"Yes, Officer."

"Judge Fostini called this morning. You'd evidently spoken to him."

"Yes, I had."

"Then I'm to escort you out the side entrance. We've already pulled your chauffeur and the car into position. That way you and the lady can avoid the press. They're all over the place. Waiting for Miss Milotte—but also to get the verdict."

"Thank you, Officer," Claudia said, extending her hand. "You're very kind."

Then she whispered to Donald, "You're a love, Donald."

Donald only smiled as they followed the man in the blue uniform down the hall to an unmarked door leading into a hallway and the District Attorney's private elevator.

*　　*　　*

63

Wednesday's newspaper and television reports of the Grand Jury investigation were fragmentary. The Jury concluded that Richard Winston's murder had been committed by person or persons unknown and that the matter now lay in the hands of the police.

Lieutenant Lamark issued a brief statement, hinting that certain suspects were under surveillance but that he was in no position to identify them.

"The evidence," he said, "remains incomplete."

Claudia and Donald Laine were having lunch at the Sutton Place apartment when the news broke.

Claudia seemed bewildered. "I don't understand it. All those people down there for hours, talking and talking. That silly young boy asking questions. What did they find out? Nothing. They don't even know what sort of gun was used or what time it happened."

"That's the system, Claudia," the lawyer explained. "Grand Jury proceedings are secret. They turn their findings over to the District Attorney, who decides whether or not to prosecute the case—assuming there's someone to prosecute. In the absence of a suspect, the case remains with the police—and that's where it lies until they come up with some sort of solution.

"You certainly wouldn't expect them to parade their clues and suspicions in the press, or trot them out for television viewers to look at. They're going to say very little about the pathologist's findings or the actual evidence the police picked up. I wouldn't be surprised if they'd located the gun.

"The police know that there were at least a hundred people roaming around the Grand-Plaza on Saturday who had reasons for killing Richard Winston. But that doesn't mean they intended to do it. Still, businessmen can be an emotional lot. Although murder isn't their bag, they're capable of it—especially guys who'd been slaughtered by the highhandedness of the Winston octopus.

"There were top European and South American executives present who pleaded to be spared the slaughter Winston had prepared for them. He grew rich just by threatening takeover; frequently our unpredictable entrepreneur never intended going through with it. But whenever Winston and Associates got on the tail of a company, the owners began running scared. Men who had founded a successful businesses sold out at a loss rather than face the pressure Winston's goons knew how to apply. Ritchie could be pretty ruthless, you know."

"It didn't take me long to find that out," Claudia said, "but I'd prefer to forget it, if I ever can. I doubt that I can; it's the kind of nasty experience that sticks to you no matter how hard you try to blot it out of your mind. I've been around that course twice, as a matter of fact, Donald. My God! All those women—a bunch of two-bit whores! But were they any cheaper than Ritchie? I don't think so. I just wonder how I've survived as long as I have."

Speculating about the murder, however, was not why Donald had invited himself to lunch. Prodded by other officials of Winston and Associates, he'd been delegated the delicate task of persuading Claudia to attend the funeral of their slain chief.

When she was asked to take part in the funeral arrangements she looked at Donald in astonishment. "Why?"

"Because you're his widow."

"That doesn't make sense. In name, yes, but not in fact. I have no intention of making a fool of myself by helping with the arrangements—or even attending the funeral.

You people do whatever you want. Fly white doves over the coffin for all I care."

Donald pointed out that in the interests of sound business it was important that she make an appearance either at the church or the graveyard ceremonies.

"Winston and Associates," he said, "are taking a beating on the market. All our issues are down and we've got to regroup and present a solid front."

"You're making me cry, Donald. The issues are down, indeed! And people who want to strengthen their control are just waiting to step in and pick up the pieces as fast as they can—you included."

Donald winced. "I don't have that kind of capital."

"You know people who do, don't you?"

"A few. None I could really go to."

"You know me."

"I doubt that you have the sort of money that would make much difference—even if I really cared. I don't. Right now I'm just doing a job."

"You surprise me, Donald. I thought you were more ambitious. I always imagined that you'd love to step into Ritchie's shoes if anything happened to him."

"Ten years ago, maybe. Today, no."

"So you're not one of the vultures, after all!"

"Claudia, don't nag me. Put it this way: I made peace with myself and my ambitions a long time ago. Now I'm just taking orders. Moreover, from your point of view, attending the funeral is a practical matter of public relations. But don't yell 'foul' afterward. Your absence will give the newspapers another batch of headlines."

Claudia's eyes looked daggers, like sharp points of jade. "My dear Donald, don't hit your head against the brick wall any more. I am not a hypocrite. I was thrown out of Richard Winston's life years ago, physically tossed out of the house like a common whore and hustled off the property by his goons. I can't forget that—nor all the torture I went through afterward. You were there; you saw it. Go tell the truth to those big shot businessmen of yours. And don't ask me again. Is that clear?"

"Quite clear, Claudia. I told the directors that you wouldn't budge. In my opinion you're right; moreover, you're laying your integrity right on the line for everyone to see—at least those who know the truth. There are very few of those. Ritchie saw to that. The newspapers will have a field day with the story, separation or not."

"I know, I know. I can see the headlines now—all about the rich widow refusing to attend her husband's last rites. Let them have my hide. I'm used to it. You know, Donald, I was a very dark person when I was a young girl; I'd brightened by the time I met Ritchie and fell in love. Now I'm regressing, I'm becoming dark again. When you have these dark feelings it really doesn't matter what people think of you.

"What's more, they forget very quickly. This week the Winston murder is everywhere you turn—the strange behavior of the widow, the 'mystery woman'—it's all in the headlines. Next week there will be another arson in the Bronx and some poor children will be burned alive. We'll have those headlines for twenty-four hours, and what happens to the arsonist will be reported months later on the back page, if at all. Life has no value these days, so why should I worry about a few hours of notoriety? You don't quite know everything, Donald. It could be much worse."

"Claudia, don't tell me now. I've had enough for one morning. I'll be here on Friday to take you to the train. Perhaps by then we'll have some information about the will."

Donald got up to leave. He glanced at his watch. "I'm late for another appointment. So damned many things to do. I'll explain how you feel."

"Keep it cool, Donald. Tell them in words of one syllable. It goes easier that way."

Claudia put her hand on his arm as she walked him through the living room to the door. "Don't be hurt, Donald, because you think I'm stubborn. It's my right—don't forget that. As for the will, believe me, I'm not holding my breath. I never asked to be rich." They were at the door. "As a matter of fact, I've never wanted to be *me*."

Donald kissed her and walked to the elevator. He rather wished she'd close the door and go inside.

Claudia stood, the door ajar, waiting for the elevator to arrive. Whenever Claudia spoke of "darkness," Donald's palms began to sweat. There had been those stories of her years of isolation after the separation. Then there were the moments when he'd encountered Claudia in a deep depression, filled with hate and thoughts of destruction. To see her now, it was impossible to reconcile the Claudia he'd known in those moments of terror with the poised, beautiful woman before him.

Standing at the door, the chiffon gown making her look extremely desirable, a teasing, taunting smile on her lips, Claudia filled the corridor with her presence. She was so vital, so alive, it was hard to believe either the anguish of her childhood or the tragedy of her marriage. Life had treated this extraordinarily beautiful woman as though she were, as the English would say, "shabby baggage." Yet Donald knew that in Claudia's life there had not been a single act toward another human that was less than kind, thoughtful and sincere.

The elevator arrived. Claudia blew him a kiss and

disappeared inside the apartment.

Donald took a deep breath, hoping to exorcise his own thoughts, which also had a way of darkening.

A wry smile crossed his lips, the handmaiden of an old, familiar, cynical thought. He sighed. It was always the same. Donald had loved no other woman and he never would. But he could not ask Claudia Milotte to either share or understand his secret. She might try—that was her nature. But she was an earth woman, born to satisfy and be satisfied by men, not to live in the half world of her own "darkness" or that of a man with shadows he feared.

*   *   *

Billy Briggs accompanied Claudia to Boston. Donald drove her to Pennsylvania Station, after thrusting a large manila envelope into her hands. "This is the will. I've written a digest of the parts affecting you. It's like the newspapers said, you're going to be a very rich woman—maybe. It depends on how things come out in probate and whether the companies or Winston's family protest the will."

"And after the court and the lawyers have taken their piece of the action," Claudia added.

"That's about the size of it," Donald said. "You've got stock in lots of companies. You've inherited all of Ritchie's personal assets—as well as his debts. Claudia, my dear, I am not being facetious, but I suggest you keep on working and don't let this go to your head or affect your spending habits."

"Donald, my dear, that's exactly what I intend to do." She turned and looked him straight in the eye. "Donald, how about you?"

His face fell. "I got what I expected—a kick in the ass. I

do hold on to a few directorships that pay a hundred dollars a meeting and a free lunch several times a year. However, I'm your executor. Ritchie wrote that into the will so the position is irrevocable. If you don't want me around, I'm quite willing to quit. There's nothing he can do about it—not from the grave."

"I doubt that's going to happen."

As they spun into Penn Plaza, Billy Briggs stood waiting. They had arrived just in time, and Billy whisked Claudia through the station to the train and into their compartment. She fell into the seat, feeling free at last, grateful that the dreadful week was finally behind her.

Billy Briggs, a round, fiftyish, even-tempered man, a pro to his fingertips, had been scheduled to leave on Friday in order to begin hanging the show on Sunday. When Claudia had heard this she had asked to travel with him. It solved problems. She'd avoid the airport where the press hung out, and there was the privacy of a compartment, even if it meant taking one of the slower trains.

Billy was a perfect traveling companion. He made conversation when that seemed to be in order, but he knew when to keep quiet.

After they had checked in at the Hotel Adams, Claudia turned to Billy and impetuously kissed him. "You're a joy, baby! I've lost twenty years of worry in four hours just being locked up in that compartment with you. Let me buy you a drink before we call it a night."

Billy separated the bags for the bellboy. "We'll be in the bar. Bring the keys there, please." He handed the boy a fiver.

"You know, Claudia," he said, as they found a table in a dark corner, "it's terrible how others ache when the people they care for are troubled and when there's not a

70

fuckin' thing you can do for them."

"Yes, Billy, I understand the feeling. But the right time does come. For example, there's this trip. Darling, you made all the difference. You were like a trouble jar; I could bounce what I felt off onto you or just keep my mouth shut. It's not that way with everybody." She pressed his hand. "Thanks a lot." The waiter arrived at their table. Claudia glanced up. "Triple bourbon on the rocks with plain water on the side. Twice."

Billy was convulsed with laughter. "You, a triple bourbon? How come you know about me?"

"Oh, Billy, don't be so naive. A lady has a way of collecting information when you hang a star on her dressing room door. You know you weren't Reg Wuthering's first choice as stage manager of our little opera."

"Naturally; Reg always uses his son-in-law, Milt Henry. I was surprised when I got the call. I never did find out why. God knows, Reg Wuthering never tells you anything he doesn't have to."

"It was quite simple, really. As soon as Anne Alexander signed her contract she got to me. Then I got to Stella Morell. We tossed a coin and I was chosen to go to Reggie and give him the bad news. We wouldn't accept Milt."

"How come?"

"You know as well as everyone. He's a nice guy but a nasty drunk. With three women stars in the play, we didn't feel up to it. Anne told me to ask for Billy Briggs. She said, 'Besides being a dear, he has a habit of limiting himself to one drink a day—after the show. Of course it's a triple and it would kill me, but that's Billy's routine.'"

"So Anne Alexander is my Lady Bountiful! She never said a word."

"She wouldn't. Anne is a cool lady. She's marvelous to work with—an actress who never makes a mistake." Claudia sighed. "I wish that in her private life she was the same stylish Anne we see on the stage."

She stopped. "Ye gods, look who's talking! Claudia Milotte—up to her ass in cops, murder, lawyers and enough legal complications to keep me running back and forth to court for the next ten years."

When their order arrived they clicked glasses and sipped first before pouring water into the drinks.

"You know, Claudia, I love this show," Billy said. "It's the kind of company you dream about—real pros. You're all stars. And the play is magnificently written—everyone has one big scene and they tear down the house with it. There's not a flawed actor in the play; maybe that's why it goes so well. The actors respect each other—you don't find the backbiting you usually come up against. How did it ever happen?"

Claudia took a long drink. Her green eyes narrowed, then opened brightly. "I took it for granted everyone knew. I guess they don't. Hell, let it all hang out. It might do me good to remember."

She called the waiter. "Some coffee, please. You, Billy?"

"No thanks, Claudia, this is fine."

"You read in the papers that Richard Winston and I separated a year ago. That wasn't true. It happened before that—three years ago. I'll skip some details. I was up in our summer place on the Cape. It was our wedding anniversary. Ritchie hadn't visited me for three weeks; there always seemed to be some excuse—meeting he couldn't get away from, business people coming in from abroad and the coast. You know, all the excuses you read about in novels and see on television.

72

"I decided to surprise him, so I drove down to our estate in the Hamptons. What I found there came right out of an X-rated movie. I didn't have one 'other woman' to compete with—but six. They were literally teenagers, and younger. One kid I recognized; she couldn't have been more than twelve. That was Ritchie's thing—kids. I'd been his shield. So were all the women he ran around with before we married.

"He was furious that I'd caught him. I was tossed out of the house by his bodyguards. They slapped a wad of bills into my hands and told me to get lost. Oh, there were a lot of things I could have done, like calling lawyers or the police, or raising a fuss in the newspapers.

"But I couldn't. It was impossible. I was too hurt. I'd been beaten—again. The reasons? They all went back to my childhood. I began to regress back into it from that minute. I was a failure again, a misfit, a freak, just as I'd been as a kid. That's a part of me I wake up nights screaming about. I wanted to think it was all a fantasy, but it wasn't.

"So I ended up living in a loft in Soho. You know what I did for nearly two years? I sat there watching television, drinking beer, growing as fat as a house, thinking only of my failures. Until that moment I believed I had done one thing well: I had managed to make a happy marriage and to keep my husband contented. But I hadn't. Now I know why, then I didn't.

"Every day Rose came to visit me. Faithful, wonderful Rose! She tried to make me eat. I refused. I lived on beer, and odds and ends of junk food. I did allow her to give me vitamin shots. They probably kept me from dying.

"One of the columnists finally broke the story. She found out about me, where I was hiding. She came to see me. We talked for a whole afternoon. Except for Rose and the kid who delivered the beer, she was the only human being I'd communicated with. Winston had me watched by detectives around the clock, hoping for evidence so he could file for divorce. He was worried that I was after his money, and a few other things I'd rather not go into.

"The columnist played it very cool. She left out all the grubby details, saying that the Richard Winstons had secretly split and that Claudia, once a star on her way to the top, was thinking of going back to work. Baby, that was farthest from my thoughts. I didn't think there were too many parts around for women to play elephants.

"Stella Morell, you don't need to be told, lives on gossip. She knows everything about everybody, and if she doesn't believe all she reads in the scandal sheets, she really wants to. Anyhow, she read about me in the Italian newspapers. We'd become friends when I made a picture for her husband, Nino Bellafiore. It was one of those things that got so mixed up in financial intrigue that it was never finished.

"Two days later I was in Capri, where Stella told me she had been waiting for years to perform *The Capri Affair* in New York but had turned down offer after offer because she needed the perfect actress to do Catherine. That actress, she had decided, was me. It sounds like bull, but there was one single point in my favor that made me a more logical choice than anyone else. That's our secret.

"Losing the weight was no problem—not when you were being dominated by Stella Morell. While I sweated off the poundage, she handled the business arrangements with Reginald Wuthering, who had been begging Stella for years to bring *The Capri Affair* to America.

"Here's a curious thing I don't believe even you know. Stella asked Reg to direct. He didn't want to. He hadn't directed a show in years, but Stella insisted. You know how she behaves when she's persuading someone. Nothing stops her. She cries. She screams. Most of all she makes the person she's working on seem the most important person in the world.

"I can hear her now 'Reg, *tesaro*, you are not too old. It is not as if it were a new work. The play's been done in Italy and in France. I need you—the play needs you. I tell you why. The other directors—they focus too much on me. They give me the lights, the positions, everything. For my own people, seeing Stella Morell this way is *magnifique, grandé*. But not for America. There they need to see the play more clearly, and the other artists. The Contessa is the catalyst; Catherine is the star. There is a big difference.' Have you ever heard of a star conning a director like that?"

"Never."

"You're so right. The amazing part is that Stella meant it. That's why we have a hit. You know the rest. We all agreed Anne Alexander was perfect for the American daughter. Keith Byrne was the only logical choice for her English son, and you brought us Robin Haywood to audition for the role of Flavian. I thought he was too beautiful to be real, and when he first read the scene where he tries to convince me of his love for the Contessa, I was in tears. I still break down now and then. He's an amazing talent. Wherever did you find him?"

"Just as it says in the program—although Wuthering takes the credit. I caught him in Ohio—Canton, I think. He was Marchbanks in a semi-pro production of *Candida*. Even for Marchbanks, Robin was too young— but, Christ, he was good. The others were young, so they balanced. But it was Robin's performance that you noticed. He was amazing. I went backstage, introduced notices. He was amazing. I went backstage, introduced myself, and got his Cleveland address and phone number. When this play came along I lent him the bus fare to come to New York to audition."

"He must be very grateful to you."

"Grateful! He's like a school kid bringing apples to his teacher. Every week I get a present—a necktie, toilet water, a box of handkerchiefs, fancy cigars. I keep telling him to save his money for the great love of his life—whoever the hell she is."

"She? I thought he was gay."

"Everybody does. Robin's given up on that one. He sends out more autographed pictures than anyone in the company—mostly to gays. But they're not his bag."

"And this woman—what about her?"

"Don't ask me; she's a 'mystery woman.' Ouch! I shouldn't have said that."

Claudia patted Billy's hand. "It doesn't worry me, darling. But I'm fascinated. Do you know who she is? Has Robin ever given you a hint?"

"Nope, nothing. He just moons and broods like a lovesick calf."

"Darling, it sounds mad. What about his spare time?"

Billy leaned back, straightened, and gave a perfect imitation of the serious, sensitive young man with the quiet, well-mannered voice. "It's this way, Claudia. Our young friend is sublimating—he's overcoming physical and emotional attractions by other activities—reading, studying languages, dancing, the piano. Lately he's taken to the guitar. I also suspect he takes a lot of cold showers."

Claudia closed her eyes. Then, almost whispering to herself, she said, "How odd! I never gave Robin's personal life a second thought. I took too much for granted. We have more in common than I imagined."

76

"That's a teasing remark if ever I heard one. You're not going to explain it, are you?"

"No." Claudia smiled.

"I didn't think so."

"You *are* a dear—a wise, wise man. I'm going upstairs."

"I have to call Jack Myers. He's in the hotel somewhere. According to him, business looks great."

In the lobby, Billy signaled a bellboy to take Claudia to her suite.

He waved goodnight as he picked up the house phone and asked for Jack Myers, the company press agent.

Jack was ecstatic. "Welcome to Beansville, old boy—and the greatest triumph since *My Fair Lady*. We're sold out for three weeks already, and we could play another three if the time were open. Christ! What a story—what a mad story...."

Billy interrupted, "Pedal it, baby. We all know none of the publicity is going to hurt the box office—even the lady. But let's not make a big thing out of it around the company."

"Christ, Billy, do you think I was born yesterday?"

"Of course not, Jack. Just making sure. We all gotta live with her."

"Any time she wants me to."

Changing his tone, Jack continued, "I'm a press agent so I act like one. That doesn't mean I'm not human. I'm crazy about Claudia. Everybody is. The press here adores her. They've all come to me and, without my asking, said that whatever interviews she accepted would be strictly business. They wouldn't ask her anything about Winston. I don't know of many stars who rate consideration like that."

"Claudia Milotte deserves it," Billy said. "Tell her that

77

first thing, when you see her. Maybe we can have lunch together tomorrow. She needs company. I came up on the train with her."

"Sure, Billy, whatever you say. Sleep well."

Billy Briggs started toward the elevator from the direction of the bar but his way was blocked by an approaching wheelchair, an electric contraption being navigated expertly by an exceedingly beautiful young woman with a serene oval face that, at first glance, looked as though it had just modeled for a Middle Ages painting of the Madonna. She maneuvered the chair his way; as she drew closer the woman said, "Mr. Briggs...if you don't mind...may I...."

"Excuse me, Miss," Billy said. "Do we know each other?"

She smiled and the face became even more exquisite. Then she laughed and it seemed to fill the lobby with the sound of silver bells.

"No, no, we've never met. I got your name from the waiter. Then I knew who you were—the stage manager for *The Capri Affair*. Congratulations on having such a fine show. I have a note for Claudia Milotte. It's quite personal and I'd appreciate it if you'd give it to her yourself. Would you?"

"Of course."

"Thank you."

"May I have your name?"

She smiled. "I don't think that's necessary. Miss Milotte will understand."

As her voice trailed away, she smiled and directed her wheelchair toward the lobby.

Billy stuffed the note in his pocket. It wasn't uncommon for a stage manager to be given messages for stars. This one could wait until the next day.

In his room, Billy sat on the edge of the bed for a second to rest. It had been a long, tiring day. He slid off his shoes, then stood up to take off his jacket. His hand crept into his pocket. He pulled out the pink envelope and stopped to notice the stylish handwriting—Miss Claudia Milotte. In the left hand corner, *personal*.

He started to place the note on the dresser but, remembering the extraordinary beauty of the girl in the wheelchair, he knew he was going to open it.

It wasn't a pleasant thought, but Claudia had become that dreaded word in show business—notorious. Artists in her position were invariably prey to kooks. The danger of a threat to her safety was very real. Billy slit open the envelope and pulled out the note before he became even more befuddled by considering the propriety of what he was doing.

His expression grew dark and worried as he read.

> Dear Claudia, I know it was you who killed Ritchie, and I'm only sorry that I didn't murder him myself when I had the opportunity. It would have spared me a life as a physical cripple and you as a woman haunted by fear of exposure. That will never happen. You will be protected. You have my word. I will speak to you personally before you leave Boston. I'm sure you recognize the name of one of Ritchie's little toys who admires and prays for you——Ella D.

Billy carefully folded the letter into its envelope, fished into his briefcase and placed it in a zippered compartment where he stored documents involving the show and its personnel.

The letter could be the aberration of a crank. But was

it? How about his own doubts—what of his fears that others in the company were trying very hard not to express their hidden thoughts? Actors were trained to control emotions on stage. Their experience in real life was usually no different from that of the ordinary person.

Billy decided a sleeping pill would prevent a restless night.

* * *

When Billy woke his first thought was the letter. It worried him, but what to do?

For the moment, nothing. But he wanted to be damned sure that Claudia was covered by someone in the company from morning until night. This was Saturday and offered no problems. Jack Myer would take her to lunch. He would show her the town tonight.

At eleven he called Claudia, asking her approval of the arrangements. She was delighted.

Sunday was something else. Like all stars, she'd sleep late and spend some time with the Sunday papers. Feature stories on the show and Claudia had all been written for the Boston papers by Jack, who assured Billy that she'd be pleased.

"I've seen the proofs of the articles. They refer to Winston at the very end, saying that he was killed last week and that Claudia had been separated from him for several years. That's fact. You can't argue it. I had to mention it, but the papers didn't enlarge on what I wrote."

Jack couldn't quite fathom Billy's preoccupation with Claudia. Sensing this, Billy offered a clue. "Remember, Jack, you were in Boston just reading the headlines about the case. You weren't living with the lady, as we were. You didn't see the press storm the stage door, read the headlines about the 'mystery woman' and hear all the snide insinuations."

"Well, the story wasn't exactly hidden in the classifieds here, but I get what you mean. She needs attention. For me tomorrow's a problem. How about Keith Byrne or the kid?"

"When does Stella arrive?"

"No one knows for sure. Maybe in an hour. You know how she is—changes her mind every few minutes. The men are here. Try them. You have to hang the show."

Billy called Keith Byrne and asked to see him in his room. The actor replied, "Of course, old boy. Shall I order you some breakfast?"

"Just coffee will be fine."

He was at the actor's door in seconds.

"Do we have an emergency?" Byrne asked.

"Sort of. I'd like you to ask Claudia to lunch or dinner on Sunday. She's at loose ends and, with all that's gone on, I think she ought to be kept busy."

"Quite right. Good idea!" Byrne said. "I'd love to spend some time with her."

"Good, then it's settled."

"Not quite, Billy, my boy. With someone else along."

"How come?"

"Are you blind?"

"Of course not. Twenty-twenty. What's the problem?"

"Her effect on me. She shatters me. I adore her. It's all I can do to keep my hands off her. You know that scene where I fall on my knees and she holds my head in her lap while I break down and cry?"

"Of course. It stuns them."

"But, man, what it does to me! Ouch! I'm supposed to be her half-brother, but the only reason I don't project

81

incest in that scene is because I'm a damned good actor."

"You're kidding."

"About being a good actor? Certainly not."

"Keith, you mean to say you couldn't have a quiet dinner with her like a friend?"

"I hate to risk it, that's all. Especially now, when she's so vulnerable. I'd end up making a perfect ass of myself. You don't know; you can't understand. You're not close to her. You don't hold her hand or touch her skin. You don't see the sadness in those green eyes—or the joy when that's how she feels. She's an incredible creature. Before I do that scene I talk my pecker out of going into a state of tumescence like a Dutch uncle. It takes discipline to be on that stage with that woman. I've never enjoyed such frustration in my life. I pray that this play lasts forever."

"Suppose I get you a chaperon?"

"Fine, then I'll have to behave."

"Is the kid all right?"

"The kid? Robin?"

"Is there another?"

"Billy, how long have you been in this business?"

"Twenty years—give or take a few."

"And you don't know about Robin?"

"What's there to know? He looks gay. The audience loves him. He gets fan letters from guys. He's in love with some mystery. . . . Oh, my God! He's in love with Claudia. That's why there's all that goddamned secrecy . . . he's afraid to talk to about it."

Billy poured some coffee. "I imagine he's mentioned it to you."

"Never," Keith answered.

"But how do you know?"

"Let me tell you a story about John Barrymore and Dolores Costello. When she got pregnant, he searched all over town to find the very best obstetrician he could. After he introduced them, he forbade his wife ever to see the man again. He insisted on another doctor. Now guess who Dolores Costello married after she divorced John Barrymore?"

"The greatest obstetrician in Beverly Hills."

"You're right. Jack Barrymore knew the instant he saw them together that they were going to fall in love. He had that extraordinary sensitivity every actor possesses to feel emotions going on around him. Now, mind you, Barrymore was Mr. Super-Actor, but I'm not exactly amateur night. Just take my word for it, the kid's out of his mind because of Claudia. My torture is exquisitely mature, so I enjoy it. His is young and romantic, therefore anguished."

Suddenly Keith stopped. "All right, I'll put it together for you. I'll do it as an acting job. God, what exquisite torture! I'll play Claudia's chaperon and save her from the advances of both of us."

"You know, Keith, and don't get me wrong," Billy said, "some real lovin' is just what the girl needs."

"Billy, don't get me wrong either, I know it. But face it. I'm the character man, ten years older than Claudia. Robin's the juvenile, fifteen years younger. We have too much pride to risk being laughed at. You can see that, can't you?"

"Claudia would never laugh."

"That would be worse," Byrne said evenly. "Claudia— and I'm not being vulgar—is that one-night stand a man never forgets. You don't need Barrymore's superintuition to imagine that."

"This is a lesson in the theater that I'll remember for my memoirs."

"Just remember where you got it, old boy. Spell the

name right. Give the show credit and make my grandchildren proud. It's a deal. Leave it to me. I'll call the lovely lady and the lovesick boy. You hang the show and I promise you Claudia will be either so bored or so entertained by us that at the line rehearsal Monday afternoon she'll positively glisten."

Billy sighed his relief. "Thanks, Keith. I owe you one."

"You're goddamned right you do."

*   *   *

On his way to the theater, Billy wondered about Keith Byrne. Why had he become so devastated about being his age? For an actor with his looks, reputation and vast reservoir of talent, Byrne was at his prime.

True, in *The Capri Affair* his classical features were lost in make-up. As Terry Thompson, the Contessa's first child, born of an English aristocrat father Keith Byrne was playing his first real modern character part.

Terry was a man who'd lost his spirit and his hope, a failure who, in better days, survived through the kindness of women who had been attracted to his looks and considerable talents as a lover. He'd married twice, lived with two other women for several years and eventually lost his privileges of bed and breakfast at the homes of all four.

Like the Contessa's other children, Catherine (Claudia's part), daughter of her French lover, and Daisy, played by Anne Franklin, born of an affair with an American banker, have converged on the Contessa's pink stucco villa in Capri to determine the extent of her fortune, estimated in the millions, and how they can pick up a piece of it to suit their immediate needs and tie up some more for the future. They are taken totally by surprise when they discover that a handsome young man, Sandy Jameson, played by Robin Haywood, has been ensconced in the villa for a couple of years as the Contessa's companion and heir apparent.

Nino Bellafiore's story was laced with Italian mysticism, cynicism and old-fashioned melodramatic devices. The art of the work was that it played well, given a suitable cast. That had been Bellafiore's intention—to create a vehicle for Stella Morell which she could revive for the rest of her life.

Keith Byrne, Stella Morell told everyone—especially the press—had been a gift of the gods. He was quite the best of the Terrys she had ever performed with.

His make-up cleverly suggested the Byronic, classical handsomeness of a man degenerated mentally and physically by having sold himself on the open market as a stud. It was a specialized field in which the rule of diminishing returns was presumed to set in as he grew older.

Terry bore absolutely no resemblance to Keith Byrne. His loose, ill-fitting clothing, his shuffle and his sloped shoulders appeared to make him shrink. Actually, Byrne stood slightly over six feet; his face was long, with sharp elegant features. His speaking voice was a marvel, equaled only in its agility in *The Capri Affair* by Stella Morell's. But he prided himself on his acting, not his looks.

Billy recalled a Shakespearian season some years earlier. Keith Byrne hated the engagement because of the tone of the reviews. He was playing major parts, *Hamlet* among them, but the critics, he complained, "Exulted for three paragraphs on my behind and my legs and gave two lines to the performance."

In Billy Briggs' eye, the legs, behind and talent were still intact in the person of Keith Byrne. He was a witty, charming, imperturbable man, very attractive to women. Billy noticed that at company parties, of which there were many, Claudia inevitably gravitated to Keith. They appeared to enjoy each other's company to the point that an affair seemed mandated.

Perhaps, Billy thought, that's what happened. Byrne may have already tested the water and found it chilly. But that had never stopped him before. Something must have happened that an outsider could not be aware of.

As for young Robin Haywood—the juvenile's problems lay beyond Billy's willingness to try to understand them. Billy had done his bit for modern adolescence by raising a son and a daughter, now in their twenties and preoccupied with their own families. Now Billy and his wife, Millie, privately admitted that grandparenthood beat parenthood by a good deal.

As he glanced down the street and saw the marquee of the Wadsworth Theater, Billy's hand slipped into his inside coat pocket where he carried his special wallet. Like it or not, he intended doing something about the letter from the lovely girl in the wheelchair.

First he stopped at the boxoffice. Jackson Ryder, white haired and distinguished, had been treasurer of the house ever since Billy had been coming to Boston. Neither his looks nor his exuberance had altered with the years. Everything was always "fine," and if business wasn't good today, it was bound to pick up tomorrow. Ryder lived on his faith and on the tips he gave the management. The Wadsworth remained a constant moneymaker because Ryder's opinion was heeded in picking the shows.

The Capri Affair, Ryder told Billy, was doing fine. "The advance is strong—exceptionally strong. Those newspaper stories from New York may account for the heavy advance, but this piece would make it in a blizzard."

"I have a favor to ask, Ryder," Briggs said. "If you get a request for a wheelchair accommodation, let me know. I don't care if it's right in the middle of a light cue, call me backstage. It's important."

"Sure will."

"Thanks. May I borrow the phone for a couple of minutes?"

Ryder slipped a key under the grill. "This opens the manager's office. You know where it is. Take your time. Relax, you look upset. You shouldn't be, not with this show. I caught it twice in New York."

Billy worried about Ryder's remark. It wasn't good when his anxieties were that obvious. The company had been on layoff during the week that Winston, the "mystery woman," and Claudia's refusal to attend the funeral, were all in the headlines. There was bound to be some tension when the actors reassembled tomorrow for the line rehearsal. Billy had to be careful not to add to it.

He locked the door to the manager's office, sat at the desk, reached into the top right-hand drawer containing a telephone with a private line. First he dialed Claudia's apartment in New York. No answer. In his telephone book he located the name Rose Derlanger, and called her number in the Village, where Rose lived with her husband, a musician, and so many kids Billy had lost count.

Rose answered.

"Good morning, Rose, this is Billy Briggs in Boston."

"Well, hello. How are... they... is something wrong with something wrong with Miss Claudia?"

"No, Rose, she's fine. We're keeping her busy up here. The Sunday press is excellent. I'll send you the clips. When are you coming up?"

"As soon as the old man gets back from some gig he's doing in Philadelphia. The end of the week, maybe."

"Rose, who is Ella D.?"

There was a silence. Billy waited until Rose framed her answer. He'd hit a vein all right—and it wasn't good.

"Is she still pretty, Mr. Briggs?" Rose asked, obviously playing for time.

"Yes, very pretty. Marvelous eyes, and you forget she's stuck in a wheelchair almost from the minute you first talk to her."

"Mr. Briggs, right now it wouldn't be wise for her to see Miss Claudia, if that's what you want to know. Or for Miss Claudia to hear anything about her. Maybe some other time, but definitely not now." Rose paused. Billy hoped she might explain why. "Does that help you, Mr. Briggs?"

"A little, Rose. But I'm still left in the dark."

"Please, Mr. Briggs, let's leave it that way for now. All right?"

"Just as you say, Rose. Thanks. You've been very helpful. See you soon."

* * *

The opening performance in Boston of *The Capri Affair* was a triumph. Stella Morell repeated her modesty of the final performance in New York by eliminating the hoke from her curtain call and sharing the stage with Claudia. Moreover, she arranged with Claudia for each of them to bring on the others individually for the final company call.

Bostonians cheered, and so did the contingent of friends who arrived from New York and other parts of the country. Robin's parents came from Ohio. Keith Bryne's cool evaporated when his two sisters arrived backstage, surprising him with the sight of his elderly mother and father. They were a sprightly pair from Maine whose eyes glistened with tears at the joy of seeing their son in the flesh.

"You know," his father said, "we'd begun to wonder if you were round any more. Television is so darned flat."

Stella's delegation was huge, and not all from New York. Prominent members of Boston's Italian colony crowded into her dressing room. Photographers clicked away as Stella was made an honorary member of various societies. From time to time she screamed for other members of the company to join her in a photograph.

Old friends who remembered Anne as an ingenue, popular in summer stock on the New England circuit, surprised her. Claudia and Stella were gracious when Anne realized the friends were eager to meet the stars.

Donald Laine arrived from New York and introduced a host of people involved with Winston and Associates in Boston. Claudia could have done without them. Winston and Associates had already become part of her past. The Boston performance was in the present, and it exhilarated her. The Saturday evening spent with Keith and Robin had been a resounding success. She'd often wondered why the two male members of the cast had maintained such a distance from her. Certainly compared to Keith Byrne, she was a neophyte in the theater, but it couldn't have been the caste system that kept them apart. Whatever, they were friends now. They'd all gotten politely high and ended up at a waterfront dive at closing time drinking boilermakers with the fishermen.

Robin, so romantically handsome, had been a revelation. He actually knew how to smile; his language was earthy. When they danced at dinner she sensed a muscular, aggressive male, quite different from the quiet, etheral blond youth whose sensitivity was taken for granted.

Billy Briggs had postponed delivering Claudia's flowers until the guests had emptied out of her dressing room, Donald among them, while she changed into street clothes.

"Here they are, Claudia," he boomed. "About seven floral pieces—pretty good for Boston."

"Damned good, I'd say. And look at how big and handsome they are. That one, I swear, came from a race track by mistake. It looks like those wreaths they put around the horses at the Kentucky Derby." She flipped the envelope open. The piece was from one of the Winston people. She recognized Donald Laine's note immediately on another bouquet but delayed opening it, after spotting a card with a less familiar scrawl. She opened the latter and, before she unwrapped the dozen yellow roses, Claudia handed the card to Billy.

"What do you make of this?" Her face had paled.

Briggs, concerned about the significance of the flowers, anxiously read the card. It was from Lieutenant Frank Lamark.

"Cher Madame Milotte: May I wish you success on this opening night? I shall be in Boston on Thursday to view your performance again. May I have the honor of your company at supper afterward? With great admiration, your friend, Frank Lamark."

"My friend? Since when has a policeman become my friend? Our only meeting had to do with the murder of my husband, a man who threw me out of his life years ago.

90

Lamark wanted to know how I'd spent the day of the killing. Billy, does that make him my friend?"

Briggs was also puzzled by Lamark's use of the words. They couldn't be accidental; they were intended to tell Claudia something. How were either of them to interpret the message? It could be a trick to establish a relationship with Claudia that might lead to serious consequences. Billy was still living with the anxiety created by his encounter with Ella D. and the letter that lay hidden among his papers.

"It beats me, Claudia. I suppose you'll have to see him, but that doesn't mean you're obliged to go to supper."

"Unless he's really trying to be my friend. How does that hit you?"

Billy shrugged. "Who knows, maybe he thinks he's Inspector Javert."

"Well look who knows Victor Hugo! And am I supposed to be Jean Valjean?"

Billy laughed. "Don't be silly, honey. I saw all the movies of *Les Miserables*. Great stuff—as long as it was a movie."

"*Et comment*! Which translates, *mon cher*, into 'and how!'"

* * *

For all her bounce and vitality, Stella Morell was not a night owl. While the others dashed off to opening night parties, she'd firmly rejected the invitations of the society people and the pleas of the Italian-American groups, saying that she needed her rest.

It was true. Stella's performance sapped her vitality. It had been years since she'd played eight shows a week and it took time to become accustomed to the strain. Now that she had, the Italian star stuck rigidly to her routine of going directly home after a show, unwinding with television or a book, and sleeping late the next morning.

Only Billy Briggs, the stage doorman and Stella were left in the theater after the photographers, the audience and the performers had gone. She'd just slipped into her street clothes when Billy poked his head in the door.

"A tremendous night, *Signora*. What can I tell you that I haven't said before?"

"Come inside, Billy, and shut the door."

Her abruptness startled him. "Excuse me. I didn't mean to talk so tough. But you know things, and you're not telling me."

"What makes you think that?"

Stella smiled. She fingered the ring on the little finger of her left hand—a golden serpent. It was a habit indicating that Stella wasn't fooling around. Billy recognized the signal. Nevertheless, he had no intention of opening up until Stella gave him the cue.

There was a moment's silence. Stella eyed him, waiting for him to start. She counted ten. *Niente*. Very well, she'd make the first move.

"Why don't you sit down, Billy? We'll be more comfortable, and I'll open the cat-and-mouse game. I shouldn't make you carry the burden all by yourself."

"It's been a burden, all right." Billy felt relieved.

"You have some information threatening Claudia?"

"Yes."

"I thought so. What is it."

Everything that Billy knew burst out of him in an incoherent flood. Stella brushed aside what Claudia had told him about her last years with Ritchie Winston.

"I know *all* the shocking details of that era. They're dreadful."

92

From his wallet he pulled out the letter and told of his meeting with the beautiful girl in the wheelchair.

"She hasn't seen it?"

"No. I called her maid, Rose Derlanger. She told me not to give Claudia the letter, and to prevent the meeting—for the moment, at least."

"That makes sense," Stella said.

She returned the letter. "Hold on to it carefully. If Ella comes to the theater make sure she doesn't get backstage."

The casual way Stella spoke of Ella gave Billy the impression that the Italian woman knew her. He decided not to ask.

Stella smiled. "I'm reading your thoughts, Billy. I've never met Ella D. but I know who she is." Her voice deepened. "I also know why she lives in a wheelchair."

When Billy mentioned the flowers and the note from Lamark, her face brightened. "I like that. I noticed, when I saw them together on the night of the murder, that he's in love with her."

Billy remembered the story Byrne had told him of the curious instincts of John Barrymore. What could prevent Stella Morell from possessing the same powers? Nothing. Absolutely nothing. Nothing except that this mumbo-jumbo perception by actors was not how Billy Briggs knew them. He went by the old rule that they were all spoiled kids—and that's how you treated them.

"Billy," Stella said, "I want you out in the auditorium on Thursday night when Lamark is there. Your assistant can handle the show. He's good. I want you to notice everything he does, every move he makes, even if he only scratches his nose or shifts his position. I want to know if he scratches his balls—everything—do you understand?"

"Yes, Stella, it's quite clear."

"I want you to remember at what point in the play he

does these things. That is very important."

She fingered her ring and pounded her fist on the table, fighting in her mind for something she didn't dare forget. When it came, she got up from her chair and clapped her hands together in applause.

"Ha . . . ha . . . of course. I smelled it that first night. He uses scent. Very faint, very sophisticated. Not those macho anti-smell things baseball players advertise on television. Whatever Lamark goes for is expensive. He sweats . . . that's it . . . he sweats. The French sweat. They consume too much liquid during the day. So watch for him to mop his brow; that's going to tell us an awful lot."

"My god, Stella, how do you know all this? It's spooky."

She flopped back in her oversized chair.

"You think that, do you? *Tesaro*, my darling Billy Briggs, you are very wrong. I am reaching conclusions born of fact. If my conclusions are right, our Claudia is in serious trouble."

"That's how I've been thinking. But I couldn't put it into words."

"Don't try, Billy, and don't speak of anything to anybody. You go on now. My driver's outside. Don't worry about me. Have a good time—you're a good man."

Being a "good man" was little reassurance, Billy thought, as he walked through the stage door and into the alley. He realized that now there were five people wondering if Claudia Milotte had been her husband's murderer! Besides himself and Stella Morell, there were Ella, who stated it boldly, Rose Derlanger, whose passionless voice said nothing but suggested much, and, most certainly, Lieutenant Frank Lamark.

*   *   *

By Wednesday, first-night excitement had passed, as well as the delight members of *The Capri Affair* company took in the rave reviews of the Boston critics. There had been universal enthusiasm in the newspapers and from the television critics. As far as Boston was concerned, the new theatrical season had reached a peak with *The Capri Affair* and anything that came afterward would find it difficult to follow.

At twelve-fifteen Claudia's limousine slid into the driveway of the hotel. Claudia was waiting by the door talking to Robin, whom she'd found wandering aimlessly around the lobby a few minutes earlier.

"What's up?" she said.

He seemed to be growing handsomer by the hour, she thought. It had started with the Sunday they'd spent with Keith Byrne. Then, when the reviews praised his performance at such length, Robin magically matured. He'd begun to lose some of that boyish petulance which had distressed her during the New York run.

Robin laughed and smiled more readily now. "I'm not up to anything yet, Claudia. There's been too much excitement, I guess. You know, I got pounced on by two girls this morning who'd hidden themselves somewhere in the hall waiting for me, God knows for how long."

Claudia smiled. "Imagine that! What did they want, your body?"

"Nope, just my autograph. Then they gave me a self-addressed envelope so I could get yours and Stella's. I'm supposed to mail them back today. How about that? It's puzzling. Am I pounced on for my art or to be a messenger boy?"

"I'd say it was a little of both. Don't knock it. When the fans don't bother you, that's the time to worry."

As she started for the car Claudia said, "I'm leaving for

the theater. Want to come along?"

"Sure, why not? It's early for me."

"Don't rub it in," Claudia said, as the driver opened the door.

Robin sat beside her. "Rub what in?"

"That all you need is to cover your face lightly with greasepaint, add a little eye shadow, and you're ready to go on. A woman's got to work at the job—especially at my age."

"That's ridiculous. With make-up or without, you're the most attractive woman I've ever met."

"Well, thank you, Robin," Claudia said. "But you have a few years to go a statement like that means much."

Robin was about to sulk, but Claudia would have none of it. "It sounds lovely coming from you, because you're one of the best-looking and most charming men I've known in a long time. You could be a heart-breaker if you worked at it."

"Well how about that?" Robin said, "Except heart breaker isn't how I want to see myself. I want someone to enjoy being with me—someone like you. How about supper after the theater tonight?"

Claudia smiled. "A date at last, after all this time! Fine. I'll be looking forward to it."

They'd reached the theater and stopped at the stage doorman's cubicle—Robin to pick up his usual large collection of mail, Claudia to get her key and a couple of letters.

She asked the doorman, "Has a package come for me?"

"Not yet, Miss Milotte. Nothing came in this morning."

"If it shows up would you send it to me right away? It's from New York; I addressed it myself. It ought to be here by now."

She turned her attention to Robin's letters. "You certainly are the matinee idol, friend Robin. How about splitting them with me?"

He laughed. "You wouldn't appreciate them."

Impulsively, Robin took her in his arms and kissed her, holding Claudia tight until she was almost brethless. His face had turned beet red, but he was laughing as he broke away and headed toward his dressing room.

"Don't forget—right after the show tonight."

"What shall I wear?"

"Nothing fancy—but no slacks. Boston's entitled to see those legs."

One of her letters was a big envelope from Donald. She stuffed it into her purse and turned to the doorman. "The package—you'll remember, won't you?"

"Of course, Miss Milotte."

* * *

Billy and Ella D. met in the manager's office.

On his way backstage Billy Briggs stopped at the boxoffice to check the sale.

"Sold out," said the assistant manager. "Jackson wants to see you. He's in the manager's office."

Billy pushed through the heavy double doors, turned left and knocked at the door marked "private." Jackson Ryder was on the telephone. He waved Billy to a chair opposite one of the two desks in the room.

When he had finished with the phone he turned to Billy. "We have a wheelchair request for the matinee today." He glanced at a slip of paper. "All it says is 'Miss Ella.'"

"That's the woman I'm waiting for. Where do you intend to seat her?"

"There's a space in the center on the far aisle, even-numbered section, where we usually put the chairs. Next to a fire exit."

Billy went backstage and arranged with his assistant to handle the second act in case he wasn't there. "I have to go out front."

He found Ella, quite alone, seated in her chair, indifferent to the curiosity her appearance in the theater created. She was wearing an expensive tailored suit and, as on the night of their first meeting, she seemed incredibly serene.

"May I speak to you after the performance, Miss Ella?" Billy asked.

"Of course," she said, smiling. "I guess you read my note. Maybe giving it to you to deliver was a mistake."

"Perhaps not."

Her smile forgave him. "We can talk about that later. Isn't this a great play? Claudia is magnificent. I'm so happy for her."

An usher led Ella D. to the manager's office while the curtain calls were still going on and before the wheelchair could get stuck in the rush of people leaving the theater.

Billy began nervously, "In view of the circumstances, Miss Ella, you can understand why I opened your note. It's a fairly common thing to do in the theater, where stars get so much mail. In Claudia Milotte's case, we're apprehensive about notes like yours. It contained a damaging accusation."

"But you didn't turn it over to the F.B.I. or the police," she said, "or I would have known."

"Of course not. I checked around as far as I could. Stella Morell knows who you are, although she said she had never met you. She also knows why you're confined to a wheelchair."

Ella's eyes stopped dancing. "Of course Stella would know that. She knows everything."

"I also called Rose Derlanger."

"You did?" Ella brightened. "What did she say?"

"She wanted to know if you were still beautiful and I told her yes—very definitely yes. But she also said that this wasn't the right time for you to meet Claudia. She urged me to do my best to avoid it. I don't understand the reason. Rose was reluctant to go into details. I didn't press her."

"If Rose feels that way, I'll respect her judgment. I won't try to see Claudia. Now, about the letter...."

"I'm keeping it for the time being."

"Good. I know it's safe. You won't turn it over to the authorities...."

"No, Miss Ella, I won't."

"I'm going to tell you part of the story. The reason I'm in this wheelchair is that Richard Winston threw me down a flight of stairs in a wild rage. I wasn't like the others."

"What others?"

"The other little girls he'd invited to his big estate on Long Island. You see, I was strong. I wasn't going to take off my dress; I put up a fight. Most girls would—when they're thirteen."

"That's the kind of thing you read about in newspapers and you don't want to believe. But you do believe."

"And then you forget, don't you, Mr. Briggs, unless it happens to someone you care about. Anyway, it happened a long time ago, about five years before Winston met Claudia."

"That makes you almost her age. It's amazing, you look so young."

Ella's eyes darkened. "We always hear that. It's a characteristic of paraplegics. My spinal cord was severed.

I went through three operations before the doctors decided the damage was permanent. The reason paraplegics don't appear to age is that eventually we make peace with ourselves. We're unable to bear any more suffering; we've already had our share.

"Moreover, we have two overriding worries to distract us from petty problems. The first we control by eating sensibly—a girl can get awfully fat sitting in one of these. The second we know is inevitable, and it makes us uncommonly fatalistic. We die young—kidney malfunction.

"Claudia Milotte may have heard about me; I imagine she has. Once she may not have believed I existed, but I do. I'm quite real. I was shipped out of New York by the Winston people and settled here in Boston. I'm well taken care of financially; I'm the vice-president of a Winston corporation. I believe I own a couple of banana boats.

"Banana boats, oil wells, a sawmill—what difference does it make? My life was taken away from me by a monster. I want Claudia to know that I'll testify to this if she ever needs me. I may loose my vice-presidency, maybe even what life I have left, but I really don't care. You see, I wish I had had Claudia's courage."

"Aren't you taking a great deal for granted, Miss Ella?" Billy Briggs asked.

The madonnalike expression returned. "You were obliged to ask that, Mr. Briggs. I understand. Do me one favor, please: tell Rose that I followed her advice, and I appreciate it."

"I will."

"Good. Now if you'll head me in the direction of the lobby I'll let myself out. There's a car waiting for me at the curb."

Billy Briggs opened the door of the manager's office

and guided the wheelchair to the lobby, where Ella signaled for him to stop. She extended her hand, saying, "Thank you, Mr. Briggs. Our conversation has been reassuring. Claudia's going to come through this all right."

"What makes you so sure?" Billy asked. He bit his tongue as he realized that implicit in the question lay the admission that a problem existed.

"She has good friends. Good afternoon, Mr. Briggs."

Ella maneuvered her chair through the open doors and out into the street, where Billy saw a handsome black man lift her out of the chair and place her gently in the back seat of a car. He folded the chair with a series of quick, experienced moves, got behind the wheel and drove off.

*   *   *

Claudia prayed that Robin would understand when she begged him to postpone their night on the town and settle for a nightcap at the hotel bar. She explained that she was bone tired, nervous and worried.

Robin did understand. His readiness to postpone their date sprang from hope that extra rest would make Claudia less jumpy than she'd become since the Winston murder. Who could blame her for being subject to spasms of nerves? Even Robin had been shaken by Stella's curious performance that evening; it was totally out of character. The matinee had gone off without a hitch, but the evening show turned into a shambles. Stella mumbled, fluffed lines, went ahead of herself and slipped out of context so often that the others had to virtually rewrite the play to keep it afloat until the final act, when Stella finally settled down.

The audience, totally unaware of the agony the actors

were suffering, cheered and applauded for a long time. That relaxed some of the tensions, but it did little to spare Stella embarrassment. After the show she fled to her dressing room.

Claudia wondered if her inexplicable behavior had any connection with the fact that she'd been closeted for almost an hour between performances with Billy Briggs. Also, why had Billy Briggs been away so long during the matinee?

Then there were those muffled conversations on the intercom between Billy and the box office. They were little things, Claudia knew, but they preyed on her frazzled nerves. Donald Laine's fat envelope didn't help, either. Besides the legal documents she was supposed to sign without understanding a word, the envelope contained a handwritten note saying that both Donald and Rose Derlanger had been visited by a policeman—not Lamark—and were obliged to go over everything they'd done on the day of the murder.

Robin drove to the hotel in Claudia's car. At the bar they ordered drinks. They avoided each other's eyes as they sat in eerie silence. When they talked, it was the idle conversation of strangers who'd just met. They avoided mentioning Stella's incredible performance.

Robin, trying to brighten things, took Claudia's hand. "So you're not up to anything tonight. It's all right; I'm not disappointed."

She stared at him curiously. "Well, I am—damned disappointed."

Robin wasn't sure whether to yell with delight at the outburst or murmur apologies. "You know what I mean. I want you to feel comfortable, that's all. And you can't imagine what it does to me when you say you're disappointed."

"Well, goddamn it, I am. I'm tired of being a wallflower—the broad who's so messed up nobody asks her anywhere. I think you're one helluva young man and I'll be one helluva date—whenever it comes off."

"How about tomorrow?"

Claudia shuddered. "You'll never believe it, but I've been invited to supper by a cop."

"Not that French-looking detective from New York?"

"Lieutenant Frank Lamark? None other."

"What the devil is he coming up here for?"

"Darling, that's what I'm going to find out. Or I expect to. He sent me flowers opening night with a note saying he'd be here Thursday and would I have supper with him."

"He's got a nerve."

"Maybe not, Robin. You don't have to duck the Winston thing. A man who was my husband got killed. He was president of an organization of worldwide importance. Lamark's investigating. He can call me up any time of the day or night and ask me questions. If I refuse, he can always subpoena me, bring me into the District Attorney's office or shove me out in front of the Grand Jury. This guy's odd; he doesn't do it that way. He invites me to supper, sends me flowers. What would you do if you were me?"

Robin grinned. "Go to supper with him. Maybe Friday, after it's over, you'll feel better."

"I hope so, Robin. I guess I'll turn in now."

She kissed him chastely. He walked her to the elevator. Then he returned to the bar and ordered a triple bourbon.

He sat drinking for three-quarters of an hour, oblivious to either the drinks or the atmosphere around him. He seemed not even to hear the music as he cradled his chin in the palm of his hand.

Robin felt a knee press into his thigh, rub gently, then slide quickly down the length of his leg. "Pardon, but do you have a match?"

He turned quickly. The youth was in his early twenties, darkly handsome, and in his eyes Robin saw the reflection of his own loneliness. How could he tell the boy this—or explain that he'd tried it once his way and it hadn't worked?

"Sure," he muttered, and tossed his matchbook toward the youth.

He looked at the clock and appeared to time it to his watch. "Keep the matches. It's getting late for me. Enjoy yourself. See you around."

He plunged his hand into his pocket, found that the key was there and not at the desk. He headed straight for the elevator and another lonely, restless night.

When the elevator reached his floor, the door slid open. He made a step to leave, then moved back and pushed the button that brought him back to the lobby. He walked into the bar. The chair he'd just left was still empty. Fear that it wouldn't be had bothered him terribly on the way down. He could hear his heart pounding when the dark-haired youth turned and fastened deep brown eyes on his.

"I guess you changed your mind," the young man said.

"Yeah, sure. Why not?"

"I'd like to order drinks. May I?"

"Of course. Thanks."

Robin liked the warm smile he saw on the man's face. His nervousness began to fade.

Part Three

Angrily Claudia slammed her room door after stomping out of the elevator in a rage. She was furious at herself for avoiding the date with Robin, angry with him for being so "damned understanding." That, of course, was ridiculous. Robin had no way of knowing her problems. Against all his instincts, he was being gentlemanly. Wasn't that in the young men's guidebook to making out with older women? What gave Claudia the right to complain?

Older women! She should be so lucky as to be in the ranks of the few she knew and the hundreds she'd read about who shuddered at the very idea of turning back the years. Even "poor" Anne Alexander, who'd given total devotion to a possessive mother, confided that her life was not quite as bleak as her friends assumed. The brownstone she owned had long housed a tenant on the third floor, a successful businessman who rented the place in order to be near her.

"I call it an intimacy rather than a love affair," Anne said. "He travels a great deal and I literally crawl into producers' offices when they're planning road companies—anything to get away from my mother. For me, that's growth. Ten years ago I couldn't imagine even leaving mother, and when I did her nurse couldn't be anyone less skilled or dedicated than Florence Nightingale. Now I find young Puerto Rican girls who are wonderful with the old woman. They know she's a fraud. When her temper explodes they only giggle. I used to get hysterical.

"When it comes to sex, our separations add excitement to my relationship with my 'intimate friend.' Eventually he's going to marry. He ought to. But it won't be to me. He's fifteen years younger than I am."

Remembering how casually Anne spoke of her "intimacy," Claudia's fury mounted. She whipped off her clothes and stood in front of the full-length mirror. She wondered if tall, skinny, angular, flat-chested Anne Alexander enjoyed the sight of her own body.

She posed and looked at herself. "What's wrong with that?" she yelled. "Nothing, not a damned thing—except me." She revolved slowly, peering back over one shoulder and finding the rear view equally intriguing. There was a nice upward thrust to the buttocks that was quite in fashion these days. As she touched herself, Claudia's flesh seemed to glow in response and she began to feel a quivering intensity.

Shuddering, but fascinated with the picture in the mirror, Claudia imagined she was seeing a wicked but strangely beautiful image of sensuous womanhood. Flushed cheeks. Lips pink and tremulous, moistly agleam from the sweep of a mercurial tongue tip. Emerald eyes shining with suppressed excitement. It was years since she could ever quite recall having seen herself so beautiful, so radiantly alive.

But as quickly as her self-approval swelled, it disappeared. She slipped into a robe and turned off all the lights to begin what had become her nightly routine since arriving in Boston. She'd moved an easy chair close to the window with a cocktail table beside it. The table held a decanter of red wine and a tray with a single glass. She filled it, sipped quietly as she stared out of the picture windows to the view of Boston Common and the hills surrounding the famous old park, wondering if there were others in those houses, some speckled with light, others clothed in darkness, who sat alone—and waited.

She toyed briefly with the idea of calling Robin, of inviting him to her room to share her wine, but discarded the idea almost immediately. Claudia had been around long enough to identify that sort of behavior as arrogance—the coy trick played by the big movie stars. She called it "summoning the pet poodle" and wished that she hadn't thought of it.

Where had all that famed French logic Claudia was supposed to possess disappeared to? Robin, obviously disappointed, had shown more logic when he wanted their first date to be free of tension. And why not? They had nothing to hide. Claudia was a free human being at last. Well—almost free.

She'd depended on her logic and French reserve to see her through these crucial weeks. This was not the moment to lose control. Nor was it the moment to propel herself into an emotional state over a beautiful young man with a boyish crush on her. The sight of him—his touch, those young lips pressed against hers—would bring the relief she needed so badly. Fine! But that would be tonight. Tomorrow all her iron discipline would have to be summoned from the deepest recesses of her psyche. It would be sheer folly to slacken the harness with emotional intrusion. Robin would not understand. Some day, yes, but not now.

She finished the wine and carried the empty glass to the bathroom, where she washed it out. Claudia sighed. The wine had flushed her face ever so slightly. She thought, "You look like they say in those dirty books—wanton. And baby, you are...."

She turned on the bath, bound up her hair. As the water reached the halfway mark she stepped into the tub. She had always enjoyed the feel of warm water, steamy and sweetly scented, engulfing and invading her body with its intimately lapping insistence.

She lay back in the tub, enjoying the delicious languor that began to pervade her flesh. Her fingers skittered up and down her body. Her mind turned on a picture of Robin. When she closed her eyes she could see him, shirtless, his boyishly robust chest covered with only a sprinkling of light, almost gossamer hair.

"A wonderful daydream," Claudia thought, half aloud. "Or does one call them night dreams?"

She quickly finished the routine of bathing and drying, and fled to the bed, where she covered herself with the fresh linen and fleecy blankets which for so many years had been her only companions of the night.

Claudia prayed no devils would visit her tonight.

* * *

"So you're going to Boston tomorrow," Sal White said to Frank Lamark as they lingered over coffee at Murray's

Deli, "and you're not sure why? For a policeman, it doesn't make sense."

Lamark smiled. "That's a matter of opinion. If you watch those TV shows, policemen often do things on a hunch."

Sal laughed. "I suppose that's one way of describing an infatuation."

Lamark shrugged his shoulders, grateful for Sondra's intrusion. She'd been overcome with delight when the two men arrived at the deli and actually waited five minutes for their favorite table to be cleared. Then, surprise of all surprises, they sat down and ate a whole dinner!

"More coffee, gentlemen?" Sondra asked, as she picked up the dessert dishes.

"Well, I'll be... Mr. Lamark actually finished his cheesecake."

"How could I resist? You've been hawking it for months."

"I always love the cheesecake," Sal interrupted. "Yes, Sondra, more coffee, please."

He waited till she was gone before he went on. "Of course, there are a lot of holes in these clips," he said, as he hauled the Winston file from the seat and placed it on the table. "Ritchie Winston's early years were protected by his old man's wealth and power; Claudia's, because she was hidden away in an orphanage somewhere in the South of France, a village near the Pyrénées, a place called Lucenay. Do you know it?"

Lamark nodded. "Yes. It's one of those ghastly small towns of France which tourists find so charming and unspoiled because time has stood still for five hundred years. If the Inquisition were to be started all over again, it would find a ready-made population in Lucenay delighted to burn heretics and witches. I can imagine the narrowness of the world Claudia found in an orphanage in that part of France. I can believe too that it affected her character in ways that perhaps even she doesn't understand."

"Then it ought to be easy for you to fit in the missing pieces, to read between the lines," Sal said. "When someone becomes famous, you, of all people, should know that embarrassing facts about his early life either vanish completely or become distorted just enough to create an entirely new image. Christ, for the last eight years we've had a fathead trying to get the presidential nomination and nobody knows how old he really is. For twenty years he's been in public life and not a newspaper in the country has been able to obtain a copy of his birth certificate. Power makes fools of the people."

"But Claudia Milotte isn't running for president," Lamark observed.

"Maybe not, but a lot of facts about her younger years got obscured naturally. World War II, the strange behavior of the girl's mother, who dropped out of society to become a hooker, and the death of Claudia's father. We only have the picture of her golden years to go by, when she landed in the care of her grandmother, who offered her a splendid education. Then we meet her as a young and beautiful movie star, sponsored by two distinguished moviemakers, Francois Smadja, who discovered her, and Nino Bellafiore, who didn't do so well with Claudia professionally but gave her a damned fine friend in his wife, Stella Morell.

"What somebody's got to find out is what happened behind those high walls of the orphanage of Lucenay in the years between her fifth and fifteenth birthday. Aren't they supposed to be the most important years of a person's life? Don't the shrinks tell us that our personalities are formed in childhood, along with our sex preferences, eating habits, the whole *geschichte?*"

Lamark was thoughtful. "Yes, that's what they tell us. If you work very long as a policeman and do your homework, you find that it's pretty accurate. Today's delinquent kid is, unfortunately, tomorrow's criminal. About sex I'm not so sure. Today, the old rules don't hold. The kids swing so many different ways I wouldn't want to predict how they're going to turn out. I'd hate to think that a woman as feminine and attractive as Claudia Milotte was suffering sexual maladjustment because of a dark decade in a French orphanage."

Sal smiled. "Man, you've got it bad! Is this trip to Boston official? Are you putting it on your expense account?"

Lamark hesitated. "I'll put it to you this way," he said eventually. "I'll decide whether it was business or personal *after* I return to New York."

Sal sighed. "I guess that's why I never heard of your being on the take. Still, it's splitting hairs very fine. Aren't you using your official position to make a date with a doll who has to accept it?"

Lamark smiled. "You're damned right I am, and if you want to know the truth, I'm not the least bit ashamed. How many traffic tickets do you imagine get torn up in the course of the year in exchange for a fast blow job?"

"My God! Lamark, if Sondra heard language like that from *Mister* Lamark, we'd be eighty-six'd on the spot."

He riffled the clips in the folder, pulled out a two-page spread and pointed to the headline: THE SEXIEST MILLIONAIRE—*How He Plays House with Dolls Who still Like Dollies!*

"It's a no-name story, but that's Ritchie Winston. His name was on the confidential list of sex offenders and

111

child molesters in every precinct of the city and all over Long Island; Christ, every place he ever went. Young Ritchie never outgrew his nickname. He liked it. He couldn't make it with girls his own age, even when he was in high school and the three colleges his father pushed him through before some two-bit college in the south, almost a diploma mill, gave him a degree."

"How does that jibe with all the stories we hear of his conquests nowadays, and of the women chasing him, including that 'mystery woman' everybody assumes was one of his current *amours*?"

"What do you think?"

Lamark's answer sounded too glib for Sal White. "I think she was a plant, a distraction to hide the real killer, a hired hit man."

"Sorry I asked," Sal said.

Lamark let the inference pass as Sal found another clip, showing a silhouette of a young woman in a wheelchair. "My information is," Sal continued, "that Richard Winston IV is a slob, a satyr, a sadist, whose kicks come from debasing women. These days he buys himself virgins under most discreet conditions arranged for him by his staff of pimps; he's gone so far that he can't haunt schoolyards and playgrounds like he used to. Besides being internationally loathed as a financier, he's internationally notorious as a pedophile. It's very simple. When his pimps can't buy him a virgin a day he gets by on the same favors cops receive for tearing up traffic tickets. Remember, it's your idea—he lives on blow jobs. This is the story of one kid who fought back," Sal continued, as he moved the clip toward Lamark. "It's absolutely correct in every detail. She gave it to me and wanted no fee. She didn't need the money.

"She was only thirteen when, along with a bunch of

other little girls, she was invited to the Winston estate in the Hamptons. It turned out that only Ritchie was home. He'd just graduated from college—or bought his diploma. One by one he lures some of the kids up to his bedroom, where he asks them to strip. Some did; others didn't. This girl was especially attractive, a beautiful blonde with lovely blue eyes, tits just beginning to sprout. She really sent Ritchie—but she wouldn't buy his game. She fought him and he threw her down a flight of steps. Her back was broken. All hell broke loose. Old man Winston got word to his lawyers and fixed things with the kid's family."

Lamark shook his head. "Yes, yes, I know that story. I read the clipping several times. Ghastly. But that's in the past. What I can't understand is how a girl as intelligent as Claudia got mixed up with Richard Winston in the first place."

"Lieutenant Lamark, you ought to know: intelligence is no substitute for experience. Claudia may look like a worldly woman who's done it all twice and is ready for the third time around, but that's her marvelous body and her acting skill sending the message. But just look at the facts of her life—what the hell did she know? She was a sheep in wolf's clothing. Can you see it that way?"

"With a little imagination I can," Lamark said. "Maybe we can call her a lamb being led to slaughter."

"However you want to say it, I'll lay it on the line," Sal said. "Claudia Milotte was a dummy as far as men were concerned. As a young actress she turns out pretty smart, but there's this big disappointment when the Bellafiore movie doesn't come off—*Schizo* or whatever it was called. She played a double role. The picture never got finished."

"I wonder if there's a print around."

"Sure. There are millions of feet of unreleased film stored in vaults here and in Europe. *Schizo's* probably in Rome. There are a lot of big stars, name directors and writers involved. The pictures got dumped once enough money had been spent to write them off as tax losses. Nothing has ever been invented that shows a tax loss faster than show business. That's how it survives. A guy by the name of Primo Franchini's the big middleman in Rome."

Lamark scribbled his name on a pad.

"Claudia got cold feet about Hollywood when they started putting the heat on her to make like a Love Goddess. That's not what she wanted. So she comes back to America and starts playing in community theaters. It's great publicity. The girl's got a name; she draws business. To everyone's surprise, she's also a good actress.

"So they're having a festival in Philadelphia—the works of a native son, George Kelly. He was a playwright, Grace Kelly's uncle. They grab Claudia for two roles, a pretty ingenue in *The Show-Off* and a big fat dramatic part in *Craig's Wife*. She knocks them dead in a role that Rosalind Russell and Joan Crawford played in the movies. The New York critics stumble in, and every producer on Broadway is pounding on her door. Richard Winston gets there first."

"How come?"

"Because Winston and Associates donated a big hunk of dough to the festival. Yeah, they only did American plays. Big outfits had to ante up some cash. Boy meets girl. Boy gets girl. Boy marries girl—and that's the end of Claudia Milotte, star."

"Then what happened?"

"You're a detective, Frank; you find out. That was about thirteen years ago. Fill in those years—that's a lot of time. Fill in the ten years when Claudia lived in the orphanage with the Middle Ages nuns, too, and you have a story that would tempt me to schedule a two-million-copy run of *The Lowdown*.

"Uncover the real reason that Claudia didn't divorce Winston, and why she turned down his offers of a settlement worth a couple of million at least, and I'll raise the run to three million. You know, Frank, that hasn't happened in the exposé field in more than twenty-five years. You'd be setting a record."

Lamark smiled. "I'll give it a good try, I promise you."

Sal White believed him. But he also believed it meant Lamark would have to pin down Claudia Milotte as her husband's killer—beyond a reasonable doubt.

*   *   *

Claudia went to the theater particularly early on Thursday evening. Her sleep had been restless. She made the best of the situation by spending a large part of the afternoon in bed. Claudia didn't believe in drugs and was given neither to tranquilizers or pep pills. When her nerves were jangled beyond sufferance, she simply made herself rest until they grew calm. She explained her antipathy to drugs by saying, "I like my nerves. Without them I wouldn't be any good."

Of course, Claudia told herself, the tensions she'd endured since Ritchie's murder were hardly the kind that could be enjoyed. Still, having avoided the drug scene for so long, she didn't feel that the present crisis warranted experimentation.

Claudia's willpower had returned with strength and new vitality after her recovery from the months of isolation in the Soho apartment. As an experience it had been invaluable, in the sense that Claudia learned there was no escape from everyday reality. One could not cure anguish by losing one's sensibilities in a bottle. Life had to be faced and its problems were handled more wisely by a mind that was neither dulled by chemicals nor brought to unrealistic euphoria by alcohol.

At the theater, Claudia inquired about her package. She was told it had not yet arrived, so she proceeded directly to her dressing room. Neither Stella nor Anne, generally the first to arrive, had come in.

She heard footsteps, voices and the sounds of a backstage gradually becoming filled with the people who would turn on the lights and perform the magic she found in every performance. She enjoyed the sounds that sneaked in through the thin walls of her dressing room.

The knock she heard was Robin's. She yelled a hearty, "Come in," and her eyes were immediately drawn to the jiffy bag Robin held in his hands.

She recovered quickly enough to smile. "Hello, Robin. You're early tonight."

"I wanted to make sure you were all right. I called a couple of times this afternoon; they told me you weren't taking calls. Then I found out you'd left for the theater."

He handed her the bag. "I found this when I went to pick up my key. They never seem to have the same doorman two nights in a row. Whoever was there asked me to give this to you. He said he'd told you it hadn't arrived. Must be the package you sent to yourself. Funny, it doesn't look like your writing."

Claudia, trying to be casual and doing it very well, tossed the package on the dressing room table and said, "Well, I got mixed up. Rose must have addressed it. You're looking pretty chipper," she added. "How did it go with you today?"

"Ouch!" Robin said, "let's not talk about that now. You have a performance to do and then you have that date with the old man—the New York gumshoe."

Lamark, an old man? Claudia let that pass. He couldn't be more than five or six years older than she was. But from Robin's young viewpoint he probably looked ancient.

"I'm being very positive about it, Robin. There's no way out of it; we both know that. So far Lamark has been extremely polite to me, God knows why. Maybe I'll find out tonight."

She'd started making up, so Robin blew her a kiss. "I'll be around if you need me. I may not look strong, but I am. Don't let that cop get fresh."

She was sure Robin really believed Lamark was too old to "get fresh."

After he closed the door she looked at the bag. That had to be gotten back to the hotel somehow before she met Lamark. She thought for a couple of seconds, then snapped her fingers and walked to the dressing room door. Billy Briggs was only a few feet away, talking to his assistant.

"Billy," she said, "when you have a minute come see me."

"My minute's right now, baby, whenever it's you."

"Liar!" Claudia said. "I know you call your wife every night you're on the road. What do you say to her?" She stopped short. "That was a leading question, wasn't it? With me still in the newspapers, you must be running up quite a bill."

Billy didn't like that. "The only time we've talked about the newspaper stories was at home in New York, when Millie said how sorry she was."

"And I'm sorry too. That was a nasty crack. But you

117

have to understand that the nastiness I'm fighting sometimes comes out—usually with the wrong people. Forgiven?"

"Of course," Billy answered. "What's on your mind?"

"You know where Lamark's sitting. Get to him before the curtain, or at intermission, and tell him that I'll meet him at the hotel—at the Sky Room at eleven thirty. I don't want him backstage waiting for me to change. Besides, I haven't anything here to wear. And I intend to be pretty devastating tonight—even if I'm damned if I know why."

"No trouble at all, Claudia. I'm going to be out front tonight. Jack's gotta handle the show once or twice on his own before we move to Chicago."

"Of course, I'd forgotten, you might be leaving. But you and Millie are coming to Capri at Christmas, aren't you?"

Billy Briggs smiled. "Millie and I know better than to argue with Stella. A great dame, even if she doesn't *invite* you to Capri, she just says, 'You be there.' I'll talk to Lamark, don't worry. I'm looking forward to tonight. It'll be the first time I've seen the show from out front."

"We'll dazzle you, baby." Claudia smiled.

* * *

Lieutenant Frank Lamark looked even more handsome than she expected as he waited for her at the entrance to the Sky Room. Claudia told herself that the Sky Room, like most smart nightclubs, was lighted by an expert who could make King Kong look like Robert Redford. But even so, there was an appealing quality to this unusual policeman that intrigued her. Beyond his looks and his cultivated speech and manners, she believed there was a man who'd suffered a great deal at some point

118

in his life and was recovering from it through control and determination. It showed in his eyes.

As they took a table less conspicuous than the one Billy had reserved in Claudia's name, she wasted no time in bringing up the murder. She had decided on that strategy the minute his message and flowers arrived on opening night. Claudia had no intention of fielding a lot of inconsequential chitchat before being clobbered with a question about Winston out of the blue.

Before the waiter had brought the drinks she asked, "How's the investigation going? Have you lined up any suspects yet?"

Lamark smiled. "You don't pussyfoot, do you, Miss Milotte?"

"Not with a policeman. If you have some questions to ask about Winston, what I imagine, how I feel or anything like that, do it now. I'm not going to play cat and mouse all evening."

"I'm sorry you have that impression of me. I assure you, Miss Milotte, I have no intention of discussing the murder. If you have something to say and want to, then say it. Otherwise we'll forget the whole nasty matter. I would prefer you to believe that I came to enjoy the pleasure of your performance under leisurely circumstances, as well as the pleasure of your company. I admit I've taken advantage of my official introduction to you. If I weren't who I am, you might probably have avoided me."

Claudia's eyes lighted mischievously. "Not necessarily, Lieutenant. And if you'll call me Claudia, I'd prefer to use your first name too, if I may?"

"I appreciate that, Claudia."

"No, I haven't anything to say about the murder. They keep throwing papers at me to sign, all involving the

119

estate. I'm not the least bit interested in it; I don't need the money. But I'm no fool—I have no intention of letting those big business manipulators get away with anything. Would you?"

"Never."

"As for Richard Winston, we were separated for quite some time before his death. It was a miserable marriage with a miserable man, and I don't enjoy being referred to as his widow. Now, Frank, have I forgotten anything?"

"You've covered the grounds thoroughly."

"And you?"

"As I told you... I've taken advantage of my position...."

"That's fine. I don't mind. I'm delighted you're here. Quite flattered, really! And to borrow an old theatrical joke, let's stop talking about me and talk about my performance."

"Claudia, it was magnificent. You were playing on nerves when I saw the show that Sunday matinee. Today it was different, totally different. You really got inside the character. I knew her—almost. You held some things back. You let the audience imagine them. That requires art."

"And Stella? Isn't she superb?"

"Yes, in a very different way from you. That's what gives the play its excitement. You are both good—and the men couldn't have been better. We really should order," Lamark concluded hastily, noticing the waiter, who was as consumed with enthusiasm as the detective himself.

Claudia settled for cold chicken, a salad and red wine. "I often wish I were a chorus girl or a dancer; they really know how to knock off a meal after a show. But I can't—I have to watch my weight."

Lamark chose a steak sandwich and salad, and his

choice of a French wine from the wine list brought a beam of approval from the waiter. Although Lamark seemed comfortable about having used his position to date her, Claudia felt that the best way to handle him at the beginning was to keep the theatrical chatter going.

"Maybe you aren't aware of it," she said, "but I've known Stella for a long time. She was the reason I came back to the theater. We met years ago when I was starting out. I'd done two French films and her husband, Nino Bellafiore, saw me. He signed me to come to Rome for a film about a girl with a dual personality. It never had a final title. We called it *Schizo*. It was a joke.

"But that's how it's still referred to. You see, the movie never got finished. The money ran out and poor Nino couldn't find any more. I guess the movie has turned to dust now. Anyhow, he was such a perfectionist that the lead players were expected to do their own inserts."

Lamark's face went blank.

"You know, those shots you see of the heroine's legs walking away from the bad guy, slowly at first, then running. Or a girl stepping into a tub. Those shots are never made by the star; a bit player does them. But Bellafiore felt that the character became more complete on the screen when the actor actually performed those little bits and pieces for himself. I wouldn't know how it came out; I never saw the film put together, just the rushes now and then. But it was so close to being finished it just doesn't seem fair."

"What about Hollywood? Why didn't you go there?"

Claudia smiled. "I don't know," she said, fumbling for an answer. "That's so long ago. I think I was afraid of what might happen to me. They might try to make me somebody I wasn't." Then she sat upright and laughed. "Ye gods! It couldn't have been worse than marrying

Richard Winston! Ouch, that's a no-no. I'm sorry. I'll shut up now, Frank, and give you a chance."

"Don't apologize. It's how you feel. I understand. Now that I have the chance to talk about it, do you know the scene in this play that impressed me the most?"

Claudia leaned back in her chair and laughed. "Of course. The card game."

"You've heard it many times before, I suppose."

"Thank God for that. It's the most difficult scene in the play, and every gesture has been worked out very carefully. Do you know, Stella and I count 'one, two, three,' in our heads to keep the timing perfect? You see, the strength of the scene lies in the fact that I deal the cards lefthanded against her right hand. With our hands we create the illusion of physical combativeness to match our verbal sparring. It took me weeks to learn how to deal! I rehearsed the scene over and over again, not only with Stella but with the stage manager, the script girl, anybody. I practiced dealing lefthanded at home until my arms ached."

"Isn't it unusual for that much effort to go into one scene?"

"Not at all. Any time an actor handles props that are important to a show he has to master using them without making a mistake. That's part of the craft."

Claudia noticed that Frank Lamark was relieved when the waiter arrived with the food. She scored one for her side, and afterward it turned out to be a surprisingly pleasant evening. They sometimes spoke in French. Lamark's was excellent considering how little time he'd spent in France. "Just a couple of years after high school," he told her.

When they separated, he kissed her and she responded

with a warm embrace. He said that he would see her one day soon.

"Tomorrow," he explained, "begins my vacation. I'm flying to Paris and, if I can take a little more time, I may go to Italy. Anyhow, dear Claudia, thank you for this lovely evening. You've been a tonic for me."

"I might say the same," she replied, as they entered the elevator.

On the twelfth floor, before leaving the lift, Claudia impulsively kissed him on the lips, a long, lingering, affectionate kiss. "*Au revoir, mon ami*," she said, gliding out of the elevator—a queen bee who had made her conquest.

* * *

Tony's Pleasure Boat had been around the Boston harbor for as long as anyone could remember. The incumbent Tony was a roundbellied, loud-talking, cigar-smoking ex-New York cabdriver named Ben who had married Tony's widowed daughter, Elena Mathea and took over the family business on the death of his father-in-law. There were also other compelling reasons why Ben had left his Brooklyn home and old friends— reasons which were unrelated to his decision to take a second wife after many years as a widower, or his total lack of interest in Boston or Boston harbor.

Running Tony's Pleasure Boat, if one possessed Ben's adaptability to circumstance, was no different from driving a cab. You were your own boss. You worked your own hours. You were out in the open air. From one day to the next you never knew what adventure lay ahead. If the people you met weren't the equivalent in numbers of those you encountered behind the wheel of a cab, they were no less wacky, nutsy, fruity, off their rocker and zany.

As Ben saw it, that's what life was all about—people. While other operators of motorboat trips closed up the day after Labor Day, Ben's pier stayed open until the first snowfall closed the wooden steps that led from street level down to his boat. Actually, it was after Labor Day that Ben drew his favorites—eccentrics who appeared to have come to him because he was there. Ben sincerely believed they were drawn by the all-knowing hand of fate.

"All my life," Ben told Elena, when she worried about his catching cold in the damp days of the fall, "I've given service to people. It's too late to change now."

"But you're fifty-five, Ben, you don't need to work so hard."

"And God willing I'll be sixty and still rendering service. You can't fool around with destiny, Elena."

Elena limited her nagging to two warnings a season. Ben wouldn't react mildly to a third. So she kept their apartment warm and comfortable, served Ben carefully prepared, healthful meals, and prayed she would not become a widow again. The years between had been lonely and terrifying.

Maybe Ben was speaking for both of them when he talked about "rendering service." Without her there would have been no Tony's Pleasure Boat. First she had cared for her father, then for her first husband, who helped him in the business. There were three boats then. Now there was only one boat, the *Elena*, and Elena watched over the captain, Ben Schwartz.

This last Friday in September was bound to be an interesting day, Ben told himself, as he slipped the canvas covering from his boat and began the systematic polishing of its brass and chrome which occupied the first hours of every morning of his seven-day week. There were only a few puffs of clouds in the sky. The weather was brisk, the water choppy. But that would never stop whoever was headed his way today.

She didn't show up until ten o'clock, when a taxi appeared on the street about a hundred yards away from Ben's pier. The driver got out and opened the door to the passenger compartment, and Ben didn't need glasses to realize that he was about to greet class.

The driver pointed to Ben's pier. He saw the lady nodding as she thrust a roll of bills into the cabbie's hand. It was done with such grace that Ben's practiced eye told him there was plenty more where that came from. Even from where Ben was situated the former taxidriver could tell that her purse was real leather, not one of those pieces of vinyl junk he saw so much of these days. He wouldn't let Elena buy one, not even for his sister-in-law, whom they both despised. "Better give her nothing than make her look cheaper than she really is," Ben warned Elena.

The cabdriver reached into the rear seat and pulled out a shopping bag. He handed it to the lady, who smiled her thanks and started in Ben's direction.

Good, Ben thought. A dumper—he hadn't had one this fall. The first of the season. Coming so soon, it augered well for the future. Ben puffed on his cigar and tried to imagine what she intended dumping.

It didn't look like ashes. But how the hell could you tell these days? Undertakers were putting them in cheaper and cheaper containers. Christ, one poor old dame showed up with ashes stashed away in one of those five-gallon containers of frozen milk they deliver to soda fountains. Ben lent her his neckerchief to wrap the container in while they carried it out to sea.

If the bag wasn't ashes, the care with which she carried

it reassured Ben in one respect. She wasn't a jumper. In the seven years he'd been in Boston Ben had dealt with only one jumper, but that was enough. Christ, he wasn't even a jumper, he was a slider—a young fellow, tall, good-looking, with half a load on. Ben should have known better. He wanted to go fast; Ben obliged. They sped out beyond the breakwater and, when Ben turned around, the guy was gone. He'd just slid into the water, God knows where.

Ben remembered the fellow with respect. He was a perfect gentleman. He had left behind a note to be opened by the police, his wallet with all his identification, and an envelope which read, "For the captain." It contained a hundred-dollar bill.

Maybe there had been other jumpers aboard the *Elena*, but they must have changed their minds. He remembered one old guy who got so fed up with Ben's chatter that he snarled at him, "Don't you ever shut up? Take me back. I'll find some way to die in peace."

There was no way Ben could be sure of that one. But why think of him now, when this vision of loveliness was headed his way?

He had started to tip his hat when Claudia asked him, "Are you free, Mr. Tony?"

The whole gismo—the "Mr. Tony," her voice, that heavenly skin and those green eyes—they were too much. Ben took off his hat.

"Yes, ma'am."

He looked up at the sky. "A beautiful day. The sea's choppy, though. I guess you want a little trip around the harbor."

"Yes, that's it," she said, "to enjoy this fresh sea air while I can."

"I guess you're from out of town."

126

"I am," she said, following Ben down the wooden pier to the middle point, where he scrambled in and fixed the ladder.

"It's ten dollars the first half hour, seven-fifty every half hour after that. We can stay out as long as you like."

"Good," she said, stepping gingerly into the boat, clutching both her purse and the shopping bag in one hand to free the other for holding on to the ship's rail.

Ben knew better than to reach for her bundle. She was definitely a dumper.

With dumpers Ben kept the chatter to a minimum. It wasn't decent to keep shouting over the sound of the motor. He limited his spiel to a few comments about the shoreline, mentioned the various boats that were in port that day and watched her expression. She was serious, maybe troubled. In a case like this Ben looked for a spot in the shadow of a big boat, where he idled the motor and leveled. It wasn't good business to let the passenger get nervous.

"Excuse me, lady, and just listen. Even if I'm outta line. You get it?"

Claudia nodded.

"It don't matter to me what you got in that bag. I figure you wanna throw it over the side. If it's the ashes of some dear departed, we can go to a quiet spot and do it serenely. It really doesn't matter to me personally. But there's all kinds of laws about throwing things into the sea—federal laws, and the Coast Guard that patrols these waters can get nasty. They prefer to grant permits for dumping ashes. Don't ask me how you get them. So if you intend to dump—pardon—I mean to throw something overboard, just say yes. I don't wanna know no more. I'll take us to a spot where nobody's snooping with spyglasses or whatever. You let the thing slide into the water, and if you'll look under the seat, lady, there are a couple of bricks there. Take one; be my guest. It makes whatever it is sink faster. Now if it's ashes and you want to scatter them...."

"Mr. Tony, it isn't ashes. It's...."

Ben held up his hand. "Don't tell me. We'll start moving now. When I slow down you just let it slide—whatever it is. Then I guess you'll want to go back."

"I appreciate that. The cab's going to pick me up in half an hour."

"That's fine. God bless you, lady."

How do we find each other, Ben asked? Destiny—it's always there and you never know when you're going to meet it.

Claudia found the bricks, lifted one into the bag. About five minutes later the boat slowed. Ben nodded his head. She heaved the weighted bag over the side, heard it splash into the water and sink into the choppy sea.

Back at the pier, Ben's oil-stained fingers wrapped themselves around a wad of bills he'd noticed the elegant lady counting out on the way back.

It came to at least a hundred. A charming and gracious dumper.

Her cab had spun into view. They shook hands and Ben heard the lovely voice for the last time.

"Thank you for being so understanding," Claudia said.

He watched the grace of her walk as she made her way to the cab. "Like a star—like a real star. They don't make them like that any more," Ben mumbled.

Inside the boathouse, he hauled out his log. He wrote the time and date and a description of the passenger.

It made sense to him to fill in everything on the page of the day book of the day before and to describe the passenger as "a Caucasian female, about sixty, wearing print dress, sneakers and no hat, with gray hair and carrying a large vinyl purse. Passenger wore bifocals and professed to be hard of hearing. Arrived and left in car driven by Caucasian male who waited on shore."

Ben closed the book, feeling the same satisfaction he'd enjoyed every time he met a dumper. Fuck the law! Let the bastards find their own goddamned knives, guns, icepicks, razors and whatever in Boston Harbor. Some day they'd learn how they goofed when they picked up Ben Schwartz's medallion because he'd slugged a cop. One tiny punch in the face, that was it. Not even a bloody nose. And down the drain goes twenty-five grand. Ten years Ben Schwartz worked to buy that medallion!

Now they could fuck themselves.

What's more, he'd rendered service to one lovely lady. Elena would like this. She always went around the rosary beads a second time when he brought home a story of a lady dumper.

*   *   *

On Saturday Robin and Claudia made love.

She'd ordered a buffet supper, which was ready in her suite when they returned from the theater. But they only nibbled at the food and nibbled at conversation.

Eventually, in one of those grand gestures Claudia accomplished with such consummate taste, she opened the door, wheeled the dining table into the hall, turned to Robin and said, "I really don't think we have much use for this any more. Or do you?"

"It seemed to clutter the room, Claudia. May I?" he asked, as he peeled off his jacket.

"Of course," Claudia answered, as she turned out the overhead lights and dimmed the two floor lamps in the living room. With the street lights peeking through the blinds and around the edges of the curtains, Claudia knew the subdued lighting would flatter her.

She hadn't "invented" it solely for tonight. It was an old habit, an actress' trick; her first order of business on arriving at a new hotel was to move the furniture around to create a lighting arrangement that made her feel comfortable.

Claudia's natural beauty, the texture of her skin, the perfect bone structure and the firmness of her body were Godgiven. She had never been vain about them, but she was careful to display them under the most advantageous conditions.

She feared she'd be nervous tonight, but she wasn't. She took delight in her calm. Robin was standing near the window. She walked toward him and flung her arms around his neck, and their lips opened eagerly. Still clinging to his tongue, she freed one hand and began to open his shirt, feeling the muscles of his chest. She broke the kiss, bent over and pressed her lips against his hard breasts, tasting the bittersweet flavor of his hot flesh. Then their lips met again; she pushed her tongue inside, flicking it back and forth until Robin could bear no more.

He led her into the bedroom. They began to undress. In a flash Robin was stripped, except for his socks and shorts. His body excited her. He had the luster of youth and that instant energy Claudia needed so badly. He seemed assured, totally at ease, as his shorts slipped down and he leaned over to take off his socks. Claudia's eyes lighted up when she saw the size of his penis, which had already begun to harden.

Gently, Robin pushed her down on the bed. Standing beside her, he appeared to inhale the ravishing perfection of her body. To him it was a vision of loveliness, the culmination of long months of anguish, fear, anticipation and hope. Now finally Claudia was his. He fell to the bed and pressed his mouth hard against her nipples. Claudia wrapped her arms around him and felt the back muscles. His hands raced to the inside of her thighs, caressing the soft hot skin. She opened for him, and they began to make love.

Robin's was the excitement of youth, but his style of lovemaking was careful of Claudia's sensibilities. There was none of the "hit and run" in Robin's technique. Passion was an exquisite event which he'd chosen not to indulge in indiscriminately—even if the need sometimes diminished his high ideals.

To recover from the first time, Robin buried his head in the pillow and Claudia believed she heard him sobbing ever so quietly. But not for long. He recovered quickly and once more his young blood rushed to his groin. The sexual energy he displayed became more sophisticated as he guided Claudia through the ancient ritual of passion like a graceful Greek god who had come to life for this remarkable night of love.

Robin's awareness of Claudia, of the ebb and flow of her body, was wonderfully sensitive. His whole being glowed with the thrill of having brought so much pleasure to the body of this creature who had seemed unattainable.

Claudia shared his joy, so different from the smug air of conquest that many men subconsciously convey to women on their first encounter. Robin made her aware, without speaking the thought, that they were sharing the priceless gift of belonging to each other, that the passions felt that night could never be counted in minutes or hours. Whatever came of the act, they would be forever bound

131

by it—perhaps not in any conventional sense, but the link had been forged and the future would interpret its meaning.

These moments, at least, were theirs. So when their passions ebbed they behaved as first-time partners generally do: they talked.

Their bodies had opened their hearts. Robin and Claudia began to know each other. Secret pentup thoughts spilled out of Robin so fast that he tripped over his tongue, and sometimes he stopped to laugh when incidents involving his romanticizing about Claudia began to bump into each other.

He carefully avoided the words "older woman" when he told her of his only other love, a teacher in college.

"My parents interferred and the woman seemed to feel that their objections were valid, so there I was all alone at eighteen, suffering my first rejection. It hurt, and I couldn't get it out of my mind for a long time. But there was work. I buried myself in it. I feel an actor needs as many skills as he can acquire—that there's more to the art than merely learning stagecraft. You need the full experience of life to draw on if you really intend to be great.

"That's what you have, Claudia. I see it every night when you step on that stage. You know so terribly much—languages, music, art—but most of all, you know about life. You know how thin the line can be between a laugh and a tear. Damn, that shows. Yet when you've finished there's always the element of mystery. I keep saying, 'we've seen part of her—how fascinating the rest must be!'"

"Wow!" Claudia kissed Robin affectionately, a brief encounter of lips. "You ought to be a reviewer. They say

132

an actress lives on applause. Well, you've given me enough to live on for days and days. I appreciate it because, coming from you, it's sincere, if still outrageously flattering. But you know how everyone admires you. That's a terribly difficult part and you play it remarkably well against characters that are very strong both in the way the roles are written and the way they're performed."

"You're sweet, and I do know people appreciate my work," Robin said. "But I wonder how many young actors have ever enjoyed the help that I have. You'd expect Keith Byrne to be a terror, with all those yards of great credits he's earned. With a flick of his finger he could wash me out of every scene we have together. But he doesn't"

Claudia was grateful that their conversation had turned to the theater. Although she longed to confide in someone, too many doubts gnawed at her mind to let her dare being candid with this young Lochinvar.

Who was he? An extraordinarily handsome young actor, slavish in his admiration. Claudia appreciated that. She was thrilled that Robin possessed skill at lovemaking that belied both his years and what appeared to be limited experience. He was probably holding something back. But was Claudia in a position to belabor that point? Hardly.

She ached to tell Robin the whole truth—that for more than two years she had lived completely without the touch of a man. No one had shared her bed, much less her body. For all those months she had fought off nightmares and dark emotions as violently as the devils that had haunted her years in the orphanage.

How could Robin ever associate the grubby truth with

133

his image of Claudia as a richly voluptuous woman capable of making love into the supreme act of human affirmation?

Would this dazzling young man understand the degradation and humiliation she'd endured during her marriage? He would try, of course. Secretly he would be horrified. Women who'd lived in Claudia's style were far beyond his ken. However sincere his protests, Claudia— the woman—would be tarnished. This was not the moment to shatter Robin's illusions.

Claudia loathed self pity. She no more enjoyed facing the facts about her life than the few who knew some—but not all—of them—friends like Stella Morell, Rose Derlanger and Donald Laine. Being a sufferer had never been her idea; her suffering was born of circumstance.

To sit down and deal honestly with herself, and with Robin, might accomplish her dream, clearing the air of the horrors of her past and the terrors of the future.

But who was Robin really? She barely knew him. He was a boy. His experience at living was just beginning. So was hers, in a way. Claudia liked that thought and allowed it to linger for a while.

No, Robin could be her friend, perhaps her young lover. He would never be her confidant. It was a pity. God knows she could use one. Imagine it! At thirty-seven there was not a single person in the world Claudia Milotte could either trust or turn to with her dark secret.

So Robin became her joy of the "now"—Robin with his dazzling smile, his even teeth, with his youthful romance that had been "interfered with" by his parents, was like a breath of fresh air in the life of a woman, closer to forty than to thirty, who was pulling together the pieces of her shattered world.

Claudia watched for signs of condescension in herself.

She made herself listen to the young man's dreams and hopes for his career with all the concentration she could summon. Essentially they were no different from those of other young actors. They could get pretty dull. But Robin would never hear this from Claudia's lips.

Robin was beguiled by Claudia's simplicity. She lacked arrogance and artifice, characteristics that he assumed were cultivated as part of a star's image. It would be useless for Claudia to explain to Robin how vividly she identified with him. They shared so much in common. Like Robin, Claudia was searching for identity, purpose and reality in her life.

Like Robin, she hoped that in finding these she would also enjoy at least a nodding acquaintance with love. But, for now, love held a low priority.

She wondered about Robin's dark patches. They seemed to be little patches of gray compared to hers. But comparisons, besides being odious, were unfair. Moreover, Claudia had learned in these recent weeks how abruptly gray turns to black. The world, alas, did not stop spinning while a mixed-up actress fumbled for luck or fate to guide her destiny. Standing still was a luxury few could afford. The only still people were in the grave.

Claudia wondered how she would deal with Robin's obvious eagerness to spend the night with her. When he raised the question, the answer would have to be "no." She offered the acceptable excuse actresses depended on—their need for a long rest on Sunday.

"You know what kind of week it's been," she said. "There will be other nights."

When Claudia put her arms around him she almost changed her mind. She felt his body pressing against her, their tongues met and held fast until the short gasps from their lips broke the embrace.

Her guard had been weakened but Claudia stayed with her decision. Robin slipped quietly away, Claudia promising to call when she awoke.

There was no reason for her to mention that it would be dawn before she slept. Robin wouldn't understand. For Claudia there remained the hours before the window, looking out at Boston Common, waiting for sleep, hoping she would be spared the "nightmare."

Robin had given her a precious gift—something to look forward to.

*   *   *

In the Beacon Hill house Stella Morell had obtained for her stay in Boston, around the time Robin and Claudia were making love, a conference was being held between the Italian star, Donald Laine, Billy Briggs and Aldo Roselli who, like Laine, was a lawyer.

The Signora loathed hotels, even if she consented to stay at them during short stands. However, when playing engagements of several weeks, Stella managed to obtain the use of a home. Members of the Italo-American colony idolized her and were only too eager to make their accommodations available to her. She was seldom fussy about neighborhoods or the economic status of her hosts. She'd lived on Mulberry Street in New York and in downtown San Francisco just as happily as she was enjoying her stay at a historic Boston mansion on Beacon Hill.

One of the unexpected benefits of a visit by Stella Morell was the presence of an irascible housekeeper-maid-companion who accompanied her. She was a bent, elderly woman who was introduced only as Assunzia. Her skin was wrinkled; she shuffled rather than walked. To

136

outward appearances Assunzia seemed only steps from the grave. Stella's hosts discovered different. With little to do beyond taking care of Stella's wardrobe and preparing light meals, Assunzia, finding herself with hours of leisure, gave each new residence the housecleaning of a lifetime.

The daughter of the Italian Ambassador in Washington had once asked Assunzia to be a little less careful in her work.

"It ruins me for months afterward," she said. "I expect our own cleaning woman to be in your class. It's impossible."

Assunzia had set up a table of cold cuts and a bar for Stella's guests, who had all arrived furtively: Laine, without letting Claudia know; Roselli, by warning his family to say that he was out of town.

"For reasons that may be clear in the future," he told his wife, "my only contact with Stella occurred on opening night when we visited her backstage."

Mrs. Roselli was used to such confidences and appreciated a husband who guided the white lies she was supposed to tell. It made things much easier for the wife of Boston's best-known criminal lawyer, who sometimes anglicized his name to Al Rose.

Laine recognized the name, if not the man, when Stella introduced him. Briggs was known to all parties.

After Assunzia had left the room, Stella pointed in the direction of the buffet, saying, "Gentlemen, please help yourselves."

At the table they filled supper plates and poured drinks, and Laine enjoyed the opportunity of expressing his admiration of Aldo Roselli.

The short, round lawyer, bald, with a fringe of white around the outer edge of his head, brightened at the attention. Roselli was far from unaware of his reputation but he nonetheless appreciated recognition, particularly from a fellow counselor high in the inner circle of Winston and Associates.

"You're not exactly a newcomer yourself, Mr. Laine. What we will be talking about tonight isn't your field, but I presume you'll get the drift of it with little difficulty."

When the time seemed right, Stella rapped a fork on her plate for attention "Mr. Laine and Billy, this informal meeting is in charge of Signore Roselli. He is going to speak in *legalese*."

She picked up a slip of paper from her lap. "You see I have to write the word down to remember it. I guess I know what it means. Anyhow, Mr. Roselli speaks for me."

She turned to the lawyer, saying, "Aldo, please."

He put down his highball and began to speak in a low, cultivated voice—not at all what Laine expected. Both his appearance and his low-key style were at variance with Roselli's reputation as a tough, ruthless counselor who knew criminal law backward and forward, as well as all the tricks that could be used legally within it. Judges stood in awe of his knowledge, and in Boston legal circles it was noted regretfully by his adversaries that a gambit by Roselli was seldom overruled because judges realized he knew more than they did.

"Gentlemen," Roselli said, "this is a meeting requiring the upmost discretion as you, Mr. Laine, will soon understand. I am referring to the remote possibility that a vital cast change might become necessary in *The Capri Affair*, which would upset Signora Morell both professionally and personally.

"I have her permission to be frank. Signora Morell is broke. This tour and the probability that the company

138

will be invited to perform in London, as well as in a film production, represent a great deal of money to the Signora. She owns the play and, needless to say, she is well paid as a co-star. You may be surprised to learn that Keith Byrne is paid exactly the same salary as Stella. It was his price, and Stella insisted that Wuthering meet it without haggling. She wanted a quality production and got it. We agree there, I presume?"

Donald Laine nodded.

"In effect, *The Capri Affair* represents an annuity for Stella and she's not about to risk that if it can be avoided. A New York detective recently visited Boston and attended a performance. Stella asked Mr. Briggs, the stage manager, to observe his reaction in case that might shed added light on our suspicions as to why he chose to look at the play again after having seen it in New York. Mr. Briggs will read his observations from a statement I have seen and approved."

Billy Briggs read from a small slip of paper he pulled out of his pocket. "The detective's reaction was impassive throughout. There was no sign of a special reaction to any particular scene. It was my feeling that he realized someone in the company was observing him. Of course, I have no way of supporting this reaction—beyond my experience in the theater."

Roselli looked at a page of notes. "So much for that. We now go into questions to Mr. Laine which he may answer privately or in front of us."

Then, looking at Laine, Roselli smiled. "Of course, he doesn't have to answer them at all."

Laine smiled back and said, "Counselor, may I have a word with you privately?"

"Of course. Shall we go into the next room?"

Laine towered over the short Italian as they left the

library and closed the door behind them. They were in a living room, a small parlor.

"Am I correct in believing that the information you want from me affects Claudia Milotte?"

"Yes, Mr. Laine."

"And it is intended to be helpful in ending what we can call ... let me think...."

Roselli supplied the answer, "Why don't we call it 'unusual interest' in her?"

"Ah ... thank you. Very good—very good indeed.

"Now, how do I phrase the next question?"

"I suggest you avoid any question about the purpose of this meeting. It's an informal conversation. Reject the questions you're sensitive about. We're certainly not here tonight to become part of a conspiracy, or to interfere with the due process of law or justice or anything like that. Wouldn't you feel that our overriding interest here lies in our concern with Stella Morell and the future of her play?"

"I know why you have your reputation, Mr. Rose, and I bow to you."

"Thank you. How do you wish to speak—privately?"

"No, not at all. We should be frank in Stella's presence. She's an old and important friend."

"Very well, let's go back."

The men poured fresh drinks, Stella sipped a Campari and soda.

"Mr. Laine," Roselli began, "there's not much I want to know. The figures, mostly. What part of the estate of Richard Winston will Miss Milotte inherit? She might wish to invest in the film."

Laine's response was prompt. "It will be in the newspapers within a week—not to the decimal point, of course. I am the executor without challenge of Winston's personal estate. After paying off outstanding notes Claudia will have access to three million dollars in cash, negotiable bonds, blue-chip stocks and other items, like savings accounts, etc."

"Before or after taxes?"

"After taxes."

"Then what?"

"She has been given the widow's share, one-third of all his holdings. They're vast, farflung and quite beyond assessing at this point. Roughly they will provide her with an income of a million dollars a year, assuming the business remains stable."

"About insurance?"

"There is a modest policy of about twenty-five thousand dollars payable to her. It was taken out shortly after their marriage. That will be the first cash she'll see."

"There is other insurance?" Roselli asked.

Laine was about to pass that one but changed his mind when he realized Roselli would have no trouble obtaining the information from another source.

"Ritchie," he said, "disengaged me from the holding company, Winston and Associates. I only keep a few minor directorships, so my knowledge of the division of his business holdings is therefore limited."

"But you've heard things?" the Boston lawyer persisted.

"Of course, his major partners—there are about four—will divide a two million corporate insurance policy. Maybe twice that if the double indemnity clause holds."

"Personally?"

"I believe so."

"Nice haul, but don't quote me," Roselli purred.

"Mr. Laine, do you think the partners at Winston

141

would prefer to buy Miss Milotte out to having her involved in a management capacity—which she'd certainly be if she retains the holdings?"

"Any corporation would prefer that to dealing with an inactive but important stockholder."

"Who is also the widow of the former head of the company," Roselli threw in.

"Legally, if not in fact."

"We would call that throwing salt on the wound, wouldn't we?"

"Precisely."

"We understand each other, Mr. Laine. Thank you for visiting us tonight."

He looked around, seeming pleased with the information he'd acquired. "Now, may I offer you a drink?"

"No, thank you. It's eleven. If the driver is up to it, I'd prefer to slip into the back seat and sleep my way back to New York."

"We've arranged another driver for you, my personal chauffeur, and what I call my 'sleeping car.' The rear seat folds out into a very comfortable bed. When you're a minor New England lawyer, a car's better than a plane to get around to the courts I practice in."

After Laine shook everyone's hand, Billy Briggs got up to leave as well.

"The car will drop off Billy Briggs a block or so away from the hotel, Mr. Laine, if you don't mind," Roselli explained.

"Not at all."

Stella saw the men to the door. Roselli accompanied Laine to the limousine to introduce him to the driver and acquaint him with the wonders of the passenger section, which served the multiple purpose of an office, a bedroom and a communications room.

"Use the phone if you wish," Roselli said as he waved the car on its way.

Back in the library and alone with Stella, Roselli's face had lost its exuberance.

He poured a drink. "Anything for you, Stella?"

"No thanks, Aldo. What do you think?"

"About the money situation, it's fine. About what I expected. I imagine Claudia will sell out, in view of how much she loathes the Winston people. I suppose you know why she wouldn't accept a settlement or consent to a divorce. She could have named her own figure. But let it remain a secret for now. The less I know at this point, the better."

"I thought Laine was very direct," Stella said.

"Yes, but as he pointed out, it will all be a matter of record."

"He's a good man. Too good for the likes of Winston," Stella went on.

"I guess now he's waking up to the fact. But you know I have a hunch he's going to enjoy life a lot better as Claudia's lawyer. Even with a settlement, there's a lot to administer. She'll need someone who cares about her. From everything I've heard—and you've confirmed it—Laine feels protective. I've heard the rumors—you know, that he's gay. Some people want to think Donald will marry Claudia. I doubt that. But he'll be closer to her than a lot of flesh-and-blood brothers I know. Without him and Rose she'd never have gotten this far. How about you, Stella? You were the real bomb that exploded her life."

"Yes, I suppose I was. But I never expected anything like this. Do you know that Anne Alexander came to me this evening not a minute after Claudia and Robin left? They're 'screwing' tonight, I think."

143

"Stella, my wife is going to kill me when she finds out all the gossip she's missed."

"Don't tell her, darling."

"I don't. She finds it out anyhow."

"Well, let me shock you with this. Anne was carrying a pair of shoes with steel heels. Mama mia! I lived with those damned shoes for a year in New York. Thank God we're on the road."

"Keep it on a straight line, Stella."

"I am, you old fool, if you'd listen to me instead of trying to memorize everything for your wife. How is Florence, by the way?"

"Beautiful, the finest woman in all Boston."

"That's a good thing to hear...."

"You were telling me about Anne Alexander and the shoes."

"They're special shoes she puts on—or rather put on when she was in New York. Her mother is deaf and Anne is her complete slave. The reason for the shoes with steel heels is to create a vibration on the floor when she enters their home. They own a brownstone in the West Forties. That way the old lady knows who's come in the door.

"But the shoes with steel heels she showed me weren't hers. She spotted them in Claudia's dressing room. She wonders if Claudia used them to impersonate her. Now she didn't come out and say, 'Could Claudia be the mystery woman?' but, Aldo, she was awfully close."

"That adds another one to the list. Christ, how many have we got now who're suspicious of Claudia?"

"Donald Laine, of course. Billy Briggs because of that encounter with Ella. Lamark. Me. You. Rose Derlanger and her whole family must have ideas, but you could kill them before they'd say anything. Anyhow, Rose's brother is strong politically in New York. That's what they tell me."

"What about the men, Robin and Keith Byrne?"

"Keith Byrne belongs to another century when it comes to women, but not to money. If I shot his cock off—and it's some cock, I can tell you. We once had an encounter in . . . now where was it?"

"Let's stick to the present."

"You've got me confused."

"Thanks."

Stella laughed. "Now I have it. If I shot his cock off he'd tell the police he'd wounded himself accidentally, because I'm a woman. But if I had argued five dollars off his salary he would never speak to me again."

"About the boy? Claudia would never tell. . . ."

"Don't say it. The thought is father to whatever it is. . . . No, I don't think Claudia's going to tell anyone anything. She can't be indifferent to what's being thought, if not said. She's no fool. She has her alibi and she won't budge from it."

"All we have is a hunch—in a legal sense one could assume Claudia had motive and opportunity. But we don't really know, do we?

"Will Anne confront her about the shoes?"

"No, definitely not. I turned on a little terror at first, accusing her of snooping, thinking evil thoughts. She's easily frightened. I took the shoes and I'll get them back inside the dressing room where they belong. Hopefully, Anne told me the right place to put them. I told Anne I would find an explanation."

"She was satisfied?"

"For now. I warned her that in Sicily she would have lost her tongue by morning for as much as breathing what she told me."

"And?"

Stella's robust laugh filled the room. "She's a typical WASP. She believed me—especially when I fingered the snake ring. That's all you have to do in this country, don't you know that by now?"

"I do, *cara*, but you're the star. I'm only a lawyer."

"So we're back where we started—wondering about Lamark. They dined together after the Thursday performance. On Friday she mentioned that it had been pleasant. She said that maybe we'd be relieved of Lamark, at least for a few weeks. He's going on vacation. I had the feeling she was sorry to see him go."

"Where?"

"To Paris is the way Claudia understood it."

Roselli made what he described as a "nightcap" and began pacing the room.

"Well, I can make two things out of that. He's so taken with Claudia that he's going to check out her background. In that case, chalk up one for our side. Or it's really a vacation."

"You'll find out, won't you, Aldo dear?" Stella growled in that persuasive voice that defied any answer but one which pleased her.

Roselli wasn't ruffled. "That's no trouble. It's what happens now that bothers me. The thing's stable. Lamark's gone. New York's not going to assign a cop to trail Claudia here or when you get to Chicago. They're chasing any number of tips and suspicions down there, from what I've been told. Winston and Associates would prefer that the whole thing be forgotten. Somebody was going to kill Ritchie one way or another. He was a hood in a gray flannel suit. The police know they can't penetrate gangland killings. Why bother? Hoods always kill each other anyhow. But there are those damned suspicions. We have to quiet them, and the only way is to confront Claudia point blank."

"That's what I've been thinking," Stella said.

"But we can't do it now."

"Why?"

"I'll explain that at the right time. It will have to be in Capri over the holiday."

"And in the meantime?"

"We keep a close watch on Lamark—and, *cara* Stella, we pray, I guess I'd better get on my way."

"But you don't have a car?"

"Of course I do. I used Florence's car."

"Give her my love, and we'll see each other soon."

Stella walked Roselli to the door. She fingered her snake ring as she closed and bolted the front door after him.

*　　*　　*

At ten o'clock Monday morning, when Lieutenant Frank Lamark had expected to be aboard a flight to Paris, he found himself seated in the office of the Precinct's inspector. That official had sent word that Lamark was to be there, regardless of any plans he might have made.

Inspector Ray Ryan, a tall Irishman with a fair complexion and clear blue eyes, respected his nickname, "Ramrod." It was a tribute to his lean, muscled body and the arrow-straight posture he showed both on the street and behind his desk. Bald since his twenties, Ryan cringed at any reference to *Kojak*, as newcomers to the precinct quickly found out. Ryan was a tough disciplinarian; one *Kojak* crack got by with a snarl, a second found the offender living in terror of all the regulations in the police manual, covering everything from the shine on his shoes to the order of his locker.

Ryan and Lamark had entered the Police Academy at

the same time. Their youthful friendship had grown into a professional association characterized by respect and the camaraderie of years of working together. Ryan, the administrator, moved more swiftly through the ranks; Lamark, unembarrassed by forever remaining Ryan's subordinate, preferred his reputation within the department as "supersleuth."

When Lamark was ushered into his office, Ray Ryan looked at his old friend with the bewildered expression of a man who has discovered that, having just dressed himself, he is still naked. The materials on his desk could involve any of the thousands of officers in the New York Police Department but not Frank Lamark, unless Frank had been seized by a mysterious malady.

"Even if medical authorities from Bellevue, Mount Sinai and Doctors Hospital combined to certify you as insane," Ryan was saying, "I would still refuse to grant you medical leave until I'd seen evidence that satisfied me. I've never known a more levelheaded, cooler policeman, including me, than this here Lieutenant Frank Lamark sitting in my office. This same Lieutenant Lamark who uses his day off to fly to Boston to go to the *theatah* to date an actress who one of these days might be indicted for a murder he's in charge of investigating. He asks no authorization for the trip, puts in no voucher for expenses, and says nothing about it when he comes back."

"It was my day off. I felt no obligation to report it, Ray."

"Balls! You know goddamned well that this is pretty irregular behavior. Only two days earlier, when I ask you for a report on the Winston murder, you tell me that the case is still wide open, and the best you can offer is that we're narrowing the list of possible suspects.

"So I feed that line of bull to the press and they buy it.

Why? The answer's obvious. Yesterday's murder just isn't news the way it used to be. Too many killings going on today. The press can't keep up with them."

"The statement was accurate," Lamark answered.

"I'm not questioning that. I believe you. But out of the blue some newspaperman calls me and asks what the hell Lieutenant Lamark is doing in Boston. I answer, 'How the hell should I know—it's his day off.' Then the guy tells me he's got word from Boston that you're tripping the light fantastic with Claudia Milotte at some glamorous boite of the night called the Sky Room.

"I call the boxoffice and I get a smart-ass named Ryder. He wants to make sure I'm me. So he calls back the precinct and, once convinced I'm a cop, he tells me you've indeed been in the theater. He tells me that a newspaperman called earlier and asked about *Monsieur* Lamark. He said he never heard of you."

"Bright man, Ryder!"

"Lucky for you. Then I call the Sky Room and there's no reservation in your name."

"Of course not; Claudia Milotte's a guest at the hotel. She naturally ordered the table. So it was in her name."

"*Oui! Oui! Hinkey-dinky parlez-vous!* One more lucky break. I call the reporter back, tell him he's all wet, and how he can confirm it if he wants to. So I saved your ass."

"I think it's the other way around. You saved yours."

"Don't get nasty with me, Lamark. I don't like that remark," Ray roared.

"I'm sorry, I apologize. But assuming that this precinct is still looking for the killer of Richard Winston, we're not going to find him among ordinary hit men. He's a smart operator."

Ryan relaxed. Lamark hadn't gone mad. He'd come up with a rational reason eventually. Now his analytical mind was working as it was supposed to.

"All right," Ryan said, "but wouldn't it be a courtesy, to say nothing of your duty, to let me in on your suspicions? The way this Boston caper looks I have to assume that you've selected the victim's widow, Claudia Milotte, as this super-bright assassin."

Lamark shook his head. "I have no substantive reason to suspect Claudia Milotte."

"Then why trot her out in the open as your date and risk the chance that the newspapers would tear you, her and the police department to bits?"

"Boston was a calculated risk," Lamark said. "The lady had to believe that my visit leaned more toward the social than official."

"Did she?"

"Yes and no. You couldn't expect more. Anyhow, she was impressed with my being open about the meeting. I didn't slip in unannounced and flash my badge. As far as appearances were concerned, I counted on one thing to protect me on Thursday night."

"And what in the hell was that?"

"Commander Ray Ryan would have the night duty."

"You son of a bitch! You fuckin' son of a bitch." Then he smiled. "How right you were! All right, give me the rest of it, and I'll give you what I have."

"People around Claudia suspect her: Laine, the lawyer; Rose, her maid; some others that I haven't talked to. But there's a pattern forming. It interests me."

"It should, because the pattern is already here," Ryan said. He tossed on the desk a photograph of a pair of shoes with steel attachments on the heel. "Ever seen anything like these before, Frank?"

"Tap dancer's shoes, maybe, I don't know."

"You've heard of Anne Alexander?"

"Sure, she's one of the actresses in *The Capri Affair*. Plays Claudia's sister."

"She brings the shoes in on Sunday," Ryan explained, "and insists on seeing someone in homicide. Look at the back of the picture and you can see the officer's name. She introduces herself, saying she's with the play in Boston and comes back to New York every weekend to visit her sick mother. These are shoes she uses in New York. Her old lady's deaf. When she goes home, the heels make a vibration on the floor that the old lady identifies."

"I've heard of that."

"Good; then maybe you can tell me why Claudia Milotte has a pair in her dressing room just like these. She's supposed to be an orphan."

"Is that what Anne Alexander said?"

"Yes. Not only that, but when she talked to the Italian lady in the show . . . whatshername?"

"Stella Morell."

"Yeah, that's it. She tells Morell she figures Claudia had the shoes made in order to masquerade as the mystery woman and maybe throw suspicion on Miss Alexander."

"Ridiculous!"

"That's not all. *Signora* Morell gives her hell and tells Miss Alexander that if she spread stories like that in Sicily she'd wake up one morning with her tongue cut out."

"Did Stella say where she'd find the tongue?"

"Knock it off, Lamark. You're not here to make wisecracks. You're not here to defend Claudia Milotte, either. You're here to analyze."

"Sorry, Ray. I retract it with one condition."

"What might that be, sir?" Ray asked.

"Level with me about the Winston murder. The heat's coming from somewhere to cool the investigation and from another area to bring in a suspect—any suspect—

even if it's a derelict that we hold for twenty-four hours. Someone wants the killing back in the headlines or, as we say, there are persons known and unknown who'd like the whole thing to go away."

Ryan fiddled with a pencil. "The point is, I don't know what to make of it. I do know that nobody's trying to hang a noose around Claudia Milotte."

"How about the mystery woman?" Lamark persisted.

"She's for real. You know that. You've questioned a dozen dames. Any one of them could have been her. You got a list in your files of four of Winston's trollops who couldn't give accurate accounts of their movements on the day of the murder."

"Of course not. They were stoned. What do you expect? Maybe if they'd been notified in advance that their playmate was going to be snuffed they'd have stayed home with their mothers. I'll grant that there was a mystery woman. She probably was used as a decoy. She could have been one of Winston's whores, but I don't buy the suspicion that the mystery woman was any more than that. I don't believe she knew she was going to be involved in a killing.

"Whoever knocked off Winston was extremely intelligent. It was planned from beginning to end to take every advantage of a set of circumstances that had to come together at a particular time—like an eclipse of the moon. If the conditions didn't occur, the killer wouldn't have struck that day. Just sift the record, read between the lines, and you'll know I'm right."

"All right," Ryan said, "let's do some reading between the lines. Reading backward, we suddenly meet this Miss Anne Alexander. Assuming the lady is a kook . . . no, give her the benefit of doubt, she's an actress with a vivid imagination . . . there are probably five dozen reasons why

Claudia Milotte has the same kind of heels on her shoes. But how about Stella Morell? Don't tell me that an answer like 'slitting her tongue' came from a smart Italian broad without being carefully calculated. Doesn't it suggest a cover-up?"

Lamark nodded. "Exactly. It confirms what I've been thinking. There are people close to Claudia Milotte who suspect her of killing Winston. Too many for comfort. Go by the book—where there's smoke there's fire. Now we add Anne Alexander and Stella Morell to the list."

Lamark leaned across the desk, "Ray, give it to me. Explain the heat."

"You're right," Ryan answered. "You usually are. It comes from two sources. You've seen Ritchie Winston's yellow sheet. It's a horror—the worst sort of morals offender. I doubt that he had changed before he died. He enjoyed terrific protection, even better than his old man could buy when Ritchie started playing games with kids while he was in high school.

"Anyhow, the Winston and Associates people have heavy influence downtown. We get hints they don't want the killer caught. They sure don't want Claudia's name involved. They've got their dirty hands into everything— oil, shipping, currency exchange, weapons, the lot. Winston's murder was a terrific blow to the companies. Their stock hit bottom. Now it's beginning to climb again. On the other side, there's the insurance situation. They're applying the heat in the other direction."

"I wasn't aware of an insurance situation," Lamark said.

"I wasn't either until some insurance investigator oils his way into my office over the weekend. You know how they operate—like worms you don't know are there until you find them in your soup. It seems there's a double indemnity on policies worth three million. There's a big difference between three and six when you add so many zeroes. It's worth putting two hundred bucks a day up front for an investigator to poke around. Right?"

"Did he give you anything?"

"Only what they'd like us to believe—that Winston's murderer was someone who would profit from the insurance. Claudia Milotte automatically goes into the line-up if you figure from their angle. But they don't buy her either. They lean to your idea that there was a mystery woman—a sucker acting as a decoy for a hit man who did the job for one of the partners in Winston and Associates, the boys at the top."

"And who might *they* be?" Lamark asked.

Ryan said, "I had to flush it out of the investigator. They want the police to drop everything in their laps and collect their piece—that's all they care about. Here are the names...." Ryan slid a slip of paper across the desk. "I wonder if they're real. Who knows, when you're up against international cartels? I guess you can pronounce their names. You know, pal, your linguistic skill."

Lamark said, "These are tongue twisters, *pal*."

"Yeah, one's French, another is German and the third is the front for an Arabian oil sheik. The last, as you can see, is a home-town boy, Donald Laine."

Lamark's face registered surprise, mild, to be sure, but any change of expression was unusual to the soft-spoken, slow-moving passive detective.

"This doesn't jibe; Laine's supposed to be the nice guy, the good fairy."

"Watch it, Frank."

"I meant it in the storybook sense. Laine's either a saint or a guy with a lot of crazy hangups. He lives like a monk.

We'd never have known about him if we hadn't routinely checked the records of everyone involved. One tiny charge—soliciting a vice officer in a gay bar. It was dismissed. Funny, isn't it, that a lawyer failed to pick up his papers after being cleared?"

"Why bother? He probably knew the big hole that exists in the law allowing first offenders to expunge their records. There's always the FBI to lower the boom. They never throw anything out."

"Or forget. Anyhow, it's an interesting angle to pursue, when I get back."

"Frank, I'm sorry to louse up your travel plans. You have an extra day at the end, of course."

"Thanks, Ray. Sorry I upset you about Boston."

"Which reminds me—Miss Milotte is the sort of woman an old married man like me would describe as 'stunning.' A guy like you, I'm sure, must have another point of view. How about leveling with me?"

"Ray, I wouldn't dare. She's every woman I ever dreamed about. She's unhappy and tormented, but how exquisitely she masks her anguish. . . ."

Lamark stood up, as if ready to continue his recitation.

"I got the general idea, Frank. Have a good trip. While you're away we'll do everything possible to clean this thing up."

"I wonder about that," Lamark said, extending his hand.

Ryan shook it warmly. "*Bon Voyage*, Frank. Have a drink for me at Harry's Bar. I'll get back there one of these days."

Ryan pushed a button on his desk, telling the switchboard he was accepting calls and messages that had accumulated.

Before hailing a cab to take him to the airport, Lamark stopped at a public telephone and dialed Sal White.

He was relieved to find him in. "Sal, I'm on my way to Paris. It's in my notes, but I don't want to unpack my bag. Can you recall Donald Laine's real name?"

"Sure; it's Gianni Daniele."

"You wouldn't add a 'junior' to that, would you?"

"That's what they say, Frank, but I never had a reason to check it out."

"The old man ought to be dead by now."

"Not on your life, baby. He lives in Miami, richer than Croesus, still the great untouchable."

"Well, I'll be damned."

"That's what people always say who don't keep up with the obits."

"Touché, my friend. Many thanks. See you soon."

"Take it easy, Frank," Sal said seriously. "You need a rest. You've been hitting it pretty hard lately. *Au revoir*."

A bright smile lit up his face as he hung up the phone. "Finally," Frank Lamark told himself, "we have another logical suspect."

Part Four

It was the Sunday of the last week of the Boston engagement of *The Capri Affair*. Claudia was up early and pleased at the return to a schedule better suited to her than the weekends that had passed since the dawn—"was that really the word for it?" she wondered—of her affair with Robin Hayward.

Yesterday afternoon, during the matinee, there had been a telephone call from Cleveland that Robin's father had suffered a heart attack. They put the understudy on—one of those ageless actors who was a master of make-up and a truthful version of that legendary actor's boast, "always working." He asked for and got top money, and it was said that even if Reginald Wuthering intended reviving *The Women* he would still begin casting the play by signing Zach Simmons.

Zach had never gone on in either of the roles he understudied, the juvenile or the character part. Only

157

Keith Byrne was familiar with his work. Before climbing the stairs to his second-floor dressing room, Keith stood in the hall of the first floor, where the women's accommodations were situated. "Fasten your seat belts, ladies," he shouted. "God help us all!"

Three female heads, in various stages of combing, popped out of doors. "What's that all about?" they screamed in unison.

"Darlings," Byrne said, "we're all going to be made into mincemeat tonight. Good luck!" He smiled at their bewildered faces as he walked upstairs, with the delight of a cat who'd swallowed a cageful of canaries.

Zach Simmons locked his door while he made up. Part of his artistry lay in his mastery of the art. Besides greasepaint and powder, he worked with fine brushes and water colors, a technique passed on to him by his father, a vaudevilian who had pushed Zach onto the stage at the age of five at church socials in Hagerstown, Maryland, where the old trouper had retired.

There were a few groans from the audience when the substitution was announced but backstage they could barely be heard. Zach took his position about ten minutes after the performance started, while the others were involved in what playrights and actors call "exposition."

It was a rare play that placed two stars and a pair of highly respected artists like Keith Byrne and Anne Alexander in a position where the exposition created extraordinary anticipation of the youth who had disrupted all their lives.

When Zach entered, slowly, languidly, the startled expressions on the faces of his fellow players cued a round of applause. The round-faced actor with thinning hair had turned himself into an Adonis. He was a statue that had just stepped off a pedestal.

Zach was shorter than Robin, but he seemed taller. Larger, perhaps, better explained the presence he created. With rust-colored hair, green eyes, full, sensual lips, he was indeed the romantic. But there was a macho quality in his stance, a masculinity that Robin conveyed in his acting but lacked in appearance. Zach's voice made poetry of the dialogue, much of it banal. He moved with such grace that Stella's eyes brightened with admiration.

After her first exit, the Italian star muttered to Billy, "*Mama mia,* I wonder what *Candida* would be like with that man! You know, if I could lose twenty years, I'd try it." She sighed. "I had to go to Germany to play it the first time. My Marchbanks was younger than this man and looked older than me."

She waited until Zach had made his exit before leaving the wings for a costume change. He walked right into her motherly arms. "*Caro,* my dear Zach, you are *bello, bello.* I love you. . . ."

Zach patted her cheek. "It's nothing, baby. I'm an old pro—like you. We survive, darling, as long as the chin straps hold up."

She smacked his bottom as Zach dashed upstairs to repair the delicate make-up.

It had been a triumph. Stella rewarded Zach with a special solo call, the actors standing back to join in the applause.

When the curtain fell, Keith Byrne grabbed him by the collar. "How did you manage to move me out of the light in Act Two, Scene One, page forty-one?"

Zach bowed his head in mock apology. "The same way you took it away from Robin, sir, as soon as the director's back was turned—by hitching up my pants and giving you the elbow."

"You wonderful old man," Byrne said, laughing, as he

pulled Zach into a bearhug. "Tell them how old you were when you did Polonius and read the precepts to a fifty-year-old Laertes."

"Seventeen, Mr. Byrne."

Byrne turned to the women. "Didn't I warn you?"

Anne and Claudia smothered Zach with compliments and kisses and everyone decided to go to Stella's for a drink.

Zach sighed. "Remember, kids, I'm not the Swan. Without the paint and the feathers I'm just the Ugly Duckling."

Anne blurted out, and then blushed furiously, "Darling, you're so wonderful I'd love to see you naked."

Keith Byrne roared. "Miss Anne, if that ever happened you'd faint dead away."

Byrne put his arm around Zach and they started upstairs. "Too bad that Miss Alexander missed us in that glorious stinker, *Muscles Preferred*. How old were you when you played Mr. America, Zach?"

Zach winked at Anne. "Your age, Keith."

*   *   *

It had been an extraordinary evening. Robin was totally forgotten in the excitement of discovering Zach. Claudia understood why: theirs was such a small group that a new face was bound to create a stir. Since rehearsals more than a year ago and a few understudy calls during the New York run, little had been seen of Zach Simmons. As understudy, his only responsibility lay in calling in every evening and matinee days to make sure he wasn't needed.

For all the approval of his tour de force of this evening, Zach was unlikely to replace Robin. In a small-cast show a young man was essential. He attracted the critics' attention; they enjoyed writing about newcomers. Moreover, audiences would have little interest in an older man playing a youth, but they'd be fascinated if Zach stepped into Keith Byrne's role. That might eventually occur after Los Angeles, where Byrne's contract ended.

It became quite a party. Assunzia produced lasagna as if by magic. The wine flowed and, since Zach was the star of the evening, he played his role to the hilt. Keith Byrne, a stuffed shirt on stage, reveled in an opportunity to be true to type—the "dirty old man" that character actors were supposed to be. Byrne and Zach performed skits from burlesque. Byrne pinched bottoms at will and sent Assunzia scurrying for safety when he turned his lecherous eyes her way.

Claudia was the first to leave and sought to manage it without a fuss. But it would be rude not to compliment Zach for his marvelous performance.

Zach used the gesture as an opportunity to take her aside. "Thank you, Claudia. I've been dying to get on that stage with you. It was divine. While we have this chance you ought to know that you've done wonders for Robin."

She started to shush him.

"Let me finish, sweetie. He's come out of his shell. Robin's a completely different person; it's amazing. I haven't had to listen to his sob story for weeks." Then he stopped and fumbled for words. "You're not going to like this, and I'm sorry. He's not wonderful for you, Claudia. In a nutshell, he's suddenly discovered talking. Robin talks too much. Please be careful about confiding in him. He's such a green kid."

Claudia wasn't upset. She remembered her exact words. "Thank you, Zach, for your candor. I appreciate it. If it makes you feel better, I've had the same feeling myself." She kissed him and held him tight, while Zach's apprehension melted away. He might be a marvelous actor, she thought, but he was as frightened as she was of laying things on the line.

Billy Briggs came out of nowhere to accompany Claudia to the company limousine. "Would you like to come along?" Claudia asked Zach.

"I'd love to, darling, I'm beat. But I'm sort of expected to hang around."

The car rolled away from the curb, the driver made a U-turn and Briggs walked slowly up the steps to the mansion.

Billy Briggs was known to hear a nickel drop on 42nd Street and Broadway at high noon. He'd listened to Zach's warning. Did it mean that one more pair of eyes was looking at Claudia and wondering?

Zach's words were the first things Claudia thought of after breakfast. She was horrified to realize that, as at the party last night, she had no feeling of missing Robin, although this was the first Sunday in several weeks that they'd missed breakfast together. He had promised to call as soon as he could, but there had been no word. In a curious if guilty way, Claudia was relieved.

On the way to the hotel this morning she'd considered Zach's warning carefully. She went back step by step in the relationship and found no place where she had slipped or shared a confidence that touched the gossip she knew was whirling around her. Robin had done most of the talking. As Zach said, he'd discovered it. She listened.

When Claudia stepped farther back into those "maybe yes-maybe no" days during that frantic first week in Boston—the night Lamark arrived—she remembered Robin's bringing her the package. Of course, that had been a slip. What had he said? "Funny, the writing doesn't

162

look like yours." She assumed she'd passed it off fairly well. Claiming that Rose might have addressed it made perfectly good sense. But not in an imperfect situation.

A cold chill ran up Claudia's spine. Could Robin possibly have imagined what the package contained? From the depths of her psyche Claudia began building the strength to reject the idea. She forced herself to find the reality of the moment—her exhaustion, the tenseness involved in playing opposite a new actor, the party and the effects of too much wine. By the time Claudia turned the key to her suite, she'd regained control. She was ready for a warm bath and bed. There would be no nightmares tonight, she told herself, and there were none.

But keeping control had begun to take its toll. Concentration was daily becoming more difficult for her. She glanced at the Sunday papers. It was no use. Thoughts of Robin would not go away. Zach's few words had opened her eyes to the truth—even if she longed to avoid it. Of course Claudia was good for Robin. Any woman would be. Claudia had been aware of it for weeks. Naturally, in Robin's eyes Claudia Milotte was not "any woman." Claudia's folly lay in being as myopic as her young lover.

That she was an actress, possibly a star, a woman with a worldly reputation she wished were true, gave their affair èlan, an added dimension. She'd become the substitute for Robin's "older woman" who'd gotten away. Like any young person, Robin based his ideal woman on his first experience. It was all understandable; so was Robin's talking. Naturally he would attach importance to everything that touched their relationship, however insignificant.

She sighed. "Oh, Claudia, you've done it again—mucked things up."

As yet no price tag was attached to her fling with Robin. It had filled a need, how deep a need she had wisely kept to herself out of embarrassment. She'd gone around that course when they went into the affair. Robin never knew that he was the first man she'd made love to in many months. To his young mind it would have sounded crazy, and no one could have agreed more than Claudia. So it remained her secret. In a week or so it didn't seem to make the difference that it had at first.

There had been glorious nights of lovemaking. They'd grown to uninhibited intimacy in hours instead of days or weeks. Claudia's sexual hunger made intimacy appear easy and natural. There was also her desire to match the vigor of Robin's youth and to compensate for her barren years.

Her lips trembled when Robin's lips touched her mouth. Her body shivered when his strong tongue glided to her throat. She turned savage under kisses that roamed the rest of her. She met each advance on her body with one of her own. When she unbuttoned his shirt, a habit that began on their first night, Robin's breathing grew faster. When he unbuckled his trousers and let them fall to the floor and stepped out of his shorts, Claudia's hand eagerly played over his body. He was lean and muscular; each touch sent waves of desire racing through her.

She stood up, opened the curtains and looked out at the Common. There were few people up and about at this hour—no couple huddling on a bench to wonder about and take her mind away from Robin. Youth—what a wonder it was, to those who possessed it.

Dear Robin, who was always so ready, who never seemed to have enough of her. She blossomed in the excitement he brought to their passion. When he pressed her tightly against him, the world faded into nothingness.

Why? Because she was wrapped in the energy of youth.

"Any old fool would have known that," she muttered, pulling up the armchair, determined to think it all out and be rid of it.

Geography, like time, helps put things into perspective, Claudia thought. Now they were separated by the miles between Boston and Cleveland. Robin could not intrude on fleeting thoughts that raced through her mind during the days and nights they'd spent together. Robin had immediately become possessive. He even sulked if she smiled at waiters. "That's what actresses are supposed to do, darling," she had told him. He resented her refusal to allow him to spend the entire night in her suite. "It's just not done, Robin. There are conventions in the theater, particularly in a company like this. We're all what I suppose you'd call old-timers. We live by the rules."

"They don't make sense," he sulked.

She could not press the difference. It would only serve to emphasize the difference in their ages.

But the gulf ran deeper than years. Robin was behaving naturally; Claudia couldn't. Only Claudia Milotte knew that she was either on the brink of disaster or a future that would compensate for the lost years—two decades out of thirty-seven years. That was a long time for a woman—or anyone—to live like a whipped dog, too frightened to growl, too weak to lick her wounds.

A couple walked into the park. Terribly young, she decided, and beautiful—even if Claudia was unable to see their faces. They found a bench in the sun and sat close together. The boy put his arm around the girl.

Claudia closed her eyes. "Don't slap him, darling, not like that nasty thing the other night. Take him as he is." When she opened her eyes the girl's head was leaning comfortably on the boy's shoulders. Claudia was pleased.

They became her guides. They were evenly matched. Claudia and Robin would never know that kind of affection. Yes, she had taken him as he was. But what had she given in return? Very little. Only an image—a shadow of what she'd been and what she hoped to be.

She was going to be rich in spite of herself. Claudia had gradually grown accustomed to the idea. In considering this probability she was able to draw strength from the strange turn of fate that had brought two riches together—the resumption of her career and the acquisition of a fortune.

Ten years earlier she might have abused both, not from stupidity but because of fear. Ten years from now it would be too late. Maybe not, she thought, peering closer to the window to make sure the kids were still there. Yes, they were. In considering her position as a wealthy woman, Claudia lost all the feelings of inferiority that haunted her even when audiences cheered her.

In her daydreams she saw no wild, giddy, carefree Claudia throwing money around like used Kleenex. "Baby, you've been around that course," she said, half aloud. "It's not going to be your road."

Ten years of marriage to Winston had made Claudia contemptuous of what her French logic called the *nouveaux*—the grabbers who produced fortunes out of the blue, usually by cheating, conniving, stealing and a thousand unethical business pratices that Winston and Associates took for granted.

She assumed Donald Laine would urge her to hold on to the Winston interests. She intended going against his advice, regardless of the loss. For herself she wanted nothing. As an actress she was assured of a living as long as she chose to perform. The fortune would be something apart; she would use it to help people. How? Claudia still had no answer, but it would come.

When her lonely thoughts turned to love and marriage Claudia blacked them out. They belonged to the realm of unpredictables—like the cloud that hung over her.

Would it ever lift?

Che sera sera!

Stella was right. They should never have written that song.

Claudia glanced at the clock. Nearly eleven. In an hour Stella was expecting her. This was the Sunday they were going to see Boston. It would be the same way as they'd "seen" New York—from the inside of a limousine.

Would Stella remember Boston as well as she had New York? Probably. The woman's memory was incredible. She'd visited America once before, during World War II, playing Italian repertory throughout the East in dingy auditoriums, movie houses converted to theaters for one night. Stella performed in Italian to Italian audiences.

"I was enchanted with this land," she said. "I walked and walked through all the old factory towns of Connecticut, all of New England, everywhere. I have seen it better and closer up than many Americans. Oh, they wanted me to stay. But the parts! My God, can you imagine it—Stella Morell spending the rest of her career as a gypsy wailing prophecies, or being that lady in the movies who always comes into the police station with a shawl around her head saying, 'Watta you do with Tony? He never make da trouble before. My Tony, he's a good boy.'"

After a busy, pleasant day with Stella—who had, indeed, remembered the Boston of her first visit—Claudia returned to the hotel around seven, looking forward to dinner in her suite and the newspapers she'd avoided earlier. And hopefully there would be one of those old "women's pictures" on television, with a great deal of suffering by Bette Davis, Barbara Stanwyck, Joan Crawford or perhaps even her favorite, Margaret Sullivan. God, how beautifully that actress suffered!

Once Claudia had avoided such films. They depressed her; she felt too close an identification with the characters. Now, as part of her therapy, she saw them all. There were many she knew well enough to recite the dialogue and, if she felt especially chipper, she acted out the scenes for her friends' amusement.

Claudia's rehabilitation program had become self-structured, after two short intervals at the recommended sources of hope for disturbed people. But it required weeks before Claudia summoned the courage to enter a confession box after so many years, although she frequently attended Mass. She'd re-memorized the Act of Contrition and rehearsed herself carefully in the opening words: "Bless me, Father, for I have sinned. . . ."

It was a lengthy confession, as complete in detail as Claudia's honesty could demand. When it was over the priest lashed into her for not telling the truth. "Let it all hang out," he said. "You know what I mean. Play square with yourself and your God. Confess the drugs that have done all this to you. That's where the problem starts. Not in your lies, made in the Holy Confessional."

Angrily, Claudia stomped out. To the handful of penitents standing in line, she pointed toward the confessional and said, "That priest is out of his fuckin' mind."

The priest followed her out, crossed himself, looked at the faithful, shrugged and said, "Heaven only knows what she's on. Pray for her."

During rehearsals of *The Capri Affair* she had consulted a highly recommended psychiatrist, who became furious when her problems failed to include sexual aberrations, for which he had evolved pat answers. To test him, Claudia memorized an orgy scene from a pornographic novel. The old boy was in seventh heaven. Through half-open eyes, Claudia watched the shrink masturbate. Although tempted to stalk out, making a fuss as they did in "women's movies," Caludia drew the narrative to such an explosive conclusion that she felt a dampness in her own loins.

She cancelled further appointments and began searching for help from other sources. Biographies proved exceedingly encouraging. One self-portrait which told of a star's agonizing fight against alcoholism explained that she began finding herself by writing everything down. In doing this she'd embarked on a new career as a writer—which, curiously, had been her first ambition. Claudia had not pursued this as assiduously as she might have, but she enjoyed writing and had labored over one account of her "nightmare," which she believed prevented it from recurring for several months.

She felt positively euphoric when she stopped at the desk to pick up her key and noticed Billy Briggs standing at the house phone. She sneaked up behind him and stuck her key in his bag. "Hello, lover," she said.

When Billy spun around his face was pale and worn.

"My God! What's wrong, Billy? Are you sick?"

"Not yet, Claudia. I was just calling you."

"That's not why you look so awful—I hope."

Billy forced a smile. "No, but we have a tentative rehearsal—just a walk-through—tomorrow afternoon at two. Robin's jumped the show."

"He's what?"

"He jumped the show. Wuthering got word somehow, but not from Robin. He's in London making a movie."

169

"What about his father?"

"Bull! His old man died years ago."

"But he came to the opening. I met him."

"Forget it, baby. That was his mother's boyfriend. He just dreamed up a background to suit the occasion. That's all I know. They're flying in a new boy tonight: Warren Rivers. Wuthering's seen him and says he's good. We want to give him the positions tomorrow. Zach will go on Monday and Tuesday. Hopefully, Warren will be ready for the Wednesday matinee. Zach and I will work with him. Anyhow, I'll confirm the call later. I just wanted you to know."

Claudia wasn't thinking of Robin, but of Zach. "What about Zach? Why doesn't he open in Chicago? We'd all feel safer, and wouldn't it be wonderful for him?"

Billy kissed her cheek. "You're a wonder. Such a nice woman. It wouldn't be wonderful for Zach or anybody else. You saw how great he was. That raises three questions. Who would follow him? Wouldn't the audience feel cheated? You musn't fool them, you know. Then there's Zach. Like he said, 'No actor my age could summon all that vigor and energy eight times a week. I'd end up playing him like Lear.'"

"Zach always has an answer, doesn't he?" Claudia said.

"Sure, baby, just mention his name in Sheboygan and you get the same feeling you meet on Broadway or Hollywood—respect."

"Poor Robin!" Claudia said, a tremor in her voice.

"Poor Robin my ass! At Zach's age he'll be pushing neckware at a department store—if he's lucky."

"I imagine so," Claudia said. "That's it, I suppose. Whatever's set up is fine with me. I'll be there."

She kissed him. "Billy, take it easy. Everybody's going to do his damndest; you know that. Keith Byrne pulled so many tricks to make Zach look great Saturday that I thought sure the audience would catch it...."

Billy slapped his thigh. "Damn! That's wonderful! You caught it too. But don't ever let Keith realize you noticed."

"I won't, Billy. Bye now."

*   *   *

When Reginald Wuthering heard of Robin's defection he was unperturbed, telling the actor's agent that his sixth sense had already warned him Robin might become a problem. A few days later he received an overseas call from the British producer, who was horrified at discovering the circumstances under which he'd hired the young American.

"I was under the impression that the boy was available. He told me he had neither an agent nor a run-of-the-play contract. I'd thrown him off the lot now, Mr. Wuthering, but I've got quite a bit invested in him, transportation, test footage, costumes—you know what it adds up to."

"Forget it. Go right ahead as you've planned," Wuthering reassured him. "I have an excellent understudy in the part now and a fine young actor is rehearsing for our opening in Chicago. We won't be needing Robin any more."

"I can't understand it. The part isn't all that good, three scenes at the outside. We were casting to type. We weren't looking for a performance."

"Forget it, my friend. You learn in this business not to be surprised by the Robin Haywoods. It's got nothing to do with the generation gap, the youth rebellion or crap like that. They've been around for years. Work him and get rid of him."

"Thank you, Mr. Wuthering," the Britisher said.

171

"You've been very helpful."

"Good luck!" the gray-haired New Yorker said, hanging up that telephone to accept a call from Billy Briggs.

"Boss," Billy said, avoiding amenities, "where did you find him? This dude's really something!"

"To tell you the truth, Billy, he found me. He came to the office about six months ago and warned me that Robin was a goof-off. He said he was Warren Rivers and wanted the part. His agent was getting work for the kid in Off-Off-Off-Broadway productions—you know, those things where they rehearse forever and play maybe two nights in a cellar. They bulldozed me into seeing Warren twice. Damned if he wasn't as good as he claimed. I was impressed enough to give him the script. He looked at me and said, 'You'll be calling me, Mr. Wuthering. I guarantee that.'"

"We didn't know what to expect, Boss, but everybody's wild about him. Christ! Anne Alexander's washing his socks. Stella's insisting on private rehearsals in the dressing room."

"How about Claudia?"

"I guess you know she had something going with Robin. Well, she's crazy about Warren too. But I think she's worried that she hasn't heard the last of Robin. You know, all the gossip. . . ."

"Billy—" Wuthering stopped him short—"I will not listen to any of those stories. I produce plays. That's my business. Nothing else. Anyhow, I'm pleased she's getting along with Warren."

"Are you coming to Chicago?"

Wuthering answered, "Of course. I wouldn't miss it. Post a notice for a party after the opening. You pick the place."

"Whatever you say, Boss," Briggs said, surprised by Wuthering's indifference to Claudia's problems. Far from being aloof, Wuthering was deeply interested in his people and usually wanted to know everything that touched them, either professionally or personally.

Warren Rivers, an easy, outgoing, lively extrovert, the exact opposite of Robin, brought vitality, laughter and great personal charm to the weary players of *The Capri Affair*. He stood over six feet, a broad-shouldered young man with a physique to match the attractiveness of his crown of golden-blond curly hair and blue eyes. He arrived immaculately dressed in a tailored suit with shirt and tie—quite a contrast to Robin, whose idea of dressing up was a clean pair of jeans.

Keith Bryne took one look at this Greek god, nodded his approval and offered Claudia one succinct observation. "Would you believe it? The big hunk of sapphire on his finger is real. He's learned his trade. He'll work out fine."

"What's the ring got to do with his acting?" Claudia asked.

"Darling, you're so naive," Byrne said. "An actor always puts his first solid piece of change into a good piece of jewelry—something he can hock easily. That ring's good for the rent and two weeks' eating. What more does a young man need if he's going to follow this crazy profession? This kid's not fooling around."

Claudia kissed his cheek. "I love you, Keith. You know everything."

"Thank you, dear. You're quite right, I do."

Warren found the model for his performance in the approach brought to it by Zach, who also directed him.

173

After the Sunday night rehearsal in Chicago, Stella Morell sent word that she wanted to speak to the entire company on stage.

When they were assembled, Stella said, "You know, when my husband wrote this play, he said, 'Stella, watcha out for whatta happen when dey play longa time.' His English wasn't so good. Anyhow, he predicted that eventually everyone would go off into the corners and mumble away until they got to their big scenes, and then they'd come on . . . like you say . . . like *Gangbusters*. Now that's happened everywhere I do the play, and it started all over again in Boston. Now we got a perfect cast. This guy Warren has given us new hormones. Look at him! If he's not worth fighting over, then we might as well give up. Right?"

When the actors looked his way, Warren smiled, nodded his head. He'd be the last one to disagree. The odd thing about it, Claudia thought, is that he's not offensive. A compliment is a compliment. Part of the game. Nothing to get embarrassed about. She was impressed.

Stella went on, "Anyhow, fighting over the kid is what the play is all about. This was a good rehearsal. That's how I want to see it tomorrow and for the rest of the engagement. *Va bene*? Okay?"

They applauded as Stella left the stage, waving her hand and saying, "Good night, thank you very much and break your legs."

The last remark was the show business equivalent of "good luck."

*   *   *

Frank Lamark was surprised at the ease with which he'd been able to arrange for a screening of the Nino Bellafiore film, *Schizo*, in which Claudia Milotte had

174

starred more than twenty years earlier.

In Paris he was able to obtain letters identifying him as the representative of a distributing company which had expressed interest in exhuming the unfinished picture, in view of the current name value of Claudia Milotte.

Primo Franchini, who leased the vaults and represented the financial interests of most of the unfinished epics in Rome happened to be in the States when Lamark arrived in Rome with his letters of introduction and authorization to represent the company.

This fortunate situation led to his acquaintance with Agosto Smythe, tall, light-haired, thin and serious, who insisted on picking Lamark up at the old hotel he preferred on Via Della Carrozze. From there they would drive to the vaults where the films were stored at *Cinecitta* several miles outside the walls of Rome.

The Albergo Merline was hardly a proper address for so prominent an entrepreneur as Lamark had been described in the letters to *Signore* Franchini. The hotel as rated as third class, but it enjoyed a good reputation among businessmen, who appreciated both its convenience to the city's commercial area and the comparative ease of entertaining. Lamark had never stayed anywhere else. It was his home.

Of the Merline, one veteran of its crumbling plaster walls and knotted mattresses was supposed to have enthused, "I doubt very much that the night porter would question a guest's arriving with a crocodile for a companion, provided the croc carried an identity card."

Agosto, Lamark was pleased to discover, appreciated the legends associated with the old hotel and Lamark discerned a gleam in his eye when they met. The young Italian observed, "I spent one night there; I'll never forget it. Her name was Anna."

Lamark, figuring that one-fifth of Rome's female

population bore the name "Anna," deduced that Mr. Smythe was a man of the utmost discretion. Lamark couldn't even be sure of the gleam, for Smythe saw the world through thick eyeglasses and from a height of more than six feet, dwarfing the Italians the detective had known in his student years.

Vitamins and fortified foods had made the difference. Squat chunky Italians like Sal White who, on native soil, would be Salvatore Bianco, had become extinct. As an American, Lamark once stood tall among the Romans, but that was a different era. How different, he quickly learned from Agosto Smythe, who first explained his peculiar name.

"My father was English, my mother Italian. The law requires that Italian children be baptized with a Latin name. I was born in August. That made it easier for Mama to remember all her kids. I was the first. There are six of us, three brothers, two sisters and me. Dad's the Rome manager for Royal Films Inc., so I grew up in the business."

This accounted for the second difference between the generations. Now audiences were "students of the cinema." They read *Cahiers du Cinema*; they knew not only the famous stars but the better film editors and script supervisors. They worshipped directors and photographers. Movies were no longer called movies. They were "films," and rated as "art." Lamark's age obviously marked him as an outsider in the rarefied climate of movie buffs, and Smythe had no intention of letting that fact go by without comment.

Lamark was barely able to get in a word as Smythe related reel by reel all the magic contained in the huge stockpile of celluloid lying unseen, forgotten and doomed to decay in the vaults.

Looking back on his experience with Mr. Smythe, it was just as well that Lamark's language had been reduced to impotent "oohs," "ahhs," and "is that so?" The names of neither the movies nor their creators made any impression on him. He was pleased, however, that the archivist's selectivity had more to do with the preservation of certain films than the capital invested in them.

"Film is perishable, Mr. Lamark. For protection it must lie in an air-conditioned vault where the temperature remains constant," Smythe explained. "Otherwise it turns to dust. It's unbelievable that millions of dollars' worth of historic films just don't exist any more—except in the form of old, beat-up, spliced-together prints collected by film buffs. The first movie whose future as a masterpiece was predetermined was *Gone with the Wind*."

Lamark managed, "Oh! Really?" and regretted it later.

They were driving on a side road to Cinecitta in order to avoid the heavy traffic between the city and the airport. Smythe pulled over to one side and explained the drama guaranteeing the perpetuity of *Gone with the Wind*.

"They foresaw that the picture was going to be a classic and that it could be revived over and over again. One theater in Paris ran *Gone with the Wind* for five years without interruption. Television was on the drawing boards. There had been many successful experiments, but they were halted because of the war. The Americans knew they were eventually going to be forced into World War II. Prints of *Gone with the Wind* were shipped to various parts of the world and consigned to underground vaults built into the mountains, where governments store documents and banks hold gold deposits and other valuables. Until then nobody ever thought of protecting movies to that extent. Television, of course, made the difference. But it was *Gone with the Wind* that began the program of preservation."

Lamark asked about the condition of *Schizo*. Smythe started up the *Cinque Cento* and a rapturous smile crossed his long English face.

"That's one of my favorites. I'm always thrilled when someone asks to see it. It's a magnificent picture and Claudia Milotte...well...you can't believe it. She gives a performance that would have won her an Academy Award. She's a great actress."

"It seems to me," Lamark ventured, "that a movie of such dimensions would attract interest."

"No, that's the sad part. No one cares. I do. I've even outlined how it might be finished. I have Claudia Milotte's personal script with her own markings. I have tagged on a finish that would work and make the movie worth millions of dollars. It's a period piece, seventeenth century, so that makes it easier. It doesn't look dated."

Smythe and his little car were well known to the lone gatekeeper, who signaled him to go straight ahead into the studio which had made movie history during the fifties, when it welcomed some of the biggest movies and film stars of the time. *Quo Vadis* was filmed there; so was *War and Peace*, as well as epics like *Hercules*, *The Bible* and dozens of others. Now the studio was virtually deserted, its grounds having become a field covered with weeds. Only the buildings, crumbling away, stood as reminders that *Cinecitta* had once been numbered among the great film plants of the world.

The exception was one building at the end of the lot which looked freshly painted and impeccably maintained. It housed the vaults, and Lamark assumed that Agosto Smythe was responsible for its maintenance. Smythe slid the car up to a door marked "Projection Room," jumped out, turned the door knob and nodded to Lamark. "Come right in; it's open. The projectionist is here. We can begin right away."

For two hours, *Schizo* held Frank Lamark's attention. It warranted Smythe's designation as a masterpiece. A simple study of a peasant girl with a dual personality, the theme was familiar and many of the situations and complications were predictable. What gave *Schizo* its special quality was the period of the story and its realistic picture of the squalor of life in the Italian South, where the land was tough, hard, unyielding, offering the peasants bare subsistence. Yet one of them, the character played by Claudia, pulls herself free of this society of ignorance and superstition by facing her own identity crisis, conquering it and becoming a whole woman. Arrayed against her determination are her family, the town's political elite and even the young priest whose advances she resists.

Schizo was the old morality drama, good versus evil, but it was magnificently done. Claudia's performance was extraordinary. Her beauty was articulated for him by Smythe, who kept up a running whispered commentary on the film's high points. "Watch her here," he said. "Claudia makes love to the camera...it's extraordinary...the Garbo quality."

After the screening, Smythe drove Lamark to a *trattoria* a few kilometers down the road. Although it was December the sun shone brightly, and for a second Lamark was tempted to suggest eating outdoors. But seeing Smythe wrapped in an overcoat, a scarf high around his throat, his huge hands encased in thick woolen gloves, he changed his mind.

Italians went by the calendar. If it was December it was cold, and one wore an overcoat. In April it rained; Italians

179

carried umbrellas. Delicious Italian water ices disappeared after September first, regardless of how high autumn temperatures might go. In November, heat appeared in a thin stream of steam in radiators all over Rome, whether it was eighty above or eight below.

Over a splendidly prepared lunch, Lamark pleased Smythe with his enthusiasm for the film. "There's no doubt about it, we must show this masterpiece to the world," he said, deftly appropriating the manner of the "film student," using Smythe as his model.

He had worried unnecessarily about requesting the material he needed. Lamark wondered if movie archivists were like assistant bank managers, who had to call the head office before allowing the police in to investigate a robbery. If they were, Agosto Smythe was an exception.

"Delighted, Mr. Lamark," he said, as he pulled out a pen and began writing down the sequences from which Lamark wished still pictures to be blown up from the film.

"Why are you interested in the letter-writing scenes?" Smythe asked.

Lamark hoped Smythe missed the moment of hesitation as he searched for the thoughts that would impress the librarian devoted emotionally and intellectually to his work. Lamark spoke slowly, measuring his words. "I found them especially fascinating because here we meet the two characters Claudia plays at their most intimate—perhaps vulnerable would explain my reaction better. It's almost as if the peasant girl were stripped naked and is searching her body hoping to find the devils that have driven her to madness."

Through Smythe's thick glasses Lamark saw his eyes shining with pleasure. "That's it! That's it exactly. I've been trying for years to describe what I feel about these scenes. You've translated my own emotions into words. Excuse me."

Lamark heaved a sigh of relief as Smythe transcribed the words exactly as they'd come from the detective. When he'd finished there remained one other matter.

Lamark asked, "Could I possibly impose on you to Xerox several of the pages of Miss Milotte's personal script, the one she made her notes in?"

"Pages! My dear Lamark! I'll copy the whole thing. What's the difference—a few minutes?"

"You're very helpful," Lamark said. "And, of course, I'll need your suggestions for completing the film." It was a quick afterthought.

Smythe beamed. "I'll have the material for you at your hotel by noon tomorrow. How long will you be staying in Rome?"

"I leave tomorrow night."

"What a pity! We're expecting a shipment of some Mexican films and will start showing them shortly," he said, with the assurance of a man who has found a fellow enthusiast. "They're primitive but fascinating. With dubbing, narrative, scoring, I'm convinced there's an eager audience waiting for them. The trouble is getting people to look at the material. It's odd. No one, for example, has wanted to see *Schizo* for years, apart from the occasions when I bring it out and show it to my friends in the Roman Film Society."

"Such a pity! It's a beautiful work. I'm going to do my best, I promise you," Lamark said.

They drove back to Rome, where Smythe decanted Lamark on Via Veneto. Lamark had said, "I know it's not the same, but I'd like to give the old street a look and remember how it was when I first visited Rome. Thank you for everything, and I'll expect you tomorrow at noon."

Lamark found himself standing in front of Donay's, the Veneto's fabled sidewalk cafe. At this hour of the afternoon he had the Veneto more or less to himself. He was free to paint any mental picture he chose, to recall the Veneto as it had appeared a quarter century earlier, when the older film stars of Hollywood flocked to Rome to breathe the last gasps of their careers and pretty young girls like Claudia Milotte stood in the wings.

Now Claudia Milotte had herself become one of the legends of the era—having given it only three contributions, a thin volume of film work, the best of it lying forgotten in an air-conditioned vault. Lamark shuddered. It was like being interred.

Sal White had once told him that his idea of the perfect way to begin a European trip was to fly first to London, arriving on a Sunday.

"There's nothing to do, you know," he said. "I hit the nearest newsstand and buy everything in sight—all those dreadful penny English newspapers, the French magazines, the German stuff and the Italian weeklies. For a tabloid publisher, it's like a dream come true. All those pages of gossip! The French murders, the English parson who buries his wife in the potato patch, and those private school teachers who get into trouble for birching their boys."

Lamark crossed to the large newsstand on the opposite side of the Veneto near the Café de Paris. It was one of those typical winter days that found the Roman sky clear and blue, the air just brisk enough to make the glass-enclosed Café de Paris sidewalk tables look inviting. The afternoon was free; tonight Lamark would dine with his old friend Inspector Luke Monzelli, of the Rome police department. Why not spend the siesta hours with a batch of Europe's crazy newspapers?

The Italian weeklies were fresh off the press. A glance at the photographs on two of them told Lamark that

Richard Winston's murder couldn't be avoided, even for a half hour or so at a sidewalk café. The face of Claudia Milotte filled the front page of two newspapers, her name in large black letters appeared on the others. Spotting Milotte on page one of the English, French and German newspapers, Lamark collected them all and stepped into the nearest enclosure.

He ordered a Campari and soda and turned to the English tabloid, *The Star*. A glance at the byline, blurb and copyright told him that the story had originated with *The Star*; the others were translations.

The headline and subheads read: YOUTH'S LOVE FOR MURDER VICTIM'S WIDOW—"My Love For Claudia Milotte" by Robin Haywood—Star Worried about Husband's Murder?—Tragedy of a Millionairess.

The first-page blurb gave the reader an idea of what to expect from Robin Haywood's so-called love affair with Claudia Milotte.

> *Robin Haywood, a twenty-year-old country boy from Ohio*, came to New York to become a star. Now he wonders. Now the handsome blond youth, who recently arrived in London to begin a film career, fears he may have permanently damaged the promising future that began when he appeared in a starring role opposite Claudia Milotte in the Broadway stage success *The Capri Affair*.
>
> Why?
>
> "Because Claudia Milotte lives in the shadow of the unsolved murder of her husband," Robin Haywood tells *Star* readers, in this exclusive story of the romance between the 37-year-old star, still radiantly beautiful,

and the youth, 18 years her junior, who fell hopelessly in love with her.

People close to Claudia openly suspect she may be the unidentified mystery woman who allegedly visited the penthouse of millionaire Richard Winston IV on the evening of his murder. Says Robin, "The suspicions are groundless, of course, but they have had their effect on the woman I still love. They have driven her into a dark corner of loneliness. I sometimes question her sanity.

"She wanted me with her at all times. I feared her possessiveness," Robin Haywood says, "so I fled from her arms, from the play in which night after night we pretended love we really felt, and from the country where I was born and hoped to make my name."

Now Robin is a lonely wanderer, "afraid to love again," he says, in this engrossing story of the leading lady and the juvenile, which reveals for the first time the sordid details of Claudia Milotte's strange marriage to a murdered man whose death may make her one of the world's richest women.

The story occupied the centerfold. Into the two pages were crammed photographs of Claudia at various stages of her life—the young nude star of French films, the actress in community theaters, the bride of Richard Winston IV, and finally in the arms of Robin Haywood— a publicity shot from *The Capri Affair*. The pictures were cleverly arranged to spotlight the age difference between Claudia and her "kiss-and-tell lover."

As Lamark skimmed through the exposé he realized

that it amounted to no more than a stunt that one might expect from an immature, poorly advised young man who assumed that getting publicity at the expense of a well-known personality was better than no publicity at all. It seldom worked, but who would warn Robin of that?

The claims Robin made about Claudia's tenacious, possessive hold on him, Lamark knew, were totally out of character. He felt that the writer assigned to the nasty piece hadn't swallowed it either. That section read awkwardly.

Libel was carefully skirted, in the British manner, by avoiding direct statements from Claudia. The reader was led through this romantic entanglement strictly from Robin's point of view.

"She gave me the impression of living with sorrow" and "Claudia was afraid of strangers" were observations one might make about anyone, the housewife next door or the First Lady of the United States.

Lamark finished his drink, folded his bundle of newspapers and began the walk toward Piazza di Spagna, along Via Sistina to the top of the famous Spanish Steps to the Piazza and the cobblestoned street of Delle Carrozze. His hotel lay close to the Corso, Rome's busy banking and commercial center.

Lamark had known nothing of the so-called affair between Claudia and Robin. How could he have? Claudia's private life was not his affair, beyond what it might offer from a professional viewpoint. But Lamark had been totally unable to separate his personal feelings from his work for so many weeks that it had seemed forever.

The infatuation that began when he entered her dressing room on the night of the murder had been heightened by the events of recent weeks. Lamark's heart had opened to the tragic life of this remarkable woman whose poise, elegance and beauty transcended the anger and bitterness she must be suffering. And now there had come this play for attention from a young man to whom Lamark was convinced Claudia had shown nothing but kindness!

Claudia had a need for love; he'd seen it in her eyes. Lamark shook with rage at the idea of a snotty kid like Robin Haywood answering a physical need in a woman, only to make capital of it when it suited his convenience. Disgusting!

Underlying Lamark's revulsion lay envy. It was there, and he'd be a fool to deny it. As his admiration of Claudia grew, so did his fury at having been placed in the position of her "persecutor"—a cop sworn to prove her either guilty or innocent of murder. In spite of this, some basis for friendship had been achieved. Claudia was interested in him, Lamark was confident. What more could he expect of their evening in Boston at the Sky Room than ladylike graciousness? In view of the barrier created by their roles as detective and suspect, Lamark was amazed at the extent of her graciousness.

On her Chicago opening he had sent her a cable wishing her luck for the engagement. What more could he have done? What could he write that one day might not rise up to haunt him, if he confided either his feelings for Claudia or the purpose behind his trip to Europe? What dark thoughts would cross her mind if he told her that he'd spent more days than he intended in Lucenay, tracing the childhood of Claudia Milotte?

As for his superiors, they would be horrified. What bearing could such an exhaustive investigation have on a case unless Lieutenant Lamark had gone ape? What had Lucenay to do with a case where the murder weapon was still believed missing, where the meager clues the police had kept from the public made absolutely no sense? They'd send him to the shrinks for observation.

Lucenay lay in the heart of Basque country, a mystery to many Frenchmen, anathema to others, colorful and unusual to tourists. What others thought of them had absolutely no effect on the sturdy, hardworking peasants, presumed to be the oldest ethnic group in Europe. Zealously they have guarded their ancient customs, traditions and even their language, which is unrelated to any other tongue.

No one has even been certain of the origin of the Basques, who have managed to remain isolated even in immigration forced on them by depressed economic conditions of the nineteenth century. Wherever they went, to South America, to California and other parts of the world, they chose to remain Basques, profiting handsomely by the simple act of being "quaint."

But pleasing tourists and selling trinkets, Lamark knew, was not a natural trait of a people who worked the land, fished the seas and dug deep into the earth for minerals in order to survive. Christianity penetrated Basque country slowly, but once it gained strength it grew powerful. Church leaders took advantage of the natural isolation of the French and Spanish provinces to assert their independence of the hierarchies of Spain and France.

With no difficulty Lamark found the decaying edifice that had once been Villa Maria. It lay outside the town in the midst of grazing and farmland. It was an ugly, fortress-type building, and Lamark had no trouble imagining the prisonlike atmosphere that enveloped the young girls who filled it during the turbulent postwar years. The continent of Europe was flooded with orphans at that time, many of them nameless children of parents from whom they'd become separated or who, more often, had been killed in World War II, a conflict which made little distinction between civilians and military.

In Paris, from research in the records and newspaper accounts, Lamark learned that ten years earlier Villa Maria had been closed by the national government, over the protests of the citizens of Lucenay, whose businesses profited from serving such a large institution. There had been scandals involving the misappropriation of funds, brutality against the children, and strong evidence of sexual misconduct by the nuns. The exposure of conditions at Villa Maria resulted in the expulsion of several nuns.

Without the precaution of having inquired about Villa Maria previously, Lamark might have spent months before discovering that there had ever been a Villa Maria, much less a scandal. The citizens of Lucenay were typical of the French peasants who warm slowly, if ever, to a stranger. Being Basques, they resented the black mark left on their community by the investigation of the orphanage.

Villa Maria had been forgotten. They pretended it had never existed. No one he spoke to would admit ever having heard of Abbess Prudentissima, one of the defrocked nuns, who, as a much younger woman, had been put in charge of the orphanage. For nearly thirty years she had maintained it as her personal fief, a community she ruled with an iron hand and will. She had been in charge in the years Claudia was one of the children.

To obtain a clear first-hand picture of Villa Maria, Lamark, with his orderly policeman's mind, hoped to hear the impressions of those with first-hand knowledge of the community. There had to be some former orphans who stayed on in Lucenay after reaching seventeen. But doors were shut in his face when Lamark mentioned the orphanage. In desperation he turned to officials in the Paris police department, who had ways of twisting the arms of their rural brothers.

A young officer, Jean-Claude Roget, was grudgingly assigned him. Lucenay authorities presumed that being young, inexperienced, and a newcomer to the area, he would also be a dullard.

On the contrary, Lamark found Jean-Claude Roget to be alert, intelligent and a diligent researcher. Moreover, he was terribly impressed with the opportunity to work side by side with "supersleuth" Lamark. In his youth the young man had been a devoted reader of detective stories. French detective weeklies assiduously reprinted accounts of crimes in which Lamark had been involved. To Jean-Claude, Frank Lamark was a storybook hero come to life.

In a few days Lamark wrapped up more information than he'd been able to accumulate by himself in two weeks. The young officer gained him access to city records and compelled the local pastor to produce those of Villa Maria—dusty, musty and virtually illegible. But they offered Lamark a clear and devastating picture of the life led by the children entrusted to difficult women in the difficult era of postwar France. It was an era of great change, politically and socially. There were shortages of everything, from flour to clothing. Places like Villa Maria suffered from never-ending overcrowding. The nuns had been through a national catastrophe which would mark them forever. However sincere they may have been when, as young women, they took vows of chastity, poverty and obedience, time and circumstance had altered them into

189

greedy, avaracious, selfish and brutal creatures who had lost touch with their calling and with the young people entrusted to their care.

Yet at the end of his stay at Lucenay, Lamark concluded that Villa Maria had been no better or worse than any other institution of its kind in France at the time. There were too many children, and too few people in authority who cared to investigate abuses. They had become immune to the suffering of others; self-preservation governed their lives.

Lamark hoped he was not being an apologist for a society that had endured privation, despair, invasion and occupation. He had talked to elderly men and women on planes and trains. They told him the simple stories of their families—four generations impaled on the swords of the Germans, grandfathers killed in the war of 1870, fathers lost in World War I, sons who died in the service of France during World War II and their sons and daughters who for the rest of their lives would bear the trauma of spending their formative years in a divided France of austerity and privation. They made him understand that need and hunger become the handmaidens of selfishness.

When he left Lucenay, Lamark understood Claudia Milotte much more clearly than he would have believed possible. He looked forward to Rome with mixed feelings. There he would either complete the portrait that could bring the Winston murder to a solution, or become the victim of his own emotions.

* * *

Like Lieutenant Frank Lamark in New York, Inspector Luke Monzelli occupied a unique position in Rome's police department. In a sense Monzelli had enjoyed more distinction because of the post created for him in the Eternal City. In recent years Monzelli supervised an elite task force in charge of crime that involved the huge number of foreign visitors coming to Rome.

Not all of them were pilgrims. Too many for comfort chose Rome as a convenient meeting place for a wide variety of criminal activities, from narcotics traffic to quasilegal manipulations in oil, currency and art objects, which often involved prominent, seemingly respectable people. Monzelli's job was to circumvent these offenses and frighten the perpetrators before they became too deeply involved, or to shoo them off into another jurisdiction, preferably outside of Italy.

Lamark took cases as they came. That was the New York system. "In many ways," Monzelli told him when they'd met two or three years earlier, shortly after his special bureau was created, "I'm going to envy you. These international hoods are cut from the same mold. They're whitewashed with corporations and personal respectability. You have to get to them subtly, then clobber them with some nasty bit of personal innuendo that has nothing to do with their illegal activities. It's official blackmail, but it works. Then we load them on the next plane out of Italy. I miss the excitement of a truly complicated murder case that keeps you dogging a trail for months before all the pieces come together like the last chunks of a jigsaw puzzle."

When they met in a quiet private dining room at Tito's, Monzelli greeted his old friend warmly. The two men even shared a physical resemblance. They were both of average height, with solid bodies. Their features were sharp, their eyes were clear and both were graying at the temples. Monzelli was a bachelor, Lamark a widower.

191

Because Luke always ordered dinner in advance, Frank was spared the impossible decision of visitors on quick trips to Italy to choose from menus on which every specialty listed tempted the appetite.

The only social amenities the two men observed began and ended with, "You haven't changed a bit. A little more gray, but otherwise. . . ."

They were policemen and the details of their craft obsessed them. Monzelli naturally expected Lamark to fill him in on all the details of the Winston case, which had surfaced so dramatically in the newspapers after having dropped from the headlines.

He was surprised when Lamark seemed reluctant to go over it.

"Something's out of order here," he said, as the waiter began preparing the table for the *ante pasta*. "I can't imagine your taking off for Europe and your vacation in the middle of a case like that. Heavens! It's a dream. A rich man with a shady reputation . . . a beautiful actress with a curious background . . . other women hidden all over the place . . . businessmen who'd drink champagne to Richard Winston's execution . . . solid signs pointing to underworld links involving Winston and Associates. . . . I'd give up a vacation for an assignment like that."

His enthusiasm, Monzelli felt, was making Lamark uncomfortable. Then he realized his mistake. "A thousand pardons, Frank. The vacation is your cover, right?"

"Fifty percent right, yes."

"So it *is* the Milotte woman! I never doubted it for a second. You're here to get the European background, yes?"

"In a way, yes."

"In a way, yes?" Luke mocked. "What kind of answer is that? It tells me that you haven't got much of a case."

Lamark's mood changed. "That's how it looks. You can't pin anything down."

"She's got to be the mystery woman. Who else? She's an actress, isn't she?"

"Yes, and a lovely one."

"There you have it. Prove she's the mystery woman, get your hands on the weapon, check out the note that she sent to her husband. *Ecco! Voila!* You have it. Her attorney pleads Crime of Passion, explains all the anguish she suffered over the years. What's the worst that can happen? A short sentence, commuted after a few months, and the lady's free."

"In theory it sounds fine, Luke. But how can you make a Crime of Passion out of a murder as well planned as this one? If Claudia did it alone she's a genius."

"So you think there was a finger man, someone who pulled the trigger for her?"

"I have no evidence either way."

"But you can't allow the poor woman to go on like this, with shadows hanging over her as long as she lives, or as long as the police fail to solve the case. That's not gallant, my friend."

Lamark laughed. "Since when does one find gallantry in American murder trials?"

Luke Monzelli sighed. "Only in cases of euthanasia. I guess Women's Lib has put the Crime of Passion out of business. That's a pity. It always eliminated, at least in my experience, men who would have gotten killed by somebody else. And God knows that's the case here. There must have been a hit out on Winston. That makes it worse."

"How so?"

"The hit man gets away. Claudia Milotte is guilty by inference."

"I never thought of that."

Luke Monzelli leaned back in his chair. He nodded approval as the waiter set down the veal scallopine and approved the chilled white wine, which would be served with the course. He leaned across the table and forced Lamark to look directly into his eyes.

"Your emotions are involved in this case," the Italian said quietly.

Lamark's eyes turned to the plate. He picked up a knife and fork and began attacking the veal.

"Ridiculous, Luke. Nothing of the sort. How? Why? That's impossible."

"Does she know?"

"No, damn it. . . ."

He stopped short. Monzelli had trapped him.

"Now we can talk honestly. Maybe I can help you."

*   *   *

After dinner the two men relaxed. They'd finished their coffee and the table had been cleared, except for a bottle of French brandy, soda and a bucket of ice.

"It occurs to me, my friend, that you've placed yourself in a pretty awkward position."

Lamark shrugged.

Luke Monzelli lit his pipe. "When I remarked that Women's Lib may do away with the Crime of Passion, I don't think I was being facetious. It seems to me that if women insist on equal rights, they may as well have them right down the line—including the right to be convicted of first-degree murder. Mind you, I'm not maintaining that it's a good thing, simply that it's another right that would

194

put them on an equal footing with men.

"I'm probably more experienced than some detectives in dealing with murder by women. Yet how many cases have I handled? Six, seven, eight—ten at the outside. Regardless of what I discovered in respect to motive, all my ladies went into court with the same defense. Their attorneys successfully maintained that their honor had been impinged, that they'd disposed of husbands or lovers—in Europe we're not inclined to make sharp distinctions between the two—because of a mad fit of jealousy, after finding the loved on in the embrace of another man. They supposedly acted from an emotional response; no self-respecting defense counsel would call it a 'sexual impulse.' Hence we have the European definition, the Crime of Passion."

"It has a more dramatic ring than the American version," Lamark said.

"It does, but my study of America's unwritten law concept reveals it to be man made and male-oriented. Am I correct?"

Lamark laughed. "Absolutely. A man comes home, finds his wife in bed with another man. He takes out the gun any American is licensed to carry, shoots one or both. Then he claims the unwritten law—the sanctity of his marriage and home have been invaded. He seldom spends even a night in jail."

Monzelli leaned across the table, "But that's not how it turns out when the killer is a woman. Why?"

Lamark seemed surprised by the Italian's earnestness. "You know as well as I do that a woman has no honor to respect but her own. If an American wife finds her husband in bed with his mistress, boom! she's a woman. She goes insane. She shoots one or both. In court the prosecutor and defense attorney plea bargain the murder charge down to homicide; they squeeze in 'temporary insanity,' enabling the jury to reach a verdict of 'guilty' and a recommendation for leniency. The judge has the discretion to pass the lightest sentence under the law. If the lady murderer is rich, she may serve a few months receiving psychiatric counseling in a minimum security compound. If she's poor, she does a little time—straight and nasty."

Monzelli nodded. "Essentially the unwritten law has much in common with the Crime of Passion except that, as I have said, it favors the man. But overlooking that, why are you Americans so unreasonably proud of the code that a 'man is guilty until proven innocent' while we take an opposite position? Americans fail to consider that we do not file charges as capriciously as you. Our preliminary investigations are more thorough. When a prosecutor brings charges, in nine cases out of ten he's certain they're going to stick.

"This has given the strength of old roots and years of precedent when a court is faced with a Crime of Passion. By the time the betrayed woman murderer enters the courtroom she's already been held for several weeks or months. So it becomes a formality. The tribunal finds her guilty of justifiable homicide. The judge, pointing out that she has already paid heavily for her crime, sets her free, and the spectators, as they do in television, applaud, cheer and hug one another in their happiness.

"The question that remains forever unanswered—the one that bothers me—is, *When did the lady decide to become a murderer? In that moment of wild, uncontrollable jealousy? Was it months before, when she first suspected her husband's infidelity? Or how about this? Did she plan to murder him on the day she became his bride?*"

196

"The law is myopic when it deals with women killers. Either a woman commits a crime that's sexually motivated or there's no murder at all. In the eyes of the law and society the female murderer is a shadowy creature even the police know little about. I suspect it's a deliberate oversight, the idealizing of womanhood—you know, the perfect mother, the dedicated nun, the girl who comes to her bridegroom pure and untouched on her wedding night. I would suggest, my dear Lamark, that we've been made suckers of."

Monzelli stopped in midthought. "I apologize. I shouldn't have said it so crudely."

"Why not?" Lamark asked.

"I am not . . . well, frankly, I'm not involved with a female murderer."

"And I am?" Lamark asked, hoping the question would remain unanswered.

It was.

"The detective who assumes a woman murderer is stupid is himself stupid," Monzelli continued. "She's shrewd, calculating, infinitely more patient than her male counterpart. Police can never avoid the conviction that the woman murders purely from sexual motives. I don't agree, even if that's how the case comes out in court. I believe they have a host of other reasons for murder—self-preservation, greed, ambition. Whatever the reason, they're clever and cunning. They show imagination, intelligence and daring, and believe me, they can be ruthless."

The Italian fished into his pocket for some papers. "Some years ago I came across this book, *Women Who Murder*. It's by Gerald Sparrow, an English counselor and judge."

"I know it quite well," Lamark said. "I can remember

asking myself the same questions you've raised. When does a woman become a killer? I can't believe that it happens overnight. Why is a gun always so convenient? Why is a knife usually handy? Even if she's got to go fetch it, the woman who wants to kill has her weapon stashed away someplace where she can get at it easily."

Lamark paused. "Very well. Here are some pieces of evidence I've assembled in the Winston murder. Tracing the gun was so simple that for a few minutes I believed I could sew up the case in twenty-four hours. The weapon was a .22. I knew that the Winstons lived in the Hamptons, that they'd spent a few years in Fairfield, Connecticut, and for two summers, when they lived in New York, they maintained a summer cottage on the coast of Maine, at York Beach. Three telephone calls later I discovered there was a Colt .22 registered to Mrs. Claudia Milotte Winston. Obviously her husband had given it to her for protection because she spent a great deal of time at the Maine cottage alone."

"So you found the gun?"

"No," Lamark said, "not a trace of it. We scoured the neighborhood. You know how quickly guns are disposed of after a murder, often within yards of the scene of the crime."

Monzelli fumbled through his papers. "Here's what Sparrow says: 'When it comes to preparation for the crime the natural aptitude of the woman for subterfuge and concealment stands her in good stead. She has always had to rely on a certain amount of convincing chicanery to make up for her lack of physical strength. The execution of murder is carried out with typical stealth and with consummate care. Most women can become actresses, if necessary, because they know that smiling or crying will be very useful in misleading any investigating team, which will almost certainly be composed entirely of men. The art of concealment presents no difficulty to a woman murderer.'"

"Quite true, but it doesn't help me. A month later I'm still without the gun."

"You believe Madame Milotte is the mystery woman?"

"Of course. She's an actress. She was described as blonde and twenty-eight. An actress with Claudia's talents could act any age she wanted, from 28 to 78. She wore tinted glasses. There she gave something away. She might act and dress like a fairly young woman—she's only thirty-seven—but you can't hide age in your eyes."

"An actress would know that, wouldn't she?"

Lamark laughed. "It had nothing to do with the investigation. Curiously, that was one of the things we talked about at our first meeting in her dressing room. She was explaining the time needed to make up. Her hair alone, she said, required an hour. She told me how carefully she worked on her eyes so her visual reactions would be perceived by the audience."

"Clearly she was building support under her alibi. I assume she claimed to be in the theater at the time of the murder," Monzelli said.

"Of course. It was Saturday, a matinee day. She volunteered all this, mind you. She explained that she always stayed in the theater rather than risk mussing her hair."

"And never went out?"

"A bite to eat at the corner delicatessen."

"It couldn't be *the* perfect alibi, could it?"

Lamark laughed. "Of course not. It was shot full of holes when I visited the theater the following week after I saw Claudia and Stella Morell...."

"What a divine actress!" Monzelli interrupted.

"On and off the stage. That's beside the point. I avoided questioning her because of the rumors—you read them. I wanted the rumors to grow; maybe we'd get something concrete. We did receive one substantive piece of evidence the day before I left New York—a pair of women's shoes with steel plating attached to the heel."

"Not exactly a novelty," Monzelli ventured. "They could be useful in a mugging or an assault."

"Yes, but this wasn't the case. In talking to the theater people I found out that the three ladies spent much more time backstage than actresses do normally—with legitimate reasons. Signora Morell, because she could rest directly before a performance; Claudia Milotte, either because she was lonely, or because she needed the time to create her make-up or to set up a pattern that would survive under police interrogation."

"Sounds fascinating," Monzelli remarked, "a pattern for murder."

Lamark ignored the intrusion, having lost himself in his compilation of evidence—all of it circumstantial and pointing to Claudia. "A photograph of the steel-plated shoes was brought to the precinct by the third actress in *The Capri Affair*, about Claudia's age, a spinster who told us they were not her shoes but Claudia's. She suspected that Claudia had impersonated her by using the shoes when she went to the Grand-Plaza Hotel as the mystery woman. The lady forgot that the mystery woman was described as twenty-eight. Anne Alexander is about forty.

"The steel heels, she explained, were useful in identifying her presence when she entered her home. Evidently when she stamped her feet, the floor vibrations reached her deaf mother and reassured her.

"I spoke to the house manager, who's known Miss Alexander for years. 'She came to the theater at all hours of the morning and afternoon to relax,' he told me. 'Anything to get away from that bitch of a mother. It seems to me the women were always around the theater. I never saw anything like it before.'"

A broad smile spread over Monzelli's face. "It restores my faith in the fiendishness of the human mind. By clomping around in steel heels, imitating this Alexander woman's steps, Claudia could come and go either as herself or as Miss Alexander."

"Exactly. Assuming this was how she planned it, she'd found a way to disarm Stella Morell, a lady of unpredictable habits."

"The time?" Monzelli asked. "The distance between the theater and the hotel?"

"Luke, she laid it out herself—fifteen or sixteen blocks, she said. She walked them the day before when she visited Richard Winston, ostensibly to discuss her refusal to agree to a divorce."

"Sounds more like casing the territory, to me."

"It does, but we'll never know. The only corroborater is dead."

"Wasn't there a note?"

"Yes, the mystery woman sent it to Winston with a bellboy who gave her the key to his suite. We found the note stuffed in Winston's pocket. We've never released this piece of evidence to the press—if you can call it evidence. The handwriting doesn't match Claudia's. The only fingerprints we can identify match Winston's. The paper could have come from any one of thousands of novelty shops."

"It's incredible that she'd leave the note in Winston's pocket."

"Perhaps Claudia had an accomplice?"

"It would make things simpler. The background of

201

Donald Laine, an attorney, the close friend of Claudia and Winston, is pretty shabby."

Monzelli nodded. "He's known to us here."

"The trouble with the accomplice theory is that it doesn't fit in anywhere else. I made the walk from the theater to the hotel and back. Allowing fifteen minutes—a half hour at the outside—for the killer and the victim to get together, the whole nasty business didn't take more than an hour. Claudia accounted for part of that time by saying she had gone to the deli for a quick bite."

"It checked out?"

"Of course. Why would she plan a murder and create an alibi if at the denouement she needed someone to pull the trigger? She wasn't in the position of a woman with a lover whom she'd convinced to eliminate her husband so they could live happily ever after. Just the opposite. I gather she was terrified of involvement because that was what Winston wanted.

"He had the money, the power—and the perverted mind—to turn her into a slut in the public's mind if she got out of line. The marriage was Winston's facade; he could hide all his dirty vices behind it. Claudia found out about them. That's why she left him. But Winston was still able to control her. He had to. The testimony she might give in a divorce proceeding or any action she took that would exhume his old police record would ruin him."

"We have Winston down on our lists as someone who goes after kids," Monzelli said. "I believe he's got an indecent exposure charge in Milan. That was years ago, but naturally it began coming back when I read about his murder."

The two men were silent for a time. Monzelli filled their brandy glasses. He sniffed the aroma, swished the fluid

202

around in the glass and slugged down half the shot.

He spoke slowly. "God knows you've got motive—and more. Someone was bound to get Winston one day. Why not his wife, who had to bear all the suffering?"

Lamark finished off his brandy. "That's not how they figure it at the precinct house. It's looked at as a gangland killing. Let it take its own course. They'll put me on something else as soon as I get back."

"I'm afraid," Monzelli said, "you're up against the kind of problem an honest cop hates."

"That's about it, Luke."

"I wouldn't worry if I were you."

"Bless you, my friend, and *grazie*. How come?"

"You know as well as I do where the weak link lies," Monzelli said.

"Of course; in the gun."

"The rest is window dressing. Beautiful, by the way. My compliments to the lady. But you know what you have to do—simply trick her into possessing the gun on the day in question. For someone with your experience, that's child's play."

"But it's also obtaining a confession illegally, without warning her of her rights."

"I know that, Frank. So you're going to face what we've all done at one time or another."

Monzelli poured a double shot into each of their glasses as he searched for the correct words—words that had been rambling through Frank Lamark's mind since the moment he had walked into Claudia Milotte's dressing room, finding a terror-ridden, broken, beaten and utterly lovely woman hiding behind a mask of stoicism that only a Frenchman could understand.

Luke Monzelli raised the glass. "Too much for

203

'bottoms up.' But face it squarely, Frank. You won't be the first cop, nor the last. For her sake you're going to have to be prosecutor, jury and judge. Good luck."

* * *

Frank Lamark would have been surprised not to have found Sal White waiting when his flight arrived from Rome. He'd written Sal the date, asking that he leave word where he could be located.

In coming to Kennedy, Sal was carrying a message which wasn't lost on the detective. Payoff time was close at hand. Sal was looking to Lamark to help him get the Winston people off his back. He either wanted to buy them out personally or he'd come up with outside capital to take over their stock. It wasn't Lamark's line of work, but for Sal he was willing to serve as middleman, providing the circumstances presented themselves. They hadn't come together, but the tacit, unspoken understanding existed. In meeting him, Sal was both firming up the deal and bringing Lamark up to date on what was taking place in Chicago.

It had nagged Lamark all across the Atlantic—even more than his recognition of the enormous implications contained in Luke Monzelli's remark about his being both inquisitor and judge.

With both Claudia's present and his own future cluttering a mind already burdened with too many questions and too few answers, Frank had not bothered to examine the contents of the package Agosto Smythe had delivered promptly at noon.

"They'll just get my bowels in an uproar," Lamark told himself, as he sat out the trip in total silence, staring straight ahead at the "Fasten your seat belts—no smoking" sign.

Sal's first chunk of news was good. "Yeah, Frank, the story broke in America, but they cleaned it up pretty good. It was capsule stuff, without all those quotes. But, Christ! The meaning was there all the same. Anyhow, I checked Chicago. It's incredible. She just stands on that stage and plays the hell out of that part. She's made of iron. At the end she's got them standing up and cheering. She must have the local press in her hip pocket. True, they ran the Haywood story on page three, but the columnists haven't picked up on it. Not even a mention of 'what a snotnosed kid Robin is'—the kinda thing I'd be inclined to go for. But for the artist, it's not so good. They've been real nice. It ran. It got forgotten."

Lamark sighed his relief. He had expected Claudia to find the strength to ride out the Haywood slurs, but damned if he knew where she found it.

As Sal spun his car into the traffic lane that would take them across the Queensboro Bridge, he said, "Frank, are you in a terrible hurry to get home?"

"No. Why?"

"I wanna stop on the other side of the bridge, hit a quiet watering hole. I got some very important stuff to show you."

"Naturally," Lamark answered. "I'm surprised you even asked."

"Well, you never know. Me, for instance, I never suffer from jet lag. I get off the plane and go about my business as easy as that. Other people . . . I've seen them suffer for days."

He pulled off the bridge onto the East Side Drive, turning off at Seventy-second Street, parking in front of one of those Irish bar-and-grill establishments whose bright green storefront once suggested drinking spas where the "special" consisted of two shots of whiskey or gin for thirty-five cents. Those days now belonged to a past the new generation didn't quite believe had ever existed.

"They gotta quiet booth in the back where we can talk," Sal said, extracting a manila envelope from the glove compartment.

Lamark ordered whiskey, a change of habit Sal quickly picked up. "How come?"

"It's crazy. I only think of whiskey when I'm in Europe and sometimes drink that awful Scotch. No kick to it. You drink brandy and I swear it gives me heartburn, even if it doesn't. So today it's whiskey."

"Same here," Sal told the waiter, as he opened the envelope. He pushed a Xerox of a clipping across the table. "You probably didn't catch this. Stinks, doesn't it?"

The clip, datelined Miami, was from the New York *Telegram*, dated December 1st. It read:

> The death of Gianni Daniele, 78, was revealed yesterday by Father Luis Trentini, retired, who described himself as an old friend of Mr. Daniele, one-time underworld figure whose connection with the "invisible empire" first came to light in the Kefauver investigations of the fifties. Like other gangsters investigated in connection with their ties to gambling, narcotics, protection rackets and the infiltration of legitimate business, Daniele claimed to be an executive in a legitimate business, president of Daniele's Fruit and Produce Company. Ill health brought Daniele to Florida ten years ago, where he lived in

comparative obscurity. The former crime king died of a stroke on November 25th. Funeral services were held privately and one of Mr. Daniele's two children attended, according to Father Trentini, who added that Daniele's wife, Angela, had died two years earlier.

"Wow! That's something. It's big news to us, Sal, but why do you say it stinks?"

"The space! Frank, look at the space! Just a little over a stick of type. Don't these dumb kids on the city desk ever look in the files! God! This man came close to being boss of all the bosses. You know what that means?"

"Of course."

"And they give him this—a couple of lousy lines from some defrocked priest who tells 'em what he wants 'em to know, and a couple of weeks after the guy dies. It's crazy. A disgrace to the newspaper business."

Seeing Sal reach for the envelope, Frank drank his whiskey straight, signaled the waiter for another. "This time with soda, please."

"None for me, thanks," Sal said, "not when I'm driving."

"I gather from what you're pulling out of the envelope that *The Lowdown* was on top of the story?"

"You can bet your ass on that one. I'd been watching it ever since you gave me a reason to remember the connection."

"Donald Laine?"

"Exactly. So I find out the old man's in bad shape; I put a death watch on him, and this is what I get."

With visible pride, Sal slapped two glossies on the table. The first was a photo taken by telescopic lens of a girl in a wheelchair leaving a handsome-looking house in what Lamark recognized as the Miami suburbs. The second photo was a close-up of the woman.

"This...this...by God! Sal, you're one helluva newspaperman. This is the paralyzed girl, the one you wrote about, the kid Ritchie Winston threw down the stairs. She's Daniele's daughter."

"Yeah. Ella Daniele is the daughter of the late Gianni Daniele and the brother of the soon-to-be-late Donald Laine."

"What makes you say that?"

"Ella."

"You talked to her?"

Sal shook his head. "Yes, it came straight from her."

"How come?"

"By playing square. Years ago she wanted the story in the paper. I don't think her old man did. We can be pretty sure Laine didn't. It was personal—between her and me. I recognized who she was but I never mentioned it to anyone. So you wait, Frank, and you get the payoff. Wonderful thing, patience!

"That Laine was Daniele's son came out through other sources. It was bound to. How quiet can you keep a thing like that? You can't. But it was held down because of the power of Winston and Associates. Anyhow, Ella levels with me about how Donald gets to be a partner in Winston and Associates. After the incident, old man Daniele holds a gun to Ritchie Winston's head while he signs over a fourth of the controlling interest to him in the name of his son, Gianni, Jr."

"Who's an eminently respectable lawyer by the name of Donald Laine and the beard for his father," Lamark added.

"That's it. That's how the old man lived all these years in Florida. As a quarter owner in Winston, who the hell needed to go around hustling stolen TV sets from

208

Kennedy or running dope across the border in planes flying out of radar?"

"Unbelievable! Absolutely incredible, how pieces tie up so neatly when they seem so scattered you wonder where they've flown to."

"I gotta ask you one thing, Frank. I'm quoting Ella. She says, 'Sal, I know you'll use this and maybe somebody else will use it too. I can't control it any more. I'm relieved it's over. But I had to persuade, to beg, my father from my sick bed not to kill Richard Winston. Maybe he was a hood, and I guess he should have been in jail. But he never killed anyone and, as far as I know, he never ordered any executions. That's why he never made it to *capo di tutti capi*. I told him to take a big piece of the Winston business and that would take care of Gianni.'"

"A good deal," Lamark said, "but now it's over."

"So what happens?"

"First I go home and get some rest. Second, I look over some stuff I picked up in Rome, and then. . . ."

"Then what?"

"We wait, Sal," Lamark said. "We wait for the Winston people to move a pawn."

"Yeah, I got it. They move and somebody gets eliminated."

Lamark knocked off his whiskey and soda. "You said it, Sal. I didn't."

*   *   *

The next morning, after a long, restful sleep, Lamark half opened his apartment door and picked up the morning newspapers. The headlines read: DONALD LAINE, WINSTON ATTORNEY, DIES OF HEART ATTACK.

Reading on, Lamark was impressed with how neatly it had been done. Laine and a group of Winston executives were flying to California in the company's private plane for meetings with executives in San Francisco. They'd flown the southern route because of weather. According to Fred Werther, the vice-president in charge of European operations, who was to be chairman of the meeting, Laine had suffered a heart attack and died instantly. Fortunately an unidentified doctor was aboard who, Werther said, applied artificial respiration and administered adrenalin in a vain attempt to keep Laine's heart going. The plane made an emergency landing at a private airport outside of Texarkana which housed one of the small automobile-parts factories in which Winston and Associates held an interest.

Said Mr. Werther, "Our local manager, Mr. Russell Temple, became the guardian angel to our griefstricken people, many of whom had been associated with Donald Laine for as long as twenty years. We mourn his loss to our company and the community he served so well."

The story noted that a brief memorial service was led by Temple and the plane took off three hours later for San Francisco.

Temple stated, "In accordance with the laws of this state, an autopsy was performed which revealed that Laine had suffered a fatal coronary attack. Death was instantaneous. The executives of Winston and Associates, aware of Mr. Laine's wishes in case of death, followed them to the letter. Mr. Laine had expressed the hope that his remains would be cremated wherever he happened to be in the final hours of his life."

Lamark laughed out loud when he got to the next line. "I believe this wish derives from the teachings of Saint Augustine."

Lamark muttered, "I don't think Saint Augustine had

murder in mind when he said that. Maybe he foresaw the high cost of dying and wanted to undercut the undertakers."

Lamark put the paper aside, went into the kitchen and turned on the percolator which he'd prepared the night before. He wondered if he should count to ten or a hundred before hearing from Sal White.

He got to fifteen.

"You saw it?"

"Nifty, wasn't it? They didn't waste much time, did they?"

"A decent interval, I'd say. I guess we can expect the confession to turn up pretty soon."

"By the six o'clock news for sure," Sal answered. "See you tonight."

The lead story on the six o'clock news told of the double life of Donald Laine—a respectable lawyer under one name, a gangster boss under his real name Gianni Daniele. Documents placed in the custody of the police by officers of Winston and Associates revealed that Laine had killed his friend and business associate of many years, Richard Winston IV.

"Behind the murder of the whiz kid of international business lay a carefully hidden battle for power," the network crime expert with an Italian name solemnly declared. "Laine, who secretly owned one-fourth of the Winston empire, believed he was entitled to a larger piece of the action because his contribution had been larger. His ties to the underworld, which also involved strong political connections, enabled Winston and Associates to violate anti-trust laws and to indulge in coercion and illegal sales practices with impunity. In killing Winston, Laine had expected to be the logical choice of Winston

211

executives to take over as president. This announcement, we discovered exclusively, was to have been made today in San Francisco. It never happened. Laine was dead, and with him died his dream of a lifetime."

Lamark thought of Sal White when he mumbled, "It stinks." What lousy reporters! Not a mention of the death of Daniele, Sr., the old mafioso who'd been Laine's source of power. No word whether the New York police had swallowed the story.

And God forbid that any of those smart-ass, even-teethed reporters on TV would ask for a glimpse of the autopsy report on Richard Winston before accepting the word of hoodlums.

How they were scoring Laine's "sudden" death and "confession" at Central Park West Precinct and down at Centre Street was still not Frank Lamark's concern.

There were seven more days left of his leave.

Part Five

Frank Lamark's one-bedroom apartment in midtown Manhattan suited his simple needs. His small kitchen was seldom used except to brew coffee according to his somewhat bizarre recipe. It consisted of Italian *espresso* allowed to boil for fifteen or twenty minutes and "settle" overnight. Frank was constantly surprised that few friends cared to sample the concoction a second time.

His bedroom was utilitarian, a room that served its purpose. He seldom went into it during the day except to change clothes. The king-size bed he'd installed served as a brooding reminder that there had been too many nights when the "supersleuth" was its only occupant. The absence of sex from his life had turned out to be less of a problem than the lack of female companionship. He was used to having women around him.

As a child growing up he wondered how the Lamarks could possibly have produced so many women. Besides three aunts who had come to America to find husbands, young Frank was spoiled by three sisters, who also found husbands and were now scattered around the country. His mother lived in Buffalo, close to his oldest sister. Frank's father had died ten years earlier.

The Lamarks for generations had been in the import-export business. A generation back they felt the family could prosper better by putting their son in charge of the American division. That brought Frank's parents to the States. As the American branch of the business grew, so did the family.

Frank served notice early that he had no intention of becoming a merchant. He aspired to law but along the way his interests became channeled into police work. The Lamarks were horrified at the idea of young Francois becoming a *gendarme*, but being devoted to one another, they rallied around and supported Frank's ambitions— expecting them to go away.

When they didn't, and Frank graduated at the top of his class at the Police Academy, they attended the ceremonies with great pride. Like other parents of the cadets, they masked the fears that families of policemen learn to live with.

Some said his friendship with Ray Ryan, whose father, a cop, had taught him the secret of rapid promotion, was responsible for Frank's quick rise from a simple patrolman to detective, with its coveted gold shield. Neither Lamark nor Ryan ever dignified the gossip by arguing that Lamark's extraordinary record spoke for itself.

His wife, Laurette, was of French extraction. They'd known each other for many years, but had waited for marriage until Frank was secure in his work and financially independent. For a policeman, he was extremely well off. He had owned stock in the family business from the day of his majority, and on his father's death the widow and children shared his estate. The business had been taken over by a conglomorate.

Before Laurette's death, Frank seldom fraternized off duty with his fellow cops. However, he avoided being an outsider by attending a set number of functions each year. He more than made up for his reluctance to live totally in a policeman's world by continuing a custom begun by Laurette. Every year he threw a post-Christmas party at a restaurant for the children of his colleagues. The thoughtfulness and the work Frank put into the annual affair earned him respect and his own special merit badge.

The party was held early in January. Frank remembered how pleased he'd been with the last one. At the end of the evening he had hoisted a glass of beer, a beverage he seldom drank, and proclaimed that his New Year's resolution was to find a wife. His pals cheered and patted him on the back. It was leap year and Frank was convinced he couldn't miss.

It was now December and the year would soon be over. He could count on two fingers the new female friends he'd made: Sondra at Murray's Deli—enough said—and Claudia Milotte.

He'd seen Claudia only a few times, under most unusual circumstances. Nevertheless she persisted in dazzling him. She hovered in his mind like a pretty cloud that picks a spot in the sky and chooses to remain there. He worried about her when gossip filtered back to him, and he longed to comfort her when the Robin Haywood story broke. But how would she interpret his interest? She'd naturally assume that he was prying and, in truth, he was. For his own sake—and hers—the truth was going to filter through the whirl of gossip, rumors and suspicions.

The trouble with all this speculation—Frank knew

very well—was that he kept talking to the wrong person, himself. He had confided some of his thoughts to Luke Monzelli and Sal White. A fat lot of good that had done!

Frank Lamark's living room was attractive. It was large and lined with books, and there was a fine collection of records, a color television set, a comfortable reading chair and a portable table he could slip in front of it when there were documents to peruse.

He arranged his reading setup before opening the briefcase where he had stored the blow-ups from *Schizo*, the Nino Bellafiore manuscript and whatever else it was that Smythe had given him. Some notes written by Claudia in connection with her role, he believed.

He glanced at the blow-ups and put them aside. They required greater enlargements, which he'd have done at the lab. In skimming through the manuscript, Lamark found dozens of notations written in French, English and Italian, sometimes in different handwritings. He returned them to the briefcase. They needed more concentration than he was able to summon now. His mind was wandering and he felt no guilt about it. It had been a rough trip.

Lamark was about to ignore the manila envelope, having decided to scan the entertainment page for a movie. But automatically he opened the envelope and out tumbled the Xerox'd copy Smythe had had made of what appeared to be twenty-odd pages of carefully typewritten material.

Smythe, in a characteristic show of meticulousness, had attached a note.

"These are copies of pages written by Claudia Milotte while she was preparing for her role in *Schizo*. My research reveals that

216

Nino Bellafiore, writer-director-producer, encouraged actors to write out their feelings about their roles, to describe how they intended approaching them and to seek experiences in their own lives that might approximate those of the characters. (Note: This technique was not unique to Bellafiore. It was also employed by Nikolas Barishinskof, the Russian director. An analysis of his theory and how it proved useful may be found in *Cahiers de la Cinematheque*, January 1971.)"

Lamark hadn't intended to give the pages more than a cursory inspection, but they became impossible to put down. He quickly became caught up in the remarkable experience of going back fifteen years in the life of Claudia Milotte. It was as though she were sitting in his apartment, confiding her most secret thoughts.

There was no date, but at the top of the first page Claudia had written in capital letters: MY BIRTHDAY. She'd filled out the line with tiny drawings—a birthday cake, gifts, and a sketch of a girl.

The text read:

"Today I am twenty-two, and it is the second of two birthdays I can remember with the same happiness. The other occurred a few months after I was rescued from Villa Maria and moved to America with Grandma Monica. I was 'sweet sixteen'—a special age, she told me—and I was given a very special party, with all my school friends there, my American family and, best of all, Grandma.

"I arrived in Rome last week to make tests and be fitted for costumes for my role in an untitled movie we call *Schizo*, being produced and directed by the great Italian neo-realist Nino Bellafiore, who is also writing the script.

"Nino is tall and handsome, with a head of thick black hair. His eyes are gray and they seem always to be laughing. His wife is the famous Italian actress Stella Morell, who will play my mother in the film. She is warm, round and wonderful, with a beautiful face, with satinlike skin that looks as though it has been kissed by the Italian sun. It radiates Stella's personality.

"I live in a small apartment close to the Bellafiores. Stella arranged that, saying, 'Because a woman is an actress it doesn't mean that she should spend her life living out of a suitcase in hotel rooms. An actress is also a woman. There are things she wants to do for herself—like cooking, and caring for her own clothes. She may also want to entertain without the whole world knowing it. Start learning this now, Claudia. I never live in hotels if I can help it.'

"Stella's right. I feel much better in my own place than in France where I made my first movies and lived, like Stella said, out of suitcases.

"Why am I writing these pages?

"Because Nino told me to. It would help me identify with the two characters I am going to play in *Schizo*. I don't know yet whether I shall play a girl with a duel personality, a real schizophrenic, or twin sisters. Nino hasn't made up his mind. It doesn't matter, for either way I will be the two personalities, symbols of good and evil. One commits a murder and the problem for the audience is to guess which is guilty, the good girl or the evil one.

"Nino told me to think of the characters this way: one girl loves, the other girl hates. He said I might have difficulty imagining myself as a young woman capable of hating deeply and violently.

218

"Grandma Monica never swore—she always stopped at 'Bull.' So will I. Why should I recite the story of my life to Nino Bellafiore? He picked me because he said that he saw both sorrow and happiness in my eyes, and because of my physical agility. Let it rest there. Some day I may tell him that he also saw a girl who knows hate and whose only regret today is that she failed to follow the inclination of the girl in the film. I could have been violent, very easily. But I wasn't, although I should have been. Now I know why. I was too weak, mentally and physically. A girl who is hungry day after day, year after year, becomes too undernourished to fight.

"It is a beautiful warm Roman day and I will write first of love—what little I know of it. Yes, I can remember very far back when I lived with a handsome man who was my father. I know he loved me. We were alone most of the time. Then, I didn't know why, eventually I found out that my mother had deserted us. Friends told me later how much pleasure I gave him. They said that when he returned to France he was going to marry again and become a father as many times as his wife was willing. But then he died and I became a ward of the state, a five-year-old piece of flesh they stuffed away in a filthy prison the sisters dared call Villa Maria.

"At Villa Maria I learned hate. It took months before Grandma Monica succeeded in restoring my health to the point where she could begin what I see now was the extraordinary task of turning a girl with a fifteen-year-old body and the mind of a frightened slave into an American kid who won honors at high school.

"That required great love, an unusual kind of love. It meant dedicating herself completely to one person—me. I guess Monica knew how few years there were left to her.

She kept saying, 'We must press on, Claudia, we must master this or that by Sunday'—whether it was history, mathematics, English or music. There was no time for love as it is usually expressed. Americans kiss with the lips; Grandma Monica only had time to buss me on the cheeks in the European fashion before she sent me to bed, after guiding me through my homework. Then, until two in the morning, she washed the dishes and cleaned the house before dragging her own tired body to bed.

"To have someone care so much was enough to inspire me to be better than even Grandma Monica dared expect. I was. She saw me graduate. That day she kissed me on the lips.

"'My work is done,' she said, 'now, Claudia, you're on your own. We've both made up for the years you were deprived of. Your body is healthy, your mind is bright. You were cheated of the joys of childhood. Don't imagine for an instant that you will ever forget it, or that it will not mark you for life. The damage has been done. But you will find your own way to overcome it. I'm afraid Monica can't help you there.'

"When Grandma Monica died I didn't cry because she wouldn't have approved. Not in public, anyhow. 'Sorrow is a private affair,' she had said. 'Keep it to yourself.'

"There was little to be sorrowful about. In the years when she was teaching me I know she stayed alive by sheer nerve. She defied death to take her before her work was finished. When that happened, her health gradually deteriorated and she died peacefully at dawn—her favorite time of day—in her sleep."

When Frank turned the next page and saw, in large letters, the word HATE spread across the top of the page, he paused only long enough to brew another pot of coffee.

"I have never mentioned the darkness of Villa Maria to

220

anyone because no one would believe it. Only Grandma Monica understood because she had come there to find me. It wasn't easy to locate a child who'd been shipped to an orphanage in postwar France. The bureaucracy, woefully inefficient at the best of times, was at its worst. Although she arrived with all the American papers required to prove her identity and her relationship to me, she had already spent weeks in Paris getting the papers approved before going to Lucenay. That her person and papers proved she was my grandmother meant nothing to the mistresses of Villa Maria or the intransigent Basque officials. Monica had to start all over again.

"She spent a week in Lucenay, visiting Villa Maria every day. As clever as they were at deceiving outsiders about how the girls were treated at the orphanage, they couldn't fool Monica, whose eyes took in everything. She had been a teacher. She knew hunger when she saw it in a child's eyes. She could tell how many girls had been beaten by the nuns the night before.

"For me, Grandma Monica's arrival was a miracle. It was difficult for me to understand it at first. I had lost what Catholics call their Faith and could envision nothing in my future but the day when I would be sixteen and, with luck, move out of the orphanage to serve as a worker on one of the farms in Lucenay. At seventeen I would own my own body. I did not accept the existence of a soul.

"All those doubts vanished when I was introduced to my grandmother. She knew me instantly, and I understood why: I'd inherited her green eyes. She was a short woman, thin, stylish, and, while her hair had been dyed red, it had the natural look I later associated with American women. Quality hair dyes weren't to be had in France in those postwar years, even on the black market.

"Although there was nothing severe in her appearance, Monica showed her strength in dealing with the sisters. Her French, impeccable if accented, often could be heard down the hall as she pressed her case with Abbess Prudentissima.

"'I have not come this far after so many months of red tape to leave without my granddaughter,' she said. 'I may not look like a troublemaker but be assured that I am.'

"Although I was excited at this sudden discovery of an American grandmother who cared so much for a girl she'd never known, I became so fascinated with her style in dealing with the horrid women who assumed they owned the 'orphans' that I felt no anxiety to get away as fast as I could. I had complete confidence in Grandma Monica. I loved her when she made the nuns squirm—especially one day when she insisted on reading some of her observations about life at Villa Maria.

"Finally, Monica's quiet, critical presence made them nervous. I was turned over to her. Within hours we were on our way to America and Monica's home in West Chester, Pennsylvania.

"Why they wanted me to remain was obvious. The five first years of my life were spent with a man who cared for his child. I was an American, strong, healthy and taller than the French children, when I came to Villa Maria. Five years of care, love, good food and vitamins had made me stronger than the others. But that was hardly a recommendation.

"Villa Maria wasn't a school, it was a work farm. Monica called it a 'page out of Dickens.' The girls worked long hours in the fields surrounding Villa Maria; classes were limited to the winter and days when the weather made it impossible to farm. The children saw very little of their labor. We lived on a steady diet of stale bread, thin soup and mush. Chicken was a rare treat, reserved for Holy Days. While the sisters lived in the spacious rooms of the old castle, we were confined to a wing consisting of dormitories. Cots crowded against one another to accommodate an ever-increasing population. A room meant to house twenty-five overflowed to fifty. One toilet on each floor accommodated two hundred children. There were no bathing facilities. We were supposed to 'sponge bathe' twice a week. Few of us bothered.

"Monica taught me how to look at those years. She made me stand in the far corner of the living room. Then she pointed to an object on the other side—a vase, for instance. 'Now, Claudia, that vase is a little girl. That's you, but don't think of it as you. Think of it as someone else—a poor, wretched, unhappy girl. You know her, know everything there is to know about her. But she is not *you*, not any more.'

"I liked the game when Monica taught it to me, and it works today. Oh, there are nightmares now and then, when I wake up screaming, terrified that I'm back at Villa Maria. But when I'm awake I don't see me, I see the vase Monica called a 'little girl.'"

Lamark whistled. The coffee pot was perking away at a rate that threatened to spill his brew all over the kitchen. He broke away from the pages, turned off the flame, filled his cup and resumed reading.

He shook his head in disbelief. "It's like Monica said—a page out of Dickens." He marveled at Claudia's clear, lucid recollections of her youth.

Frank found that the material had been divided into sections. Across the next page Claudia had written, LITTLE GIRL.

"The little girl is five years old when she is driven to Lucenay and Villa Maria by some men who have picked her up at the railway station where she has arrived, maybe from Paris, with a little tag on her coat. The men on the train take good care of her. She doesn't understand when they whisper every now and then the word 'orphan.' She does understand 'poor.' She knows she is a poor little girl but she isn't sure if that's a reason to cry. So she doesn't cry—not then, nor ever afterward.

"From the outside, Villa Maria is like a big palace, a page right out of a picture book. It is high and wide, with bars on the windows and big heavy doors that make a lot of noise when they open. She knows the woman in the long dress is a nun—a sister, they call them in France. They tell her that the big woman, huge, fat and ugly, is Abbess Prudentissima and that her name means "Mother Most Prudent."

"The little girl is in the school for three years before her mind is able to understand all the things that have happened to her. She knows now what Abbess Prudentissima meant that first night at Villa Maria when she pulled the little girl away from the table screaming, 'Gauche! Gauche! The child is gauche! She is a devil.'

"She remembers she is made to sit at another table where for the first few days she eats alone. She is not allowed to sit with the other children or to speak to them. The nuns smell of perfume. The smell is sweet and sticky; it makes the little girl feel sick to her stomach. Every now and then the nuns come to where she is and watch her—when she eats, when she washes her face, when she tries to dress herself.

"They mumble words she cannot understand. From their sound she knows the words are evil, that she is bad. 'Sinister' is one of the words that sounds most dreadful. They tell her she has brought a curse to the sacred house, Villa Maria. They slap her wrist until it turns red. The

224

little girl wants to scream, the pain is so great. But the little girl does not scream. She does not cry.

"This makes the sisters angrier. They pull small whips from their pockets and slash them across her body. When her hands race to her face to protect her eyes, Abbess Prudentissima yanks her arm away and pulls it behind her, screaming, 'Now, little girl, hold your arm in that position until I give you permission to change.'

"Finally the little girl understands the terrible difference between herself and the rest of the girls. No one has told her. They scream when she comes into view. The children place hands over their eyes; the nuns cross themselves and hold their scapulars before them to blot out the tiny vision of evil.

"The little girl's sin is that she uses the wrong hand—her left one, the hand that God says is dirty and impure. She will learn to use the other. It is difficult, but she tries, and when she tries the others laugh and make fun of her.

"She grows older and she lives with the dreadful names the girls have given her—gauche, sinister, shifty, crooked and, of course, she-devil.

"The little girl knows the terrible significance attached to the word 'devil' among the French. It is strong and terrifying, an accusation filled with shame and terror. It is as though the little girl has been stripped naked and stands before the sisters and the other orphans totally exposed as Satan in human form. Sometimes she feels her head, wondering if the devil's horns are really there.

"Learning to write is painful and when the little girl sometimes forgets and uses her left hand, Abbess Prudentissima pounces on her with a ruler, slapping the little girl's wrist until it bleeds.

"Abbess Prudentissima invents a leather contraption

225

which the little girl is forced to wear from morning until night, and if she is bad she must sleep with it. It holds her left arm behind her back.

"In the fields she learns to work with both hands, but the sisters say nothing. She becomes the best worker in all the school. Yet it is forbidden ever to use her left hand inside the villa. There are new punishments now that she knows how to read and write. "'These are God's Words,' Abbess Prudentissima says, 'write them in your *cahier* one hundred times so you will never forget the evil that possesses you.'

"So the little girl writes the Word of God.

"From *Leviticus*, she reads the instructions given to the priest for the cleansing of lepers: 'The priest shall take some of the blood of the trespass offering, and the priest shall put it upon the tip of the right ear of him to be cleansed, and upon the thumb of his right hand . . . and the priest shall take some of the log of oil and pour it into the palm of his own left hand, and shall sprinkle the oil with his fingers seven times before the Lord.'

"From the *Psalms*, the little girl writes: 'At the right hand there are pleasures for evermore. Savest by thy right hand them which put their trust in thee. The Lord is thy keeper; the Lord is thy shade upon thy right hand. If I forget thee, O Jerusalem, let my left hand forget her cunning. . . .'

"For her drawing lessons, which are very few at Villa Maria, the little girl is given the same assignment over and over. She must draw the Garden of Eden, showing Adam accepting the forbidden fruit from the left hand of Eve, who is always shown at the left.

"With the years the little girl outgrows her habit of using her dirty left hand, and the nuns have new younger children to torture. The little girl is now too important a worker in the fields to be abused or injured by the sadistic sisters.

"She gloats because she is now true to the nature they have given her. She is indeed sinister, cunning and shrewd. She knows her worth. She can stand in the broiling sun. She learns the secret of making other girls do the work while she pretends to be the Abbess. The nuns play her game. They turn away from the little girl, they no longer persecute her, because, as they say, 'the she-devil is a good worker.'"

On the next page Claudia's handwriting again appeared. This time it read: LOOKING BACK.

"Separating the little girl from Claudia Milotte was useful—at the beginning. Monica was wise. She knew that in modern America my tales of Villa Maria would never have been believed. I would lay myself open to being called all the names again, but this time in another language. Now they would be more brutal because they would not come from the mouths of bigoted, medieval nuns or parroted by small children who knew no better.

"So I remained silent as I'd learned to use my right hand. Monica went to extraordinary lengths to strengthen my confidence in what I really was, ambidextrous. She took me to a baseball game where the star was a left-handed pitcher. She got us seats at a nightclub in the front row where she made me watch the left hand of a jazz pianist.

"Afterward we were introduced and he gave me a lecture on how hard he'd worked to strengthen his left hand. 'That's where the heavy stuff is, kid, you play the melody with the right. A pianist with a bad left hand's goin' nowhere. Count your blessings.'

"Well, I have counted my blessings, but that doesn't mean I've really forgotten Villa Maria, nor have I lost the

227

ability to hate. It will be interesting to see how Nino develops the two characters. I shall play one of the personalities lefthanded, the other righthanded. I don't know yet which girl will be the killer. It's interesting: being ambidextrous was one of the reasons Nino hired me. I wonder if he'll follow the stereotype and make the left-handed girl the killer."

Lamark paused for another cup of coffee. This young lady could be sneaky, he thought. Was she waiting to lay Nino out if he accepted the stereotype and made the left-handed girl the killer? Nino hadn't—at least from what Lamark had seen of *Schizo*.

Looking at the next page, which Claudia called MURDER, he found a young woman who knew how to express herself dramatically in drawings as well as words. She'd decorated the page with sketches of a gallows, the electric chair, guns, bodies—unmistakably those of nuns—and even a gangster shootout with touring cars and hoods splattering machine-gun bullets at bodies lying in the gutter.

Claudia had begun her inquiry into murder with a question.

"When does a woman become a murderess?

"Monica disliked 'ess' when used to describe a person. She said, 'One thing this young generation has done that I like is to get rid of the word 'mistress' and replace it with 'lover.' She felt that this feminine form degraded women because it usually described animals—lioness, tigress, etc. I wonder what she thought of 'murderess' and 'abbess.'

"For me, they are one and the same. I remember Abbess Prudentissima telling me, 'Unless you change, *jeune fille*, you will become a criminal like all those afflicted with your handicap. You'll become another Jack the Ripper.'

"Jack the Ripper was lefthanded. If his experiences as a young man were anything like mine, I understand how he became a murderer. I wonder if he hated his victims. He must have. I know that I would have to hate in order to kill anyone.

"I hated the smelly, bigoted teachers at Villa Maria. Teachers? They were slave mistresses, warped and demented creatures who thrived on sadism and perversion. I know I would have murdered one of them had all the circumstances come together to make sure I would get away with it.

"Is that how a woman thinks? I guess so. I see this girl as plotting and planning her murder very carefully. I don't think I would ever confide in anyone. I would have to do it myself; I can't imagine a woman trusting anyone with such an awful secret.

"I must have begun to think this way when I was at Villa Maria, after I'd grown and could work in the fields. I bullied the other children just as the sisters did. But no one ever saw me steal food; I made sure of that. When the other girls tried it there was always someone who gave them away.

"I imagine this is the greatest danger in any crime, especially murder: having someone else be a part of it.

"I don't know how the script will deal with this; maybe Nino will want to read these notes. He can if he wants to. They've amounted to therapy for me. Writing it down is reassuring. I see it on paper and I know it's in the past. The nightmares are never going away; Monica warned me. But you wake up, you shake them out of your head and they're gone. You forget them right away."

Then Claudia had written "Thank God" in three languages: French, Italian and English.

Lamark put the papers aside, touched by the girl's

faith. "In a place like Villa Maria," the detective told himself, "I could never have believed in God."

*   *   *

After he'd finished reading, Frank sat and simply stared at the wall. It was difficult for him to separate the emotions that crowded into his brain—thoughts that seemed to be darting in and out, one taking over the other as soon as he began to look at a particular point objectively. These words from the past should have put it all together for him. In another case, under different conditions, he would have been elated.

But there was no excitement in his heart as he fingered the pages spread out on the table, picking out a fragment here, a sentence there that had impressed him vividly in his nonstop first reading. He felt as though he'd been snooping on Claudia Milotte, intruding on her most secret thoughts. It was eerie.

He had been right all along, from the very beginning. The autopsy, only fragments of which ever reached the press, had revealed that the bullet which killed Richard Winston had traveled in a leftward path to his heart. There was no room for doubt that the murderer had used his left hand in firing the .22. Experience, however, taught Frank that in itself the finding was meaningless. He'd come across ambidextrous killers many times in his career. The clever professional hit man learned to fire his weapon accurately using either hand.

His suspicion of Claudia began with the mystery woman. She had to be Claudia, because none of Winston's enemies would have been stupid enough to hire a decoy. Any woman *but* Claudia would be a decoy and the first to run to the police once she felt cornered by the realization that she'd been a conspirator in murder, and as liable under the law as the man who pulled the trigger.

Lamark had employed the full resources of the department's public relations facilities to wipe the lady out of the speculation, presuming that Claudia would relax her guard. She didn't. He had discovered this on seeing her in Boston. Claudia had no intention of changing her alibi. It had been too cleverly worked out and it would survive, even if here and there it cracked a trifle.

There had been his discovery of how adroitly she used her left hand in dealing the deck in the card scene. Her left working against Stella's right strengthened the impact of the scene. Confrontation. It was done with such subtlety that Stella and Claudia were halfway through the dialogue before Lamark caught it.

He had been tempted to sit bolt upright, but resisted, aware that Billy Briggs was watching him so intently that the detective was tempted to lean across the aisle and ask him how he was enjoying the show. Billy might be a clever stage manager, but he hadn't worked enough mystery plays to master the art of surveillance.

Then there was Claudia's quickwitted reaction to his comments. That happened at the Sky Room. The explanation came so fast that he wondered now if it had been rehearsed. Of what interest was it to anyone except a woman trying to establish her righthandedness, to go into extraordinary detail about how hard it had been to master working the cards lefthanded?

He got up and prowled the section of his personal library of books on criminology. He opened a few, glanced at the contents, closed them.

Like young Claudia Milotte, all he knew of "handedness" in respect to crime was the case of Jack the Ripper, the mass murderer, who committed thirty-nine murders at the end of the nineteenth century. Despite the best efforts of Scotland Yard, he was never caught. All his victims had been stabbed with a weapon believed to be a bayonet, and at every inquest it was established that the wounds had been inflicted by a lefthanded man.

It dawned on Lamark how little attention detectives paid to "handedness" as a clue to crime. What, for example, represented his own knowledge of dextratility?

The detective pulled out a yellow pad and began scribbling notes. His mind rambled on, often racing ahead of his ability to put down the words.

"The tendency to prefer one hand to another probably is a significant fact in human behavior. But what do I know about it? I know about superstitions, such as throwing salt over one's left shoulder for good luck; the words 'dexterous' and 'sinister' suggest that the Romans associated skill with the right hand and harm with the left. That must have been something I picked up in a history class."

Lamark recalled owning a medical book, one of those indexed encyclopedias where you could find a brief description of a wide variety of ailments, from hookworm to Beurgers disease. He glanced through the index and found "Sinistrality." It was part of a section on handedness dealing with the history, myths and superstitions connected with the tendency to favor one hand over another.

The opening of the article bore out Lamark's attitude—which, he assumed, was fairly commonplace.

> The origin of our preference for one hand
> over the other is still a mystery. Some
> authorities believe it is wholly due to heredity;

others, that it is entirely acquired through training and social conditioning. The trend today is toward the view that in most cases children have a natural (congenital) tendency to favor one hand over the other, whether or not that tendency is inherited. Preference is therefore implicit in the body itself, perhaps because of the dominance of one hemisphere of the brain over the other.

A few paragraphs into the piece, Lamark found references to the Middle Ages thinking that Claudia Milotte had experienced.

Sinistrality has a relatively higher incidence in persons with certain characteristic conditions. These include mental defectives, delinquents, criminals, psychopaths, epileptics, psychotics and neurotics; also individuals with developmental disorders (language) like stuttering, specific reading disability and motor awkwardness. It is more frequent among males as compared to females.

A derogatory, unfavorable personality implication has always existed toward the lefthanded person, at best being that he is gauche, awkward or unusual; at worst, that he is deficient mentally and physically. The inference has been that the sinistral is more than just physically atypical in his special lateral approach to various tasks. But the question is: Can we define the personality characteristics of a sinistral in a more definite and meaningful way?

The author, Lamark noted with relief, became more optimistic toward the end of his text when he concluded:

> The retraining of the sinistral in early childhood is generally not a hazardous procedure and does not produce ill effects if carried on with tolerance, sympathy and an understanding of the personality needs of the individual. It seems that many of the alleged effects of retraining are primarily due to the underlying personality disturbance or to the unfavorable training attitudes of the parent or teacher and not to the change of dominance.

He snapped the book shut, but not before noticing a line that lefthanded men preferred having a woman on their left, for caressing with the right hand.

"A big help!" Frank snarled, as he walked to the closet, pulled out his overcoat and hat and raced downstairs, where he took a cab to the precinct house before he could change his mind.

* * *

"You're looking great," Ray Ryan said, when Frank walked into his office. "What brings you here a week ahead of schedule? Devotion to duty?"

"What do you think?"

"Sit down, Frank, relax," Ray said. "Someday you'll learn to let go of things. You can't let one case consume you forever."

"I suppose you're speaking of the Winston case."

"Well, I was thinking in general terms but, yes, Winston is the one we have on our minds today."

"You're buying Laine as the killer?"

"That's a direct question, pal. Jesus, give me some time. We threw that one down to Centre Street."

"Where they'll say the evidence looks authentic. It might, with investigation, check out. No further comment at this time."

"I'd lay my money on that. How about you?"

"I guess I have to. But there used to be a policy that a capital crime stayed open until it was solved beyond a reasonable doubt."

"Frank, it's still there. If some evidence ever turns up that proves different, we'll act on it. What are the police for?"

"To solve crimes beyond a reasonable doubt."

"You're pushing, Frank."

"No, Ray, I'm not pushing. Just trying to get a handle on things."

"You wouldn't like to go on duty today, would you? We got a bitch of a...."

"I heard it on the radio—the lesbian triangle?"

"Yeah, how about it?"

"No, thanks, Ray. You're being too kind. The patrolman ought to wrap that one up. I'm up to my ass with women mur..."

He stopped short, hoping the floor would swallow him up.

Ray's cool eye told Frank that his superior had caught it. "You were saying?"

"Nothing, Ray. Forget it. I'd better get going. I just wanted to check up this Winston thing."

"Sure, Frank, sure."

Ray walked him to the door. He extended one hand, placed the other on Frank's shoulders. "Enjoy your holiday, and if you ever get around to finishing that sentence, here's the place to do it. Right?"

"Sure! Right, Ray, and you have a good holiday too."

It had been the wrong day for Frank Lamark to "get a handle on things."

"I'd really like to kick myself in the ass," he mumbled as he raced out of the station, hoping to avoid anyone who might want to wish him a Merry Christmas.

*   *   *

Anyone who read the theatrical section of the newspapers or the gossip magazines was aware that the season's fabulous road show, *The Capri Affair*, was going to celebrate the Christmas holiday on the spot—in the Capri villa of its star, Stella Morell.

Arrangements had been in the making for months. Although Reg Wuthering fumed about the mounting costs of the all-star junket, he found reassurance in estimating profits when the company resumed its national tour in Los Angeles after the first of the year.

Meanwhile, Wuthering was playing it cool about selling the film rights. When *The Capri Affair* had opened cold on Broadway there had been virtually no interest. The publicity had been phenomenal—even if frequently distasteful. But if the rumors and innuendos about Claudia Milotte attracted many sensation buffs, they left *The Capri Affair* convinced they'd seen a fascinating play featuring ensemble acting seldom found in the American theater.

The players, respected inside the profession but far from stars, had become personalities in the eyes of the public. Stella Morell was delighted to find that she was enjoying the same affectionate response she'd been accustomed to in Italy.

The Christmas party had been Stella's idea. Reg had

gone along with it reluctantly, but now he realized that Stella had been on the right track all along.

"*Caro*, Mama knows! You spend some of the profits from the play and you'll make it back many times over in the movie rights. Maybe it will be a first—a film with the original stage cast."

Now and then Reg dreamed of putting out a second company. It would be a gold mine. But Stella was obstinate; she would not allow another actress to play the Contessa while she was still performing it.

"Some day, Reg, but not until the film has started. Then you can line up those big tit ladies from television. And do you know what the critics will say?"

"Of course," Reg said. "No one has boobs like Stella Morell."

"You bet."

Stella was right. Her twin adornments had been world wonders for years. They'd lost none of their firmness, and she still wore costumes without a brassiere.

"But only for comedy, my dear," she told an interviewer. "At my age my breasts may be remarkable, but they're not for exhibition. There's a difference, you know."

Stella's guests had been given their plane tickets and were invited to fly to Rome and then to Capri at any time during the holiday week they chose. "It's not going to be one of those guided tours," the hostess told them.

"You're all scattered in various hotels or villas. You have a good time. Fool around with your wife, your husband, or whatever's going this time of year in Capri. We have only one formal engagement—a post-Christmas dinner on the twenty-eighth at my villa. That's the press party."

Only Claudia and Keith Byrne were staying in the

Morell villa; Claudia because she wanted to be close to Stella, Keith because he enjoyed the company of both women, a feeling they shared.

Warren Rivers had managed to convince Anne Alexander that her mother would survive without her. Moreover, Warren had guided Anne through a short visit to Rome on the way. His attentiveness to Anne was another reflection of the gentleness of this talented young man. Yet he had been as attentive to Claudia, with no strings attached. She turned to him for company when Robin's vulgar story appeared in the Chicago papers.

"She never mentioned it," he told Billy Briggs. "We had supper and talked about everything else under the sun. She's an extraordinary personality. I often wonder if she's real."

As Warren became the ladies' favorite companion, Claudia's affection for Keith Byrne had grown. She'd found a quality in him that could only be described as "humanity," a word that would appall Keith, who cherished his reputation as a cynical sophisticate.

Unlike Anne, who sometimes appeared to peer nervously at Claudia through thick, hornrimmed glasses looking for signs that horns were sprouting, and Stella, trying hard to avoid comparing her years in the gossip mills with Claudia's, Keith remained her quiet, imperturbable friend.

Keith's respect for himself would not allow him to make a pass at any woman he wasn't sure of. It was a quirk in his ego, but Claudia discovered that it had not affected his capacity for friendship. He lured Claudia out into the daylight of public scrutiny when she longed for the protection of isolation. He never warned, "It's for your own good." He simply took it for granted that Claudia would accept his after-theater supper invitation unless she had another engagement.

With Keith at her side, Claudia felt strength. She'd been cornered by a reporter when word was received of Donald Laine's heart attack. When Keith gripped her arm, Claudia knew better than to launch into a lengthy tribute, as she'd done after Ritchie's murder.

Instead she said very simply, "Donald Laine was a good friend. I'm sorry, but I have no further comment." Keith whisked her away and she noticed that, with a glance, he'd made it clear to the reporter that the interview was terminated.

Keith never articulated the confidence his presence was meant to give her, but Claudia understood. He was telling her, "Hold on, baby, you're a survivor. That's the best any of us have a right to hope for."

*   *   *

Lieutenant Frank Lamark may not have been aware of his new prominence. If he was, he paid scant attention to it. Since the Winston case he'd entered the jet-set blue book, another name in the curious list of celebrities who create news and arouse curiosity. The list ranges from faded movie stars, television personalities, writers, some newspaperpersons, sports stars and eccentric million-aires. Old guard society and noneccentric millionaires have virtually disappeared from the pages of newspapers and magazines. The sudden emergence of a good-looking, talented and marriagable detective as a name to notice among the celebrity watchers ranked as pretty close to a first. One had to go back to the days of Walter Winchell for a precedent. Winchell had made celebrities out of FBI agents, giving them their nickname, "G-men."

Murray's Deli had long been aware that the two men

who frequently met and always occupied a table in the rear were Lieutenant Frank Lamark, the guy with his eye on Claudia Milotte, and his friend Sal White, editor and publisher of *The Lowdown*. Sondra's mouth was as big as the rest of her.

It shouldn't have been a surprise, when Frank Lamark arrived at Stella's party, the uninvited guest, that preparations for his arrival had started twenty-four hours earlier, literally from the moment he booked his reservation to Rome and a connecting flight to Naples.

The news came by way of a telephone call from the public relations man for the airline, an old friend of Stella's. She went into a rage. "How dare he? This affair has been settled. It's all over. Claudia's suffered enough and so have I. I'm not going to allow him to take one step inside this house—or to see Claudia."

Keith happened to be in the living room when the call came; hence he'd been Stella's audience for her tirade.

"Calm down, Stella. You have nothing to say about this. It's Claudia's affair. The one thing I'm grateful for is that Laine died before you and Aldo Roselli went through with that absurd summit conference in which you intended confronting Claudia. By what right, may I ask?"

"How did you know about it? It was a deep secret; we swore it."

"Secrets went out of style with Watergate. Haven't you heard?"

Stella calmed down. She respected Keith Byrne and had admired his steadfast refusal to take part in discussions about Claudia's implication in Ritchie Winston's murder.

"All right, Keith, what shall I do?" She couldn't resist one note of sarcasm. "Shall I hold a special invitation for our friend Lieutenant Frank Lamark, the international

240

persecutor of helpless women?"

"Do nothing beyond telling Claudia that he might show up. You know, Stella, we're not sure of that. Just because a detective's flying to Naples...."

"Don't tell me he's going to visit Pompeii. You know as well as I do why he's coming here—to ask more questions of Claudia."

"Granted, but let's make it easier on everyone. Claudia's not going to avoid him. Tell her, and leave the rest to her. She's handled Lamark before. I'm sure she's quite capable of doing it again."

Stella nodded weakly. She fingered her serpent ring and went in search of Claudia.

* * *

When Lamark arrived at Capri on the first flight from the mainland he'd deliberately avoided phoning in advance to give the visit an official complexion. Yet he couldn't honestly call it official anyway. Like the man who climbs a mountain because it's there, he had contrived to extend his vacation to visit Capri because Claudia was there and the compulsion to know the truth overrode all his feelings, even his secret affection for her.

They chose to climb down the cliff to the shore, where Claudia knew of a cove where they could sit on a bench and talk. She looked radiant. The crisp winter air of the island agreed with her, and the noon sun gave tone to her skin as flattering as any spotlight smothered in amber and pink.

When they were seated, Claudia turned her green eyes toward him as if to give encouragement. "Where would you like to begin, Frank?"

"At the end, I guess," Lamark said, "or nearly the end.

241

Do you believe Donald Laine killed Ritchie?"

"Why shouldn't I?"

"I put my foot in it, didn't I? An obvious question gets an obvious answer. I'll start again. Can you accept that a man who took such care of himself suffered a heart attack without the slightest warning?"

"It's not the first time it's happened, Frank. But in view of the strange company he was in, I'd say it was highly unlikely."

"Considering your doubts about Laine's death, why are you reluctant to question his so-called confession?"

"I know that seems strange, but Donald had many reasons for killing Ritchie. You must know them by now. His sister, for one."

"But that was long ago. It was settled. Donald became Winston's partner because of it."

"I didn't know that," she said, and for the first time Frank heard strain in Claudia's voice. Tenseness began to show in her face.

"There was a brief period when I suspected Laine. Then I wondered if he had been your hit man, the fellow who pulled the trigger."

"You're talking nonsense."

Lamark stood up. Claudia remained icy calm, but Lamark sensed there had been no long-time rehearsals for this encounter.

"I guess not. You made that clear a long time ago."

Her face flushed. "If you're expecting a question about that remark, Lieutenant Lamark, don't wait too long."

"Don't be in a hurry to get angry—not after all the months of planning you gave the murder. Maybe even years. I know a great deal more about you, Claudia, than I did a month ago."

She'd regained her composure. "Favorable, I hope."

"Yes, every bit of it, right down to the tiniest detail. You've had a terrible life."

"That's no secret. Lots of people know it. I try to ignore it, especially now with this play, and my career reviving."

"Is that why you killed Ritchie?"

"Come off it, Frank. I didn't kill him and you know it. Where's the proof? Nowhere. Just a lot of gossip whirling around me—and now it's beginning to stop."

"I adore you when you rattle on like that. Those lines—they're perfect. They come so naturally, with such marvelous spontaneity. But there was nothing spontaneous, spur of the moment, unpremeditated about the murder. You worked out every point in advance, and even if you slipped up here and there it wouldn't really matter as long as you stuck to your alibi and fooled the police."

"I really don't understand you, Frank. If you have evidence, some proof, show it to me. Don't lecture. I'm in no mood for that."

Frank's hand had been resting on the pocket of his overcoat. He pulled it out and held up a revolver, "Do you recognize this, Claudia? A Colt .22, registered to you, the gun that killed Richard Winston on the night of November eleventh?"

"That's not the same gun. It couldn't be. I threw it in the harbor. . . ."

Luke Monzelli would have admired the tactic. Frank wanted to throw up. If they had counted the seconds, it must have been a minute before Frank spoke.

"I guess you weren't aware that we put a hold on all your mail within hours, Claudia. You've been the only suspect from the beginning."

She wasn't going to break, and Frank's heart began to beat more slowly. He was grateful for her composure.

"Very well, you've got the gun, and I suppose you put

in a phony one in case I opened the package. Well, I didn't. I just took it to the harbor, hired a boat and dropped in the envelope. That's all."

Although Lamark's eyes appeared to be fixed on the sea, they saw nothing. He was getting what he had come three thousand miles to learn; now he wasn't sure that he cared to hear the rest.

Tonelessly, he said, "The box contained the rest of your props—the tinted glasses, the wig, the little raincoat. We photographed everything. You were wonderfully methodical, even eliminating the possibility of gunpowder odor on your clothes. When I opened the door of your dressing room I could smell the wet dress hanging behind the shower curtain. What did you do—dive in and out of the shower while you were wearing it?"

"Yes." Claudia laughed. "It's an old trick when you're playing a sleazy gal, a character who wants to appear sexy. You shower in the dress just before the scene. It clings tighter.

"Well, here we are," she went on, "you've got the gun, you have a wet dress in my bathroom, and my admission that I threw the wig in the bay—or whatever you left in the package. You still don't sound as though you can prove I fired the gun."

"Maybe not, but we can prove you're the mystery woman."

"That's crazy," she said. "How?"

"By the note. Remember when you and I were at the Sky Roof and we talked about the scene where you deal cards with your left hand?"

"Vaguely," she answered. The light had gone from her eyes. Her expression turned sullen.

"You also told me how difficult it had been, how hard

244

you rehearsed. Actually you're naturally lefthanded. You became ambidextrous. The shot that killed Winston was fired with the left hand. You were too sure of yourself."

"What do you mean?" she snapped.

"Why didn't you remove the note to Winston you'd written to get the penthouse key?"

Claudia started to speak.

"Don't try to explain, Claudia. You're not a liar. You thought the writing would never be identified as yours. In Rome I saw *Schizo*. You're marvelous, you know. It's a great performance. I saw how you played the two parts. One girl was lefthanded, the other right. So you used your left and right hands to write the inserts—the letters in the picture. You told me yourself that Nino Bellafiore always made the actresses perform their own inserts."

"Yes, I remember my telling you that. It just tripped off my tongue—it seemed so unimportant. You know, it's a part of show business that people like to hear about."

"But the handwriting in the inserts is identical to yours, both in the scenes you played righthanded and those you performed lefthanded."

Claudia smiled ever so faintly. "Well, nobody's perfect."

"Did you hear about Anne Alexander and the shoes?" Lamark asked.

Although she could no longer face him, Frank was sure there were no tears in her eyes. "Only what Stella mentioned very casually."

"Anne brought them to the police station," Frank said. "She feared you'd impersonated her. She seemed quite sure you were the mystery woman."

"She was right, wasn't she?" Claudia said, raising her eyes, and the green was stormy.

"I would have done the same thing myself. It looked terribly incriminating. I can understand exactly how Anne felt."

"Would you have done the same thing?"

"Hardly, Lieutenant. I'd face the person. But we're not all alike and, after all, it was a murder."

"Then you did use the shoes to confuse anyone who might be in the theater?"

"Of course. I created my alibi. I must have rehearsed it eight times before the day it happened. It just all came together, and I shot him, and for the first time in years and years and years, I was free!"

"It must feel wonderful. I can understand, Claudia. You see, I also went to Lucenay."

"My God! You didn't!"

"I had to know everything."

"To convict me?"

"Maybe. I found out where you learned to hate and why you hated so much. I guess that's where you learned you were capable of killing."

It was all over. Claudia had confessed to murder. She was curiously composed and relaxed. The color returned to her cheeks, her eyes brightened and she spoke without fear. "It's interesting you should mention that. You know, Nino asked us to write how we felt about our parts. I wrote quite a piece about love and hate. I thought so, anyhow...."

"Claudia, I read it. Believe me, it *was* quite a piece. It told me many things that I needed to know—things that brought me to Capri today."

"To arrest me?"

"No, Claudia, I can't do that."

"Why not?"

"Oh, there are many reasons. First, I have no authority

here. I'd have to go through the local police, get the consulate involved, have a warrant issued in New York. It's not possible."

"I can see all that. But you get me when I come home."

"That raises legal questions that I fear, Claudia, involves me as deeply as they involve you. We have some choices. We can look at this meeting as though it never happened. From the legal point of view, in a sense I've tricked you into an informal confession of having murdered Richard Winston, but I committed an oversight: I didn't advise you beforehand of your rights. You were not given the privilege of refusing to make any statements or consulting a lawyer."

"The Miranda thing . . . yes, I see what you mean," Claudia said.

"Also, we're on foreign soil. That raises new complications. But I don't think they outweigh my responsibility to warn you. What you've told me is simply not admissable evidence. No court is going to permit me to testify."

"Then. . . ."

"Let me finish. Claudia, I'm also guilty of a crime. I've withheld evidence. I never turned this gun in to ballistics, I tested it myself. It's the right gun. It killed Richard Winston. And there's one more charge—the most serious one. I'd say that I'm guilty of obstructing justice. I should have hauled you in weeks ago."

"And now?" Claudia asked.

"Unless you want to confess to someone, there's not much I can do about the case now. It's closed as far as I'm concerned. On the books they've laid it on Donald Laine. For the time being, of course. Until something else turns up. That would have to be you."

Finally Claudia's eyes brimmed with tears. "Why, Frank . . . why?"

"Because I felt you had to do it."

"Did you read the hospital reports?" Claudia asked.

"Rose Derlanger did a great job on those. She had everything down in a notebook—all the times Winston slugged you senseless—all the hospitals you'd entered in the middle of the night."

"Under assumed names, you know."

"Rose gave the cop who interrogated her not only the hospitals, the dates, but also the phony names. They were checked out and the story verified."

"Thank God for that," Claudia said. "That was going to be my last line of defense if this thing ever broke. You can see—well, anyone could see—how powerless I was. Whatever I wrote fifteen years ago, I'm no killer. Who wants that hanging over her head the rest of her life? Nobody. Not me. God knows, I didn't want it to be me.

"But it was me or Ritchie. While his father lived I was safe. He liked me and he appreciated the respectability our marriage gave his crazy son. Then there were Rose and her family. Her brother would kill for me. But I never even considered that. Ritchie went wild when I returned to the theater. He threatened my life again and again. I have it all on tape."

Lamark started to interrupt.

"Darling Frank, don't tell me I should have gone to the police. Gangsters' wives don't do it that way—and I was no different from them. I had to come to terms with that. Once I did, I was able to kill.

"But now . . . now . . . ."

"Now what?"

"It seems to me that I've wrecked you. Maybe it would be better if we worked something out with the District Attorney. I've heard of arrangements being made."

"Plea bargaining, they call it," he said. He laughed. "I

thought you were smarter than that, Claudia. The D.A
would go mad with joy. Imagine having his name in
headlines linked with Claudia Milotte and the murder
case of the year?"

"But he'd believe me. I've got my facts, my figures, my
evidence."

"You bet you have, and he'd go easy on you. The jury
would free you. The D.A. would see to that, no matter
how stupid an attorney you got."

Lamark paused, searching for the words to sum it up.
"I suppose it's because I knew all these things that I took
the law and bent it a little. A Crime of Passion—you know
how a Frenchman looks at that? I was struck with my own
emotions, I guess . . . as well as the way I felt about you."

"Why do you say 'felt'?" Claudia asked, drawing closer
to him and putting her arms around his shoulders.

"A slip of the tongue," he said.

"Let's find out." Claudia's voice was husky.

Their tongues met, and it was quite a while before the
embrace broke.

"Whew! I waited a long time for that. It was worth it."

"Thank you, Frank. I did some waiting myself."

There was a long silence as they stood side by side
staring out at the sea.

"What happens now, Frank?"

The detective smiled. "God knows, Claudia. I don't. I
have one favor to ask before I forget."

"Anything," Claudia answered.

"How are you settling with the Winstons?"

She laughed. "Baby, for every goddamned penny I can
get. I decided that the minute I heard about Donald
Laine's death. I suspected he was Ritchie's partner—but I
also called it right. Donald was someone he couldn't get
rid of. When I discovered he was gay, I got the rest of

it—about his gangster father and that poor girl in the wheelchair. That's why I was so devoted to Donald. We were more than friends; we had ties no one else could understand. He was afraid to enjoy his sexual instincts because of scandal. I had to turn off mine because I needed to remain Mrs. Richard Winston. Of course, Donald never imagined how much I knew. There was no need to tell him. What would it accomplish? Only more embarrassment. Anyhow, I'm going to take all the money."

"And do what?"

"I'm going to establish a foundation to help women like me—wherever they are, whoever they are."

"And who are 'women like you'?"

"Women who are trapped. That's my only description now. When it gets organized we'll make it clearer. I don't need Winston's dirty money. I can make my own." She paused. "But that has nothing to do with what you asked."

"Except that I'm happy to hear about it," Lamark said. "As for the favor, it has to do with a tabloid called *The Lowdown*. The controlling interest is owned by Winston and Associates. My friend Sal White is the publisher. He was a terrific help on this case and he wants to buy back control."

"That's all?"

"Yes," Frank said, "that's all. Do you mind?"

"Of course not. Consider it done. Okay?"

They said very little afterward. They climbed back to the villa, where Claudia's expression told Stella that the meeting had gone well.

Frank glanced at his watch. "I'm afraid I have to go. The aquaplane leaves pretty soon. If you'll excuse me, *Signora* Morell."

"For a little while, *Monsieur* Lamark. I imagine we'll be seeing you again."

Frank glanced at Claudia, whose face lighted up with a warm smile.

"I imagine you will, *Signora. Arriverdeci.*"

*   *   *

Luke Monzelli laughed. "So you tricked me to find out the best way of trapping the lady. Thank you, Lieutenant, that's quite a compliment."

Inspector Luke Monzelli and Lieutenant Frank Lamark were seated in a tower in the center of the Leonarda Da Vinci Airport in Rome which served as the airport security office and police station. Monzelli had ordered supper for his American friend. Lamark was taking a late flight back to New York.

"I didn't know whether to begin, with the handwriting or the gun, so I left it to you."

"I'm pleased to have been of service," Monzelli said. "But what led you to conclude that she mailed the gun to Boston? It would seem a terrible risk."

"A hunch, that's all. Two of my aunts were actresses before they married—very unimportant. They sang in nightclubs. I remember their mailing their costumes back and forth to each other. They wore the same size. It was pretty common among theatrical people. So I took a chance, that's all."

"I'm astonished that the postal inspectors allowed you such easy access."

"Luke, they have so much mail fraud to contend with, they're years behind in their work. When a cop comes in they pay no attention. I used their facilities to photograph the label and the props, substituted another Colt and

251

turned the package back to them for delivery. Nothing to it."

Monzelli laughed. "It's crazy. I'd never have believed it: Frank Lamark withholding evidence and obstructing justice! There must be a couple of other charges they could dig up, too."

"A dozen more, if you start digging into the police manual."

"Why, Frank? Is it because you're fed up and want to take your retirement, or is it the other reason?"

"You mean the way I feel about Claudia?"

"Don't be silly, Frank. I have a few years' seniority on you but I don't make a point of it. There's a tremendous difference between the experiences of a New York cop and a Roman policeman. But that doesn't mean you can fool me."

Frank began to object. . . .

Monzelli put up his hand, "*Basta*, Frank! You've said too much already. But it occurs to me that a very rich and beautiful lady is going to need someone close to her she can trust to make sure the money is spent wisely. Now, Frank, don't tell me the same thought hasn't entered your mind too."

Monzelli scrutinized his friend's face carefully. Ever so slightly Lamark's tongue moistened his lips.

"I wouldn't answer that question, Frank, if I were you."

Lamark grinned. "I'm not going to, Luke. You don't expect me to."

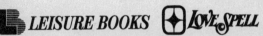